I0600975

THE
BURNING

Book I of The Burning Trilogy

From The Ages Series

PATRICK JEAN-PAUL

Volume I

ISBN: 692892954
ISBN-13: 978-0-692-89295-4

CONTENTS

Acknowledgments   i

Chapter One   1

Chapter Two   22

Chapter Three   37

Chapter Four   55

Chapter Five   76

Chapter Six   85

Chapter Seven   106

Chapter Eight   110

Chapter Nine   122

Chapter Ten   139

Chapter Eleven   151

Chapter Twelve   168

Chapter Thirteen   189

Chapter Fourteen   203

Chapter Fifteen   225

Chapter Sixteen   244

Chapter Seventeen   265

Chapter Eighteen   287

Chapter Nineteen   303

Chapter Twenty   317

Chapter Twenty-One   335

Chapter Twenty-Two   353

CHAPTER ONE

The deafening ring in my ears is the first thing I notice when I come to. The tone drowns out the sounds of the gunfire all around me; it sounds like a sharper version of the emergency broadcast tone from television. I lie there, trying to regain my composure, but my system is in shock. I feel pain shooting throughout my body. It feels like the weird pain you get when you fall asleep on your arm, and then, when you wake up, your arm just throbs. It must have been a rocket-propelled grenade that hit us!

"Aw!"

That hurts, I think. I try turning to my side, but I cannot move, so I lie down flat on my back. I look up at the sky, and the beautiful blue that I remembered is all but gone. This haze is everywhere. I cannot even remember the last time I saw green on the trees or green grass. Everything I took for granted is now gone.

I have to get up! They must be closing in on us right now. I try to turn to my right side this time, but the pain forces me to lie back down. My hearing is slowly returning. I can hear gunfire all around me. It sounds like the attack is coming from the opposite direction from where we came. *I have to get up*, I think again.

I turn to my left again. My vision clears up some, and in the distance, I see Jeremy firing his SKS rifle from behind a tree. He loves that gun, but he is only thirteen. We are all children! We should be playing video games and texting, but instead, we are out here shooting at each other. We are just kids! I have to get up, I have to help, and I have to survive. I cannot let them down, and I have to be strong. Everything hurts, I cannot move at all, but I have to move. *They might launch another grenade in the same position.* I have to move. I try getting up but fall back down. Why does the sky have to burn? Why do we have to fight to survive? We are only kids.

"Ahhh!"

The ringing in my ears is like a bad case of déjà vu. I know we are under heavy gunfire, but this terrible ringing reminds me of the last good memories I had in this life before everything changed. That was the day when life as we knew it ended. When you are young, enjoying the summer is part of what you do. You look forward to the day you grow up, leave home, and go off to college. Those dreams were taken from us, and we were forced to leave our homes. We did not leave to seek higher education but to fight in a war for survival. Why did that day have to come? The day when the sky burned and humanity changed. The day we were playing touch football, and Nate tackled me. I do not remember the hit, but when I woke up, Nate was apologizing profusely.

***

"Is he going to be ok?" Nate asks as he hovers over me. Next to him stands Cassie with a concerned look on her face.

"Ouch!" is all I can mumble. I do not have the strength to talk.

"He's coming back," she says.

The blue sky creates a silhouette around her. The wind blows her golden hair across her face. It must have been a hard hit because Cassie looks very beautiful to me at that moment. Then I think, *That's Cassie, gross!*

Nate grabs me by the arm and gets me on my feet. "Are you ok, Lance?" he says. "I'm sorry, man. I didn't think you would go down that hard."

"Sir Lancelot," Cassie exclaims as she lifts up my hair to check for wounds, "don't you ever scare me like that again!"

We've lived on this block ever since we were kids. Maybe it was because of the plastic sword that I was wielding when we first met, but she's always called me Lancelot.

Nate and Cassie help me into the house. Nate continues apologizing for hitting me all the way to my couch. "Sorry, man. Are you sure you're ok?"

Cassie brings me a cup of water. She teases me a lot, but she is a good friend.

Soon after, Jeremy walks in the door, holding the football.

"We're not playing anymore?" he exclaims.

"Can't you see he's hurt!" Cassie shouts.

Jeremy drops himself on the couch and turns on a video game.

"He's so annoying," she hisses.

"Chill out, Cassie," Nate implores. "Jeremy's my boy."

My ears are still ringing, but the dizziness is gone now. Nate is clinging to his cell phone. He must be on social media again. I don't know what he would do without his phone. He spends most of his time outside playing football or on that thing. One time, he tweeted about how much he disliked his date in the middle of the movie he was watching with her. She never spoke with him again after that.

"When are you going to hook up with Becca?" he asks. "Because she keeps commenting on your post."

"She is out of my league."

"Captain of the girl's soccer team and the girls fencing team," retorts Cassie. "I can see the musclehead kids you two will have now."

"Why do you dislike her?" I ask.

"I don't dislike her!"

"Sounds like you're a hater to me too," adds Nate.

She shoves the glass of water, spilling it on my shorts.

"Oh," laughs Nate, "she got you good."

The ringing in my ears has stopped, but now I hear rumbling. "I think I have a concussion."

"A concussion is a serious condition," responds Nate. "The coach told us so."

"Maybe you should call your mom to take you to the doctor," suggests Cassie.

"No, I'll wait till my parents get home to tell them."

Cassie walks to the refrigerator. She places some ice in a Ziploc bag and hands it to me. "Here, put this on your head."

"You got anything to eat?" asks Nate. He opens the pantry, pulls out a pack of cookies, and begins eating.

Simultaneously, the emergency alerts on our cell phones start ringing. Nate grabs his phone, followed by Cassie and then Jeremy.

"It says that we should seek shelter and stay inside," says Cassie.

"What's a solar flare," asks Jeremy.

"Don't you know anything?" nags Cassie. "It's when the sun shoots out energy from its surface."

"Turn on the TV," I suggest.

Nate turns on the TV, and the emergency broadcast system is on.

"You must've hit me hard."

"How many times you want me to say sorry?"

"Something is still wrong. I can hear rumbling."

Cassie runs from the kitchen and stands next to the TV. "Do you guys hear that?"

"Hear what?" asks Nate.

"I can hear it, too!" exclaims Jeremy.

For a moment, I feel better about the fact that I am not the only one who hears the rumbling. My dad has wanted me to quit the football team for a while now because of the concussions and recent deaths. He is always telling me what to do. My father is a brilliant person, and so he thinks he knows everything. *This time, he may be right about me getting hurt.* There is no time for me to dwell on it now. I need to figure out what is going on and what is causing the rumbling.

"Is it an earthquake?" asks Cassie.

"This is Virginia," replies Nate. "We don't get earthquakes in Virginia."

The rumbling is getting louder.

"Turn back to the news!" yells Cassie. "They might be talking about what's going on."

"No, I'm playing," complains Jeremy.

Cassie, in her big sister fashion, looks at him, and he tosses the game controller to the other side of the couch.

"You always get the TV," he says.

He gets up and walks into the kitchen. Cassie walks to the

couch and picks up the remote. She steps back and aims the remote at the TV. All the lights in the house and the TV go off.

"What did you do, Cassie?" asks Nate.

"Relax, musclehead, a remote can't cause that," she replies.

I get up and walk to the window. I look outside, and it looks like the entire neighborhood has no power. "Nate, open the door and check the rest of the area!" I shout.

Nate gets up, walks to the door, and opens it. "Ahhh!" he shouts.

He quickly closes the door.

"Yo, it's hot as hell out there. It feels like a million degrees out there."

He is sweating profusely.

"It started to get hot as soon as the lights went out," says Cassie.

I walk over to the door and reach for the knob.

Nate grabs me by the arm. "Don't open it, man. It's hot out there."

I push his hand aside. "Let me see."

I place my hand on the door and immediately feel the heat on the doorknob, and I pull my hand off of it. "You're right."

Nate takes out his cell phone and franticly presses his finger on the screen.

"Do you think there's something on the internet about this?" I ask.

"My cell phone," he replies, "it's not working."

I reach into my pocket for my cell phone.

Nate snatches it from my hand. "Give me that!"

I lean over to look at the phone. It is not powering on. "It's dead, too!" squeals Nate.

Jeremy walks back to the living room from the kitchen with a pint of ice cream in one hand and Cassie's cell phone in the other. "Cassie," he calls, "your battery is dead, and the water is out, so don't go in that bathroom."

The temperature is getting hotter, but we do not know why or what is going on. We are all perplexed at the heat. I walk over to the thermostat, but it's not working either. I run upstairs to get my father's mp3 player because it has an FM radio that we can use to listen to the news. I run down the hallway, past a mirror, and I glance at myself and notice that I am drenched in sweat. I stop in front of the mirror and look at my face. It is unusually red, with beads of sweat all over it. My mind begins to race. *What is going on? What is happening?* I step back to the wall as I stare at myself in the mirror. I slowly unbutton my shirt and remove it. I become dizzy and then stagger backward and lean against the wall. *I must take it slow so that I do not pass out.* I look at the closet and begin strolling towards it.

"A towel, that's what I need, a towel," I mumble.

I open the closet door and grab four towels. I turn and walk down the hallway to my parent's bedroom. I open the door, and the heat is unbearable in their room. I walk to the nightstand and pick up the MP3 player. I press the power button, but nothing happens. It is at this point that I realize we are in serious trouble. I begin to smell smoke, and I walk over to the window and peep out of the shades. I see some homes on fire in the neighborhood. *This is bad* is the only thought running through my mind.

"Think, think!" I mumble.

"Lance!" calls Cassie. "Where are you?"

"In here."

She walks into the room. "What are you doing?"

I peep through the shades and point out the window. "Look!"

"Oh my God!" she exclaims. "What's going on?"

"Whatever it is, it's not good."

"What are we going to do?"

I look at the towels hanging in my parent's bathroom. "Come on, I have an idea."

We walk to the master bath. I turn on the water in the sink, and a stream of water comes out and then stops.

"Your brother was right. There is no water."

"What are you trying to do?"

"Hold on."

I open the toilet's water tank, and I dip the towels in the tank to soak them.

"Here, take these."

I pass her the towels, and she takes them as I soak each one.

"These should keep us cool," I continue.

I close the tank, and we go back downstairs.

"Don't flush the toilets!" I shout.

"Why?" asks Jeremy.

"Because that's the only water we have."

"Jeremy put the rest of the ice cream back. We may need it later," says Cassie.

We go into the kitchen to the refrigerator. I open the freezer, and a blast of cold air hits me. I think about putting the water in the freezer to keep it cool. I walk over to the pot rack and grab one small and two large pots.

"What are you doing?" asks Cassie,

"Come with me."

We go into the bathroom, and I take the cover off the water tank. I take the smaller pot, and I use it to fill the larger pots with water from the tank.

"We'll put these in the refrigerator to keep them cool."

"Great idea! Let me do the other bathroom."

She runs downstairs to get some more pots. I come out to the main area.

"Guys, don't run unless you have to!" I shout. "The more we run, the more dehydrated we will get, and this water has to last."

We take the water and go back downstairs. We place the pots in the refrigerator. Nate comes out of the pantry holding two six-packs of Gatorade.

"I found these in the pantry."

"Great! My mom must've brought them."

Jeremy walks into the kitchen. "Oooooh, let me have one of those."

"No! We're going to need that for later!" says Cassie.

"How many do you have there?" I ask.

"Twelve," Nate replies.

I take one of the six-packs from Nate, and I hand the Gatorade out to everyone. "Here, we each can have one right now," I say. "But don't drink the whole thing. We might need it for later."

The rising temperature has made us very thirsty, and we open the Gatorade bottles and drink them. Jeremy quickly guzzles his down.

"Don't drink all of it, stupid!" screeches Cassie. She lightly slaps him on the back of the neck.

"Stop that!" he yells.

"We're all thirsty, but we have to conserve whatever we have to drink," she tells him, "because we don't know how long this heat will last."

It must have been thirty minutes or so since the heat started. It has drained the energy out of us, and we are exhausted. Cassie seems afraid, but we are all unsure about what to do or how to interpret what is happening. I want the heat to stop, but it keeps getting hotter by the minute. *My father wanted me to quit the football team because he feared that I would die of heat exhaustion on the field, but how ironic would it be if the captain of the football team died at home on his sofa of heat exhaustion. Nate is looking at me as if I know what to do, but this is not a football game, and he is not my running back. The captain of the football team is out of plays, just like everyone else, and I have no idea what to do. Right now, I wish I was Cassie's Sir Lancelot. He would probably take charge and come up with a game plan.*

I take the last sip of the Gatorade from my bottle and set it down. My mind is racing, but I cannot figure out anything else that we can do to help us cool down. The water and the towel idea was a fluke. I do not know how I even thought of it.

"I hear more rumblings," says Cassie.

The ground underneath us shakes.

"It must be another earthquake," she continues.

Cassie takes off running towards the door, with Nate and Jeremy in tow.

"Stop, don't open the door," I say. "It's a small earthquake, and it is too hot outside to be outdoors."

"What the heck is going on?" asks Cassie.

"We're not supposed to have earthquakes," I say. "We all need to get in between the doorposts."

The house shakes harder than the last time, which makes us more afraid. You can tell we're scared by the way we're just gazing at each other with deer-in-the-headlight looks. My heart is racing, and I look around, wondering when the shaking will stop. It feels like the ground has been shaking forever, but the earthquake finally ends. I notice how tightly I'm gripping the doorknob, and I release it. No one says a word; we are all frightened at the prospect that it is not over and that another earthquake might hit.

"Is everyone ok?" I ask. I look around, and they all nod, yes.

"I think everyone is fine," says Cassie.

"What the hell was that?" asks Nate.

"I think it was another earthquake," I reply.

"We're not supposed to have earthquakes in Virginia, man."

"It is getting hotter. We're going to need a lot of fluids to stay cool," I say. "Jeremy, help Cassie fill up the pots in the downstairs bathroom."

"Sorry, man," he says. "I already flushed that toilet."

"Nate, give me a hand getting the pot into the freezer."

Nate takes the pots into the kitchen. He opens the freezer and tosses the meat from inside onto the floor.

"Wait, don't do that."

"We need the space."

"It'll go bad if we leave it out. There's no telling if we'll be able to get more food soon."

I stand at the refrigerator for a moment, thinking about how we're going to make everything fit. Then it dawns on me.

"Leave the meat in the freezer. We can move the condiments out of the fridge and make room for the last pot."

I open the refrigerator and quickly dump the non-essentials out, making room for the pots. As I put the pots into the fridge, Cassie and Jeremy appear with another pot.

"Give it here quickly," I say.

Jeremy hands me the pot, and I place it into the refrigerator, close the door, and lean against it.

We make our way back to the front, nursing our Gatorades as we go. Nate is still trying to get his smartphone working again. He stares aimlessly at the phone as he continuously taps the screen.

"That's not going to make it work," says Cassie.

"You never know until you try," he responds. "Why aren't the phones working? I charged my battery before I came over."

"Maybe it was an EMP," says Jeremy.

"EMP?"

"You know, an electromagnetic pulse that messes up technology, like the EMP devices in *Call of Duty*. We use them to blind the enemy. It stops everything from working, cars, phones, video games."

"You're such a geek," says Cassie.

I sit there, wondering, *What is happening. What is going on outside? What is happening to our friends and other people? I wonder if our parents are ok?* Then Cassie interrupts my thoughts.

"Do you think our parents are ok at work?"

She must have been reading my mind.

"Do you think this is only happening here or all over the world?" she continues.

She goes into a panic. "My mother and my father are at work in the city, and my sister's in college. Are they ok? Oh, my God."

Jeremy walks over and sits next to Cassie. "Mom and Dad are going to be fine, and Leslie's fine too."

"I'm scared."

I look up at Cassie. I stand up to walk to her, but my head starts spinning, and I get dizzy again. I sit down and sigh.

"Are you ok?" asks Nate.

"I don't know, man. I'm feeling dizzy again."

My dizziness seems to take everyone's mind off what is going on outside momentarily, and they turn their attention to me. Cassie picks up the Ziploc that had the ice. I reach for the bag from her, but the ice is all melted, and the water inside has heated up. It is now a heating pad instead of an ice pack. We are all in shock from the event, but we still do not understand the gravity of the situation. I am still worried about my parents. We are all worried about our parents, our families, our friends. We have no news, and we do not know what is happening out there. Nothing works, no cell phones, no radio, no electricity, and no water. The air is hot. It's hotter than anything I've ever felt. If there is a hell, I would imagine that this is what it would feel like. I am not sure how hot it is; the thermostats are not working. *Wait!* I think. *Dad has a thermometer in his turkey fryer. Maybe I can use that to tell me how hot the temperature is.*

"Be right back."

I get up and walk to the basement door.

"Where are you going, bro?" asks Nate.

"To the basement. My dad's turkey fryer has a thermostat. Maybe it can tell us how hot it is."

"Well, let us know what you find."

I do not go into the basement very often. When I was a kid, I used to think that it was where the boogie man lived. I know it's silly, but I stayed as far away from it as possible when I was younger. My parents mostly use it to store our junk. I open the door to the basement, and a blast of cool air rushes past me. The air itself is not that cool, but compared to the air we've been sitting in, it feels like the North Pole to me. The air cools the sweat on my face and cools me down. It even cools the sweaty t-shirt that is clinging to my body. *Oh, my God.* I slam the door shut, and I go back to the living room. I have to get everyone into the basement if we're going to survive this heat.

"Hey, guys," I shout, "the basement is cooler than up here. We should probably wait it out down there!"

I turn to go back to the basement door, and they get up and follow me. I open the door, and we go downstairs. The basement is dark, and all of my childhood fears of it resurface. But I'm grown now, so I just smile and keep going.

"This feels so much better," exclaims Cassie.

"You ain't lying," responds Nate.

Jeremy is the last one in, and he closes the door behind him. The basement looks almost like a junkyard. Our things are all over the place, piled up in mounds, one next to the other. There is a small section of the basement that is without any of our junk. We go straight to it and sit down. We all lean against the wall and slide our bodies down to the floor. We sit there silently, not a word coming out of our mouths. I soon realize that we left our drinks upstairs.

"We left the drinks upstairs," I say. "We will have to go back up and get them later."

Cassie turns to me. "What are we going to do?"

"We are here. It's not as hot down here as it is upstairs," I tell her. "With the water we have upstairs, we will be fine. I promise."

I don't know why I made the promise because I can't guarantee that we will be ok – or even if we will survive, for that matter. It seems appropriate, though, for me to have said it to reassure her. We always read about these tough kids in books, and now I realize that they were only strong because they were born into the situation and had faced a lifetime of hardship. Our situation is all-new for us. It's the biggest challenge of our lives so far, and I don't blame Cassie for being concerned.

I place my head between my knees, and I turn my head slightly and look at our things. There is a box that my dad uses to keep his mementos sitting on one of the piles, inside a plastic container. I get up and walk to the pile. I stand in front of it and gaze at the box for a moment. The thought of never seeing my parents again is now front and center in my mind. I need to shake these thoughts and think of something else. I open the plastic container and slowly reach for the box, and I lift it closer to me with the hopes of keeping my mind occupied. I blow off the tiny bit of dust that's settled on top of the box, and I open it. Inside is a photo of my grandparents and my dad. I pick up the stack of photos and lay the box back on the pile. I look through the pictures, one after another, flipping through them until I get to my parents' wedding picture. I stop to examine it, moving it closer to me. I rub my mother's face with my thumb. As I rub the picture, I happen to see a gold wristband in the box, peeping from underneath some papers. I move the papers aside to expose a watch.

"It's Grandad's watch," I whisper.

I pick up the watch and rub the surface of it with my thumb. To my surprise, the second hand is moving, and the time seems to be correct. The watch is working. It makes sense since it's not an electric watch. It is a mechanical watch that does not use batteries.

I place the watch on my wrist and snap the golden band closed. I turn my wrist back and forth, looking at the watch. I look around and see the turkey fryer, which is illuminated by the light that is peering through the small window on the opposite side of the basement. I walk to the turkey fryer, and I pick up the thermometer. I look at the temperature, and it reads 117 degrees. This explains why it feels so hot. I lift up my head and look around for anything we can use. There is a lot of junk down here, and I wonder if any of it might be useful in our situation.

I go through the junk, and I see a flashlight. I pick it up and turn it on, but nothing happens. I turn it off and on a few more times, but it does not work. I open the flashlight case to look at the batteries. I turn it on again after placing the batteries back in, and it still does not work. I put down the flashlight and begin lifting the dust covers off the piles. I find a bunch of old books on physics, which surprises me because both of my parents are biologists. I trip over an old Apple Macintosh computer that is next to the books and fall on a pile of clothes that are neatly packed in vacuum-sealed bags. I get up and pull the cover off the third pile, and to my surprise, there are two stacks of water and Gatorade bottles, along with a variety of snacks.

"So, this is where she keeps them," I mumble. I grab a case of water and quickly rip off the plastic wrapper. I take an armful of water bottles and rush over to the rest of the group.

"Guys, look what I found."

Nate gets up, walks to me, and takes a few bottles out of my hands. "Great find, man!"

Nate and I distribute the water to everyone.

"Drink up! We have a lot more over there."

"We have a lot at my house, too," says Cassie. "Too bad, we can't go outside."

"I don't think we can survive out there. It is twice as hot out there as it is in here," says Nate.

"Eventually, it will get hotter inside than out there, and we will have to leave," I say.

It appears as if we are losing daylight. I look at the watch, and it is only four o'clock. I wonder why it is getting dark so early in the middle of summer.

I notice that the smell of smoke is stronger than earlier and cannot help but wonder if the entire city is burning. I look at the small window and notice there is an orange glow mixed with the smoke. The smoke is everywhere. I have never seen the sky like this before. It is the middle of summer, and it almost looks like twilight at four in the afternoon. *This cannot be good.* I walk to the window and place a crate in front of it to stand on and look outside. As I'm standing there, gazing outside, I hear another rumbling. There is a sense that it is the end of the world, a sense that we are all going to die.

"Another one!" exclaims Cassie.

"Get under this table!" I shout.

I jump off the crate, and we get under the table and huddle together. The shaking is light, but it scares us just the same.

"Is the whole world burning?" asks Jeremy. "What if Mom and Dad never come home?"

"Don't say that," replies Cassie. "Mom and Dad are going to be fine. As soon as it is safe to go outside, they'll be home. You'll see."

"They will all come home," I say.

The rumbling is short this time, but we do not move from underneath the table. I go back to the window and gaze out. It is eerie outside, and the sky looks ominous. We sit there and talk until it gets dark outside. I look at my grandad's watch, and it says nine fifty-two p.m.

We have been sitting here quietly for hours because we are too weak to keep a conversation going. Every time we try to talk, our mouths get dry. It is making it very difficult to carry on a conversation, so we sit, drinking as much water as we can, while we stare at each other. We are all worried about our families and our friends. We do not know what caused this besides what we learned from the quick news feed that we saw before the television went out. The world is burning, and we are terrified. Even though we have each other, we are terrified. We are worried and scared.

CHAPTER TWO

I slowly open my eyes and look around the basement. It is morning, and light is once again coming through the small windows. It still feels as hot as it did before I fell asleep. I do not remember falling asleep, but I am happy we survived the night. My mouth and throat feel like I have been walking in a desert with no water for a few days. I try to lick my lips, but my mouth is so dry that I can barely move them. I look at everyone, and they are still asleep. I look down, and Cassie's head is in my lap. Her golden hair is covering most of her face. I reach for a bottle of water, open it, and take a couple of gulps. I try to move Cassie's head off my lap, but she rolls over and wraps her arm around me. I roll my eyes and put my head against the wall. I don't mind, though; the heat took a lot out of us. I wonder what is going on out there, what other people are doing to cope with the heat. If only I could go outside to see what everyone else is doing to stay cool, then we would be able to do the same. *Yuk, is that drool?*

"Cassie! Cassie!" I whisper.

She does not wake up. Who could blame her? She had a rough day yesterday; we all did. I lift her head and slowly slide from under her, and I gently lay her head on the floor. The orange haze that is coming from the window catches my attention. I slowly stand up, climb onto the crate, and look outside. Although it is hot, it must have cooled off overnight because it is not as hot as it was yesterday. It is a good thing that the temperature dropped, or else we would not have survived the night.

I drink some more water. I look at my watch, and it still works. The time is eight eighteen a.m. I get down from the crate, walk over to my dad's turkey fryer, and pick up the thermostat. The temperature is ninety-six degrees, though it is only after eight in the morning. *It is going to be a hot day.* If we are going to go outside to check on our friends, neighbors, and families, we have to do it while it is still cool enough. I turn and bump into the table, and a box and a piggy bank full of change drops and shatters all over the floor, disturbing Nate and Cassie. I quickly walk over and shake Nate.

"Guys, wake up. Wake up."

I turn to Cassie and shake her. They both slowly wake up. I open up bottles of water for them. "It's cool enough for us to go outside. You guys need to check on your houses, and we can see if everyone else is ok. Maybe we can find out if anyone knows what is going on."

"What time is it?" asks Cassie.

She turns and sits herself up, and I hand her a bottle of water.

I look down, and my shirt is soaked again. *Why is the heat so intense?*

"Man, my mouth is so dry," says Nate. "It feels like I slept in the desert."

"Drink up," I say to both of them.

Cassie gulps down half of her bottle. She sighs and looks over at Jeremy. She places her hand on his forehead and pushes back his hair.

"Jeremy! Wake up! Wake up, Jeremy!"

Jeremy wakes up and licks his dry lips but gets no relief. Cassie hands him a bottle of water.

"Come on, we have to go check on the house," she exclaims.

They get up and slowly follow me up the stairs. I open the door, and the temperature upstairs feels about the same as the basement. I shut the door behind me, and we walk into the family room.

"Do you think it's safe to go outside?" asks Nate. "I don't want to feel that heat again."

I walk to the door and place my hand on the doorknob. It is cooler than it was yesterday. As I slowly turn the knob, Cassie grabs my wrist.

"Wait, we should take some water with us," she says. "We don't know how hot it is going to be out there. We might need it."

"That is a good idea," I say.

"We also need a plan," she continues.

"A plan, why do we need a plan?" asks Nate.

I return to the basement, grab some bottles of water, and then go back upstairs. The others are standing there waiting for me to return.

"We don't know what is going on out there. We need to stick together. We'll go to my house first and check to see if my parents made it home," says Cassie.

She turns to Nate. "Afterwards, we will go to your house and check. If everything is ok, then we can all go home."

"That's fine with me," says Nate.

"Jeremy, why don't you go downstairs for some more water?" asks Cassie.

Jeremy slowly heads to the basement.

"We can wet the towels we were using to keep us cool outside," I say.

"On it," replies Nate.

He goes into the kitchen. Jeremy comes out of the basement with four bottles of water in his hands. Nate comes back with moist towels. We each grab a towel. We look at each other, and I nod my head. We each take a bottle of water, and we walk to the door.

"Ok, let's go," I say.

I open the door, and I am immediately blinded by the sun. It feels much hotter outside, way hotter than the temperature in the house. You can feel the heat from the sun on your skin, so we cannot spend too much time outside because we will get a sunburn. I place the towel on my head, and everyone else does the same. We stand there, looking at our neighborhood, which is in flames. Jeremy quickly shoves his face into Cassie's shirt. She grabs her mouth and begins sobbing when she sees our neighbor Mrs. Dunlap, an elderly woman lying on her lawn in front of her burning home. We can tell she is dead because her eyes are open. For the first time, Cassie's not annoyed at Jeremy, who is holding onto her for dear life. She does not shove him away or complain.

"Damn," says Nate.

I know just how Nate feels. It looks like the whole world is on fire. Many of the homes are burning, and it appears that fires have raged all night and are burning themselves out in some cases. Standing there, I feel insignificant because there is nothing I can do even If I wanted to. I feel the heat of the sun and realize we have to move on, but I am afraid about what we are going to find. We just stepped out of the house and have already seen death. Mrs. Dunlap was a nice lady; she did not deserve to die like this. I wish there was something I could do for her. Maybe we can cover her up on our way back, but for now, we have to go.

"Come on," I say.

We slowly walk down the street towards Cassie and Jeremy's house, looking at the homes, taking in, and assessing the situation. Many of the houses are gone. They did not burn down in any particular way; they burned one, two, or three in a row, skipping some in between. I don't know what to think about all of the destruction. I am just hoping that Nate and Cassie's house is okay. It will be a greater tragedy if their homes are burning like these.

"Do you think our house is on fire, too?" asks Jeremy.

"I don't want to think about it," replies Cassie.

I understand Jeremy's nervousness about the house. I am starting to feel very lucky that my own did not burn. I can't help but wonder what sparked the fires. We turn the corner to see that Cassie's house is still standing.

"Thank you, thank you, thank you," she babbles.

We are relieved that her house is not in flames. In the distance, we hear an explosion, which startles us.

"What the hell was that?" asks Nate.

"Sounds like an explosion. Come on," I reply.

We reach Cassie's front door, she opens it, and we all walk into the house. It is hot and dark inside, but we expected it to be. Cassie places her hands on the light switch and sighs.

"I almost forgot that we do not have any electricity. Come in, come in."

Jeremy drops himself onto a couch, and just as quickly, he hops off of it.

"Ahh!" he screams. "The couch is hot! The couch is hot!"

"What? You've never been in a car with leather seats in the

summer?" asks Nate.

"We don't have much to eat in the house," says Cassie. "My mom did not go food shopping yet this week yet."

Her house has an open floor plan, and from the family room, I watch Jeremy go upstairs and Cassie goes into the kitchen. She turns on the faucet, pushes the knob back and forth a few times, and places the back of her hand on her forehead. Then she walks to the pantry and comes back with an armful of water bottles and lays them on the center island in the kitchen. She is home, but she looks defeated, and I know exactly how she feels.

"Here, guys. There's more where they came from. We don't have food, but we have plenty to drink."

We take the water bottles and place them in a pile. We sit there for a while because the short walk in the heat has exhausted us, and we do not say a word. We need to go to Nate's house, but the exhaustion makes it impossible to move. Things do not look good outside. I guess, in a way, we are trying to avoid going back out there. *We only walked to the end of the block, to Cassie's, and we've already seen a dead body and carnage all over the place.* Cassie interrupts my thoughts.

"Hey, has anyone seen Jeremy?" she asks.

"He went upstairs," says Nate.

"What is he up to? He should have been back down by now."

"Go and check on him," I say.

Cassie goes upstairs. Nate grabs the last of the water bottles off the counter and sets them on the coffee table. I wonder what is taking Cassie so long; she should have been down by now. I head up the stairs after her to see what is keeping her and Jeremy. I walk down to the end of a long hallway, and I see her run from her room into Jeremy's.

"Jeremy!" she screams.

I run into the room after her. Jeremy is passed out on the floor.

"Help me!" she shouts. "Help me!"

I run to his side and shake him gently to see if he will wake up.

"Jeremy, Jeremy!"

Nate must have heard Cassie's scream because he walks into the room. "What's wrong?"

"Jeremy! It's Jeremy!" cries Cassie. "I came into the room and found him like this."

"Help me get him to the bed," I say.

Nate walks over and grabs Jeremy's legs. I take him by the arms, and we lift him and place him on the bed. *He is probably dehydrated*, I think. I run downstairs to the coffee table, and I grab a bottle of water. I rush back up the stairs, down the hallway, and into the room. I hand the bottle to Cassie. She opens it up, lifts Jeremy's head, and gives him some water. He is barely conscious, but he drinks a sip. I am sweating from running downstairs. I start to feel faint, and I stagger to the wall and lean against it. Then I slide to the floor. I am an athlete, and the heat is taking its toll on me, so I can imagine what it is doing to Jeremy.

"Lance!" says Nate. "Are you ok?"

Cassie hands Nate the water, and he puts it to my lips. "Here, man, drink!"

I take the bottle and drink the water. "Remind me not to run like that again. It took a lot out of me."

Cassie places her hand on Jeremy's forehead. "He's burning up. We need to get him to a hospital."

"How?" I ask. "We don't have a car, and the hospital is too far to walk in this heat."

Jeremy moans and grabs the sheets. He looks like he is in pain. I don't know how he went from being fine to this so quickly. He just walked with us to the house, and now he is lying there, barely conscious. It can't be just the heat; there must be something else wrong with him. If this could happen to him, it could happen to any of us.

"How come we're not sick?" asks Nate.

"He is younger than us," I reply. "That is probably why the heat is affecting him the most. Do you have any aspirin you could give him?"

"Yes!" Cassie says. She takes off down the hallway towards the bathroom.

"Slow down!" shouts Nate. "You don't want to end up like Lance."

She comes back into the room with a bottle of pills. She takes out a couple and puts them in Jeremy's mouth.

"Take these."

Jeremy manages to take the pills and then lays his head back down. His skin is not looking too good. He looks as if he has a sunburn. The redness on his skin appeared out of nowhere. *The sun might do the same thing to us if we go back outside. We probably need to put on some sunscreen.*

"We need to get him some help," says Cassie.

I know, but how?" I ask.

"We could knock on people's doors to see if anyone can help him," says Nate.

"That's not a bad idea," I reply. "Someone will have to stay here with him while we go, and we need some sunscreen."

"You two go. I'll stay with him," says Nate.

"Are you sure?" asks Cassie.

"Yes, I'm sure," replies Nate. "Just go."

"Take good care of him," she says. "We'll be right back."

Cassie walks into her room while I stand in the doorway. She goes into a drawer and pulls out a tube of sunscreen. She rubs it on and then hands the tube to me, and I cover my arms and face with it. I turn to leave the room and see Nate. He reaches into his pocket and pulls out his cell phone. He sits at the edge of the bed and tries to turn it on. I smile and shake my head as I walk away.

We go downstairs, and I open the front door and walk out onto the street. I cannot help but notice the sky. The blue is gone, and an orange haze now pierces through the smoke. The smell of the smoke is potent. It's so bad that I can almost taste it. The orange sky overshadows the homes and cars that are on fire; the weird orange glow is everywhere. It actually feels like the end of the world, like the apocalypse. The shock of it all makes me numb, and I am at a loss for words. My heart sinks; I'm afraid, and I can't hide it. I do not want Cassie to know, but I think she can see it in my face, so I reassure her.

"Everything is going to be ok."

"Is it? I mean, look around! People are dead, and everything is burning. My brother's dying."

"I just meant that…"

"I know what you meant. I am scared."

"It's ok. Let's get your brother the help he needs."

We walk down the street to the Hendersons'. Mrs. Henderson should be home since she does not work. She is a good friend of both my mom and Cassie's. If anyone is willing to help us, it will be her. We get to her house, and we knock on the door, but no one answers. Cassie bangs on the door.

"Mrs. Henderson! She should be here. I saw her in her garden right before I came to your house yesterday. Mrs. Henderson!"

I turn the doorknob, open the door, and walk into the house.

"Mrs. Henderson!" I call out.

"Mrs. Henderson, Mrs. Henderson!" shouts Cassie.

We slowly walk into the foyer, calling out her name, but we get no response. I walk into the kitchen and find her lifeless body lying on the floor. *This day is getting crazier by the minute. Mrs. Dunlap is dead on the lawn, and now Mrs. Henderson is dead. What are we supposed to do?*

"I found her."

Cassie begins walking towards me, but I walk back out of the kitchen and stop her.

"No, you don't want to see this."

She slowly moves me out of her way, walks towards Mrs. Henderson, and sees her body on the floor. Mrs. Henderson has reddish blisters all over her body like she's been cooked in a fire. Cassie places her hand over her mouth and sobs with grief. She runs out of the house, and I follow after her. She throws up in front of the house. I rub her back as she releases. She takes a few steps, and then she drops to her knees and begins to sob heavily.

"Is that what's going to happen to Jeremy? Is that what's going to happen to us?"

"No, we're going to be ok. Jeremy is going to be fine."

"How, how is any of this going to be ok? I don't even know if my parents or my sister are alive. Have you seen the sky? It's orange, orange, Lance! Nothing is ok. We're all going to die like Mrs. Henderson."

"No! We are not going to end up like her, and neither is Jeremy. Now, come on, we need to keep looking for someone to help us so that Jeremy does not end up like that."

I'm talking a good game, but deep down inside, I have no idea what will happen. I have to do something, and I do not want Cassie to just give up. I put my hand out to her. She looks up at me and then slowly takes it. I help her to her feet, and she leans into me. She lays her head on my chest and wraps her arms around me. This is a first. We've been friends since we were kids, but besides the quick birthday hugs, we've never hugged before. This level of affection is new in our relationship. It feels awkward, but I slowly wrap my arm around her and hold her.

I speak softly into her ear. "We're still alive, and Jeremy's still alive, and as long as we are alive, we're going to push forward. We are going to do everything that we can to stay alive. I know you are scared. I am too, but it's the fear of dying that is driving me. Don't let it stop you. Use it as your driver to push forward. Now, let's go save your brother."

We slowly release each other. I slide my hand down her arm and take her by hers. It seems like the right thing to do. She used to take me by the hand all the time when we were kids, and now it's my turn to return the favor. We walk for a short distance, and then I let go of her hand. As we continue side by side to the next house, we begin to sweat from the intense heat. I pull the water from my back pocket, and I give it to Cassie. She takes the bottle and takes a swig as we reach the next house. We knock on the door, but no one answers.

"Help!" cries Cassie.

No one comes to the door.

"Come on, let's go."

We walk to the next house and knock on the door. We can see someone inside, but they do not answer the door. I guess some people are not willing to help others in these situations. I can't blame them because I would probably do the same thing – not because I'm a bad person, but I would want to take some precautions. The house next door to this one is on fire. We leave and move on to the next house. I look around again only to see that there are so many more fires burning and so much destruction. We turn the corner and see people out of their homes, walking about in the streets. There is a woman in front of her house, tending to a boy who is suffering the same symptoms as Jeremy. I stand there and stare at the kid, and I just know that if she cannot get help for him, there is a high probability that we will not be able to get Jeremy the help he needs.

Cassie runs down the street, shouting, "Help, help me! Is anyone a doctor or a nurse?"

Everyone just looks at her without saying a word. They probably are looking for help too, because many of them have the same blisters as Mrs. Henderson. No one here can help us, so we keep walking. Everyone is in distress. There are no police officers, no fire trucks, no ambulances, and no help that we can see. *We are on our own*, I think. It could take forever for help to get to us if this is happening everywhere.

"Why is this happening? What did we do to deserve this?" asks Cassie.

As we get closer to the woman and her child, I notice that the boy is dead. Cassie takes off running, going from person to person.

"Help me, please! Are you a doctor? Please, can anyone help me? My brother needs a doctor."

She is franticly trying to get help, and I just stand there, staring in shock. The realization of how much trouble we are in dominates my mind. These people can't help us; they can't even help themselves. The world I knew is over. I look over to the left of me, down the street, and I see Nate's house. It is a smoldering pile of collapsed debris. Cassie stops and stands there. I walk over to her and stand next to her. We look at each other for a moment without speaking.

"Come on, let's head back," I say.

I take her by the hand, and we turn back towards her house.

CHAPTER THREE

A feeling of dread has taken me over, a sense of complete hopelessness. Walking back to Cassie's house, I begin to think about everything I wanted to do in my life, all of my dreams, all of my hopes, which now seem so distant. Reality hits me, and now I am afraid that Jeremy will die. *I've known him since he was a baby. What are we going to do? The government has abandoned us, and we have no help. It is not their fault; they are probably in as much trouble as we are. The whole world is drowning in this heat, this fire, this burning.* We walk the whole way back to Cassie's house without saying a word. When we reach the house, we open the door and go straight inside.

"What are we going to do?" mumbles Cassie.

"We need to keep him cool."

Cassie picks up a few bottles of water, and we head upstairs. We walk down the hallway and go into the room. Nate is now sitting on the floor with his smartphone next to him. "Did you find anyone to help?"

"No, none," replies Cassie.

Cassie opens a bottle of water, and she tries to give it to Jeremy to drink.

"It is bad out there," I say. "There are a lot of sick people. There are a lot of people who need help."

"Let me go to my house," replies Nate. "My dad has some painkillers for his back. Maybe that will help him."

"Nate, I saw your house," I say, "and it is burnt to the grown."

Nate jumps up and runs out the door. Cassie places the bottle down. "Wait!" she shouts.

She runs after Nate, and I lean over Jeremy.

"Jeremy, we're not going to leave you," I say. "We're going to find you some help, ok."

I walk out of the room and follow them.

"Daddy!" Jeremy whispers.

I turn back and look at him, and then I continue after Nate and Cassie. I walk downstairs, but they are both gone. *They should not be running outside. They're going to get heat exhaustion.* I grab three bottles of water, and I open one to drink as I go after them. I can see Nate and Cassie turning the corner, heading to his house, and I follow. As I turn the corner, I see Cassie pulling Nate by the arm. He is trying to go into his house. I quickly walk over and stand in front of him. I hold him by his shoulders, preventing him from going into the burning home.

"You can't go in there, man. You'll get hurt or even die."

"It's my house! Everything I have is in there."

"I know, I know, man," I say. "Here, drink this."

I hand them each a bottle of water. Nate is in distress, overwhelmed with sadness. I have never seen him like this before. He is a beast on the football field. I'm not used to all of this emotion. It is affecting me, and I need to block it or channel it differently. This is like my grandparents' funerals: everywhere you turn, someone or something is making you sad. It took time to deal with their deaths, but at least they made sense – they died of old age in their nineties. This, though, is senseless death and destruction. How do you cope with that?

"You can't go into the house. It's burnt out. Even if you were able to make it in, you would not be able to salvage anything."

While we stand there, Eric and his brother, Ethan, walk down the block. They are identical twins, linebackers on our football team. They are like brick walls that you do not want to run into on the field. Eric is mischievous – we call him "Evil," and we call Ethan "Twin." You can tell when Eric is up to no good from the smirk on his face. I think Eric likes it when we call him Evil; he relishes it.

"Lance!" shouts Eric.

We wave at them, and they walk over to us. Both Eric and Ethan are sweating profusely.

"Hey, guys," says Ethan.

"Hey," we reply.

"What the hell is going on, man? We were in the house, playing video games, and all of a sudden, the heat came. We stayed in the house because it was too hot outside. We just saw people outside and came out to see what was going on, but no one seems to know what happened."

I look them over, scanning their bodies, but they do not look like they have any blisters on them.

"We heard on the television, right before it happened, that there was a massive solar flare that burst from the sun and was heading towards the earth," I say.

"Is that why everything stopped working?" asks Eric.

"We are not sure. We think it has something to do with a magnetic pulse," I reply.

"You mean an EMP, like in the game?"

"Yes, like that," replies Cassie. "We should go back to the house. We can't leave Jeremy alone."

"We were on our way to find you," says Eric.

"I'm glad to see you guys are ok," sighs Ethan.

"You too," says Nate.

"Hey, sorry about your house," I say to Nate, "but we need

to get out of this sun."

We walk back to Cassie's house, and on the way, I drink the last of the water I have. Walking the distance from Nate's to Cassie's has made us exhausted. Even though it's a slow walk, the heat makes it feel like a marathon. I'm happy to see Ethan and Eric are ok. We don't need any more of our friends dying. Ethan is six feet four inches tall and three hundred pounds, but he is as gentle as a bunny.

"I can't take this heat," says Eric. "We need a way to keep cool."

"We used wet towels," I say.

"Why didn't I think of that?"

We finally reach Cassie's house after what seems like a long trek. We go inside, and Cassie rushes up the stairs to Jeremy. I follow her upstairs to see how Jeremy is doing. As we walk into the room, Jeremy opens his eyes and looks at Cassie.

"What's wrong with me?" he asks. "I'm thirsty. Can I have some water?"

Cassie takes a bottle of water, opens it, and puts it to his mouth. "Here, drink."

Ethan, Eric, and Nate walk into the room.

"What's wrong with him?" asks Ethan.

"We don't know," Cassie replies, "and we can't find a doctor or nurse to help us. We looked everywhere."

"What about Mr. Jenkins?" suggests Ethan.

"Mr. Jenkins?" I ask.

"You know, the one Cassie's mother had us take the pumpkin pie to last Thanksgiving."

"Wasn't he a medic in World War II or something?" asks Eric.

"Vietnam," replies Cassie. "You're right. If anything, he may be able to give us some ideas on how to help Jeremy."

"Twin and Evil, you two carry him," I say.

"Dude, what if it's contagious?" ask Eric.

"I think it's too late for that. We've all been exposed," I reply.

Ethan and Eric lift Jeremy off the bed, picking him up by the shoulders and by his feet, and they carry him downstairs.

"Grab some water," I say.

Nate and I gather up some water bottles, and we all leave the house to go to Mr. Jenkins's house. Ethan and Eric carry Jeremy down the street. The chaos on the street is getting more and more intense. There are more people out and about, adding to the bedlam.

"We need to hurry up," says Nate. "Things are not looking good out here."

"They're fighting over there," adds Cassie. "We need to go."

I look down the street, and there's a crowd forming around two men fighting. There is a group of people trying to break it up. We pick up the pace and quickly walk to Mr. Jenkins's house. Cassie approaches the door while Ethan and Eric lag behind with Jeremy. Cassie bangs on the door.

"Mr. Jenkins!"

The door opens, and Mr. Jenkins steps out, holding a twelve-gauge shotgun. His grey hair softens his demeanor. The orange glow of the sky illuminates his brown skin.

"What do you kids want?" he asks. He looks down and recognizes Cassie. "Cassie!"

"My brother needs your help! He's sick."

"I'm not a doctor. I can't help you with that! Now, you kids get home where it's safe."

"Please, Mr. Jenkins. You used to be an Army medic in the war. The hospital is too far for us to take him, and I'm afraid he's going to die!"

As she finishes speaking, Ethan and Eric reach the front of the house with Jeremy. Mr. Jenkins looks at Jeremy and his face changes to one of compassion.

He opens the door all the way. "Bring him in quickly!"

Ethan and Eric carry Jeremy into the house, and we all follow. Mr. Jenkins looks to either side to make sure no one else is coming and then closes the door. He leans the shotgun against the wall, next to the door, and he locks the door.

"Quickly, put him on the couch."

Ethan and Eric lay Jeremy on the sofa. Mr. Jenkins grabs Jeremy's arm and checks his pulse. He looks at Jeremy's arms and lifts his shirt to examine him.

"He's suffering from radiation poison."

"Radiation poison, what is that? Can you help him?" asks Cassie.

"Maybe! You kids stay here. I'll be right back."

Mr. Jenkins opens a door and disappears into his basement.

"You think he can help him?" asks Nate.

"We don't have another choice," replies Cassie.

Cassie kneels in front of Jeremy, and she takes him by the hand as she strokes his hair. "Everything is going to be all right. You're going to get the help you need."

Cassie pours some water into the palm of her hand and slowly taps her fingers to Jeremy's lips. As much as they fight with each other, they actually love one another. That is the great thing about family: in times like this, you will have each other's support. Eric has Ethan, Cassie has Jeremy, but Nate and I don't have any siblings, so we will have to rely on each other. I can't shake the thought of seeing that boy in his mother's arms like that. I guess family can be a double-edged sword; they are simultaneously your greatest source of comfort and grief.

"Ahh," Jeremy moans.

"What is taking so long?" asks Cassie.

"I'll check it out," I say. "I'll be right back."

I walk into the kitchen and towards the basement door. I quietly walk down the steps and peep around the doorway. I don't know what possessed me to go into Mr. Jenkins's basement. I guess I did not think when I got up to go look. I do that sometimes: I get caught up in the moment and don't pay attention to what I'm doing. Mr. Jenkins sounds like he is coming out of a room in the basement, except he is coming out of a trapdoor in the floor. I realize he may not want me to see it, so I quickly run back up the stairs. He comes up with a bottle in his hand, and as he walks towards Jeremy, he looks at me with disapproval.

"Did you find what you were looking for?" he asks. "Let me have that bottle of water."

Cassie hands him the bottle that Jeremy was drinking from. Mr. Jenkins takes it and measures out a little bit of the powdery substance he brought upstairs. He pours it in the water, shakes the bottle, and hands it to Cassie.

"What is this?"

"Iodine."

"What does it do?"

"Radiation poisoning attacks the thyroid. The iodine will go into the thyroid and protect it from the radiation. It should also purge the radiation out of his system. Give it to him and make sure he drinks all of it."

"If there's radiation, how come we're not sick, and where did it come from?" I ask.

"It's solar radiation from the solar flare. Everybody reacts differently to radiation poisoning. For some, the reaction is immediate, and for others, it takes some time to show. But a very few will not get sick at all. It depends on how much exposure you get."

"Does this mean we all might get sick?" asks Nate.

"Eventually, you all might come down with it, but don't worry. I'm thinking if you all take a few doses of this for the next couple of days, it should prevent you from getting sick."

"Do you have some to give to us?" asks Cassie.

"Now, since you're not sick, you can take a much lower dosage than I gave him. Here, this should last you a few days."

He hands me the container he was holding, and he grabs my shoulder firmly. "Let me be abundantly clear. Do not share this with anyone or tell anyone where you got it from."

"We won't," says Cassie.

"Now, you all just stay here till it gets dark. I don't want you roaming outside in the street."

"Thank you, Mr. Jenkins, thank you, thank you, thank you!" babbles Cassie.

"Now, grab yourselves a bottle of water out of the case over there and just sit tight. Make sure he gets plenty to drink and do not skip his next dose in four hours."

Mr. Jenkins goes into the kitchen and through the basement door, disappearing out of our sight. The twins sit on the sofa, and Nate goes into the kitchen and grabs two chairs for him and me. Cassie sits on the floor, next to Jeremy.

"Have you guys heard from your parents?" asks Eric.

Ethan shoves Eric. "You idiot! How are they going to hear from their parents when the phones are not working?"

"Yeah, tell me about it. I can't even get on social media," adds Nate.

Mr. Jenkins is very kind to help us. He gave us medicine to keep from getting sick, and he is letting us stay at his place until dark. While no one else is willing to help and chaos is causing people to fight on the street, he has opened his home to us. He did not have to do that; I guess it's in his nature to help people. I am sure glad he was there to help with Jeremy. I don't know what Cassie would do if something were to happen to Jeremy. *I cannot stop wondering how his basement lights are working.*

"I saw a light coming out of a room in the basement. I wonder how's Mr. Jenkins able to get his lights to work."

"Why don't you just ask him," says Nate.

"If you come with me, I will."

We get up and slowly make our way down the stairs and into the basement. The basement is dark, so we take it slow so as not to trip. There it is, the light coming from the far side of the basement, where I saw Mr. Jenkins emerge from the ground. Mr. Jenkins asked that we stay put, but curiosity got the better of me. We slowly walk towards the door from where the light is emanating. As we get closer, we hear the sound of a CB radio. Nate and I look at each other. We are confused as to how Mr. Jenkins has both light and a working radio while no one else can get any electronics working. We get to the edge of the trapdoor and peep into a sub-level underneath the basement. We hear Mr. Jenkins talking on the radio.

"Blue Eagle out," he says.

We see Mr. Jenkins sitting at the far end of a room opposite the staircase leading down from the trapdoor.

"Mr. Jenkins!" calls Nate.

We hear a chair move.

"What are you doing?" I whisper.

"I just wanted to know if he was down there."

"We're not supposed to be down here. He told us to wait upstairs. Come on before he sees us."

I turn around and walk towards the stairs, and Nate follows. While I can be impulsive sometimes, it's Nate's normal operating mode. If we'd wanted Mr. Jenkins to hear us, we would not have been as quiet as we were. We can hear Mr. Jenkins on his way up the stairs, and we quickly walk to our seats and sit down. Mr. Jenkins comes out of the basement and into the kitchen. He walks into the living room, where we are sitting, and he does not look thrilled.

He looks at Nate and me, and he says, "It's impolite when someone has invited you into their home, to go snooping around while they're not looking."

"No, sir, we weren't snooping, sir," stammers Nate.

"We're sorry, Mr. Jenkins!" I say. "We were just looking for you to find out how it is that you have light and a working radio when no one else can get them to work."

"That's it. You all have to go now!" says Mr. Jenkins. He grabs me by my shoulder and pushes me out the door. "Leave, leave now, all of you!" he shouts.

"Mr. Jenkins, please, Mr. Jenkins," pleads Cassie, "my brother is still sick. Please let us stay until the sun goes down."

Mr. Jenkins looks at Cassie, and his temper cools down. He has a soft spot for Cassie since her mom is a friend of his. She seems to get through to him, and right now, I'm hoping we have not messed things up for Jeremy with the only person who is helping us.

"All right, but you stay put. If I find any of you snooping around again, I will throw you out."

"We'll stay put. Right, guys?" says Cassie.

"Yes, yes, we will," I reply.

Mr. Jenkins picks up his shotgun. He turns around and looks at us, and then he goes back downstairs. Now I feel bad for sneaking around his house. He invited us into his home, and we violated his trust. I don't blame him for being upset at us. I just hope he does not stop helping us. Cassie is annoyed at us, and who could blame her; we could have gotten her and Jeremy thrown out of the house.

She turns and stares at me with a piercing look. "Guys, please don't do anything to get us kicked out! I can't take Jeremy back out there."

"It's ok. We won't," says Nate.

"We haven't taken the iodine he gave us. Why don't we all take a dose for now?" I suggest.

"I'll grab the water," says Ethan.

That was the best I could come up with to calm the tension. Cassie was upset that Mr. Jenkins wanted us out of his house. She would probably never speak to me again if something were to happen to Jeremy. I decide to stay put this time; we can't afford to have Jeremy on his own without help.

Ethen has several bottles of water from the cooler, and he gives one to each of us. We measure the iodine, and we each pour it into our water. We shake the bottles and drink them. I look at my watch, and it is almost twelve o'clock. I take another bottle of water to drink, and then I walk over to Jeremy. I stand there and look at him; I place my hand on Cassie's shoulder.

"How is he?" I ask her.

"His fever is going down. He is not as hot as he was earlier."

"So, is he getting better?"

"Yes, and now that he's getting better, I can't stop thinking about my parents and my sister. I am so worried about them. I wonder how they are doing."

"I think we're all worried," says Ethan. "There's no way to talk to them, no way to find out if they're even still alive."

"Don't talk like that, man! Right, Lance?" says Nate.

"Yeah, I'm sure our parents are going to be ok," I reply. "We can't lose hope! We have to believe we will see them again."

"Look outside! Everyone is sick and dying," says Cassie.

She lays her head on Jeremy's chest, saddened by the whole ordeal we are facing. We all sit back, and no one says a word. We are coming to grips with the situation through Cassie's eyes. We are now in the despair phase, a group of lost kids, and you can see it all over our faces. What do we do? Where do we go from here? How do we cope with what is going on? We are hot, drinking bottle after bottle of water to keep cool. The side effect is that we are constantly running to the bathroom to empty our bladders.

Am I being overoptimistic? I feel that we may yet see our parents. I have to believe that; they are the only family I have. My grandfather was an only child, and so was my dad. My mother's family is from California. She has a sister, but her sister has no kids. I have met some of my third cousins, but we don't know each other well. *If I lose my mom and dad, I will have no one.* My thoughts are interrupted by Ethan.

"I have to use the bathroom again," he says.

He leaves the kitchen to go to the bathroom. I look over at Nate, who is swiping away on his cell phone. He is pushing the power button harder and harder as if it will make a difference.

"I've had enough of this," he says. "There's no internet and no computer. I'm hot and bored out of my mind."

"You know, people did things and survived before

computers, the internet, and social media," says Cassie.

"How about board games?" suggests Eric.

"Yeah, that's not a bad idea," I reply.

"I can run to my house and grab some board games and bring them over," Eric exclaims.

"It's dangerous out there," says Cassie.

"Maybe Mr. Jenkins has some," I say.

"Why don't you ask him to see if he does?" suggests Nate.

"No way, man. I don't want to get us thrown out," I reply.

Ethan walks back into the room. "What are you guys talking about?" he asks.

"We're trying to figure out who is going to ask Mr. Jenkins if he has any board games," Nate replies.

"That's easy. Send Cassie. He seems to like her," says Ethan.

"Yeah, Cassie, you go! He does like you better than the rest of us," I say.

"Me! Why me?" she asks.

"Because he likes you, and he's not going to throw us out if you do it. Just go down the basement stairs and call his name. That way, he won't say that we were snooping around."

Cassie gets up and begins walking towards the kitchen. She turns around and looks back at us. "I'll do it, but if this backfires, it's on you guys."

She continues to the top of the stairs, sticks her head into the basement, and shouts, "Mr. Jenkins, Mr. Jenkins, Mr. Jenkins!"

She backs away from the stairs slowly, and a few moments later, Mr. Jenkins steps out of the basement.

"Mr. Jenkins," she mutters, "we were wondering if you have any board games that we can play while we wait for time to pass."

"Sorry, Cassie! Unfortunately, I don't have any board games."

"Oh, do you mind if a few of us go to our houses to get a couple to bring back? It will help us pass the time."

"It's probably not a good idea because it is hot, and a lot is going on out there."

"We'll be careful."

"I don't want you kids getting into any trouble out there."

"We won't. We will be as careful as possible,"

"Well, it sounds like your mind is already made up. Go, but be careful out there. People act crazy during times like these."

Mr. Jenkins turns to us and asks Cassie, "Which one of these guys do you think is the most responsible?"

"Well, Lance is the captain of the football team," Cassie replies.

Mr. Jenkins walks into the living room, and he stares at us. "Now, which one of you is Lance?"

"I am, sir!"

"Come here, Lance."

I get up and walk to Mr. Jenkins. He lifts his shirt, reaches around to his back, pulls out a revolver, and holds it in front of me.

"She tells me you're the captain of the football team."

"Yes, sir!"

"Now, it's crazy out there, and I want you kids to be safe." He walks towards me and hands me the revolver. "This is not a toy. It is dangerous. It is only for your protection out there in case something happens. Take it!"

"I've never held a gun before."

Mr. Jenkins places the gun into my hand.

"If anything happens, you can lift it, point it, and pull the trigger. Now, stick it into your pants and cover it with your shirt

CHAPTER FOUR

I slowly reach for the gun and then stop midway, hesitating to take it. *This is surreal. Has it really come to this? Mr. Jenkins is overreacting.* I look at Cassie and then at Nate and Ethan. None of them see a problem with Mr. Jenkins handing a gun to a bunch of kids. *This is not normal. Then again, nothing that's happening is normal.* I reach out and take the gun. I look at it for a brief moment, and then I tuck it into my waistband.

"Come on, guys. Let's go."

Ethan, Eric, and Nate stand up, and we head to the door.

"I'll stay with Jeremy," says Cassie.

"Now, you boys, be careful out there, you hear me?"

"Yes, sir!" we reply.

Mr. Jenkins unlocks and opens the door for us to leave. We step out one by one, into the blistering heat. While we were in Mr. Jenkins's house, it has become hotter, way hotter. The heat is difficult to explain unless you've been in a hot sauna before. The heat is intense; it makes you feel like you want to rip your skin off. We're already sweating, but we just step outside. The sweat pours down our faces. Mr. Jenkins locks the door behind us.

"Come on, let's hurry up and do this," I say.

We walk down the street in the direction of Ethan and Eric's house. Many of the homes and cars that were on fire earlier are still in flames. We've been at Mr. Jenkins's place for a few hours, but the streets have erupted into pure chaos. Many of the homes are being looted, and people are running up and down the streets with all kinds of things in their arms. I did not think it was this bad out here. In just a matter of hours, things have gotten out of control. We rush to Twin and Evil's house as fast as we can, not wanting to spend too much time on the streets.

"Thank God no one broke into our house," exclaims Ethan.

"How long do you think until they break into all the homes?" asks Eric.

"Eventually, they're going to run out of supplies," I reply. "They're going to get them any way they can. You can never tell."

Ethan and Eric go into the house while Nate and I stand outside, looking around.

"I wish my house hadn't burned down," says Nate. "I could use my bike to get around quicker."

"That's a great idea! I have two bikes at my house. We can stop by there and pick them up when we're done here."

Ethan and Eric walk out of the house with their backpacks strapped to their backs.

"Why don't we just stay here?" asks Eric.

"Do you see what's going on in the streets?" I say. "It's safer to stay at Mr. Jenkins's place for now. He has that shotgun in case we're attacked."

"What about the gun he gave you? Can't we keep it with us?"

"I don't want to have to use it, and besides, we cannot leave Cassie and Jeremy."

"Ok, but when we leave his house tonight, we're keeping that gun," barks Eric.

"Where are your bikes?" I ask. "We can use them to get around quicker."

"They're in the garage," says Ethan.

"Quick, grab them. I will stop by my house and pick up my bikes."

"I'll get the garage door."

Ethan goes back inside the house and opens the garage door. Eric grabs their bikes and rolls them out of the garage. Ethan closes the garage door and locks it. He comes out of the house, he and Eric hop on their bikes, and we head towards my house. Nate does not look good. He is sad about his house burning. From the look in his eyes, you can see that he is not taking it well. He is probably holding it all inside and not saying anything. I have to get him to talk about it, or he is just going to bottle it up until he explodes.

"I'm sorry about your house, man," I say.

"It's burned down to the ground. I have nothing left. The clothes on my back and this dead cell phone are all I have." Nate looks at me, and he stops walking. "What am I going to do?"

"Look, we're the same size. You can have some of my clothes, and you can stay at my place."

"Thanks, man. I really appreciate it."

We continue walking toward my house. The more we look, the more destruction we see. There is a foul smell in the air. I cannot figure out what the smell is, but it is everywhere. The smell was faint this morning, and now it's potent. Whatever it is, it smells like the smoke is mixed with rubber from the burning houses. I wonder if they smell it or if it is just me. They haven't said a thing about it, but then I realize that I haven't either.

"Do you smell that?"

"Yeah, what is that?" asks Nate. "It is foul."

"A lot of people died yesterday, and with the heat," says Ethan, "their bodies are decomposing faster than usual. What you smell is the smell of death."

"How do you know that?" asks Nate.

"Our mom worked downtown Manhattan, and after 9/11, back when we lived in New York, we went downtown with her once, and the same smell was in the air. That is the only thing it could be. So many people are dead, and it's scorching, so they're decaying faster."

We get to my house, and I open the door. We enter the house, and I turn to Eric and Ethan. "Stay here with the bikes, so no one takes them."

"I'll keep an eye on them," says Eric.

"Do you have anything to drink?" asks Ethan.

"In the basement," I reply. "Bring some up for us too."

I go upstairs to my room with Nate. I take my backpack and empty its content onto my bed. I go into my dresser, grab a handful of T-shirts, and stick them into my bag. I take off my T-shirt and put on a fresh one.

I toss a T-shirt to Nate. "Here, man!"

He changes into the shirt I gave him. We go back downstairs as Ethan comes out of the basement with a stack of water bottles and snacks in his arms. I take some of the bottles and snacks and stick them into my bag. I strap on my backpack, and Nate and I go into my garage. I open the garage door.

"Nate, grab this bike." I push one of my bikes to him, and he takes it out of the garage.

"Do you have another backpack?" he asks.

"Good point. I didn't think about that."

I drop my backpack on the floor and head back into the house. I go upstairs to my room and into my closet. I grab another bag and empty it onto the bed. Then I grab a handful of undershirts and a pair of pants and place them into the bag. I go back downstairs, into the basement, and fill the bag with water and snacks. Then I walk to the turkey fryer and take the thermometer. I go back upstairs and into the garage. Nate has already taken out both bikes.

I toss the backpack to him. "Yo, grab this."

I close the garage door and come around to the front of the house.

"Hey, do you think we should ride around the neighborhood to see what's going on?" asks Eric.

"I don't know if that's a good idea with all the chaos that's going on," I reply.

"We probably should go and see what's happening around the neighborhood, so we know what kind of dangers we're facing," says Nate.

"Ok, but keep an eye out. At the first sign of trouble, we head right back to Mr. Jenkins's house."

We take the bikes and begin to ride around the neighborhood. The scene is the same as we saw before. Homes and cars are smoldering. People are sitting in front of their burnt-out homes with nowhere to go. Still, others look like they have the same radiation sickness that Jeremy has. We continue down towards the main road of the neighborhood, and there we encounter a group of men that we've never seen before. They are shirtless, shouting, and beating on another man in front of his home. This is strange to us; until today, we've never seen anything like this in our neighborhood. But these guys don't live in the area. They are probably out taking advantage of the police being incapacitated. A few members of the group are coming out of the house with jugs of water. They are well-armed, carrying shotguns and handguns along with bats and other blunt weapons.

"Come on!" I say. "We need to get back to Mr. Jenkins's house."

As soon as I say we should leave, the men turn and see us. One of them points at us, and they stop beating the man and turn their attention to us.

"I think they're coming after us. Let's get out of here!" I say.

"Let's get their bikes!" shouts one of the men.

Three of the men take off running towards us.

"Let's get out of here!" I yell.

"You don't have to tell me twice," says Nate.

We turn around and race down the street. As we speed away, the distance between us gradually increases. They eventually give up chasing us. We ride as fast as we can until we reach Mr. Jenkins's house.

"We need to put the bikes in the backyard," I tell the others. "If they weren't looking for them before, they are now."

I make sure we are not being followed. We take the bikes

around back and lean them against the house. I look at Mr. Jenkins's lawn and realize that in just a short time, the grass in the whole neighborhood has died. I reach and touch the leaves on the tree, and they feel brittle, like leaves that have fallen in autumn and dried out on the ground. It's unbelievable what the heat has done in just a day. We walk to the front, and I knock on the door.

"Cassie, Mr. Jenkins, we're back. Let us in."

Mr. Jenkins opens the door with his shotgun in hand. He sticks his head out and looks around before opening the door all the way to let us in.

"Some men are chasing us," Eric says. "They wanted our bikes."

"We saw them beating on people and stealing their things," I say.

"That means it's started," Mr. Jenkins exclaims.

"What do you mean, it's started?" asks Cassie.

"Yeah, what has started?" adds Eric.

"The chaos. Statistically, within fifteen days of a natural disaster, when food and water run out, neighbors will kill each other to get their hands on their resources," Mr. Jenkins explains.

"But it hasn't even been two days," I say.

"Well, the fifteen days is based on a disaster that's happened over time and when people are somewhat prepared for it. In this case, with the system shutting down, no law enforcement, government, or military, it will get bad quick."

"Well, what we saw outside was bad," says Nate.

"In this case, the system shut down without any warning, and no one's prepared. Those who did not have bottles of water or extra food in their homes are now desperate. They've accelerated the fifteen days."

"What are we going to do?" I ask.

"They are breaking into people's homes and taking their things already," says Nate.

"Where are your parents? Were all of them at work when this happened?"

"Yes, we're all alone," replies Cassie.

"It will be better for you kids to stay together in one house when you leave here later. That way, you can help each other out."

"I don't know how much help that's going to be with what's going on out there," I say as I pull the revolver from behind me and hand it to Mr. Jenkins. "Here you go, Mr. Jenkins."

He places his hand over mine. "You hold onto it in case anything happens while you guys are at your house later."

"Please, Mr. Jenkins, can we just stay here for the night?" begs Cassie.

It is now well into the afternoon. Jeremy finally wakes up while Cassie is talking. He is in a daze. I'm not sure he knows where he is or what's happening. "Cassie, Cassie!" he mumbles.

"Jeremy's awake!" shouts Cassie as she runs to his side. "Jeremy!" She kneels down by his side and places her hand on his forehead.

"How are you feeling?"

"I'm thirsty. I need water."

I take a bottle of water from the water cooler, open it, and hand it to Cassie. She takes the bottle and puts it to Jeremy's mouth. Jeremy gulps down the water.

"What happened?"

Cassie strokes his hair away from his face. "You had radiation poison."

"Am I going to die?"

"No, Mr. Jenkins gave you some medicine. You are going to be fine."

"Make sure he continues the medicine around the clock," says Mr. Jenkins. He turns to walk away.

"Yes, sir!" replies Cassie.

Mr. Jenkins stops. He turns around and looks at us. "Now, you kids stay here for the night. I don't want you running around outside with all the chaos."

Cassie gets up. She runs and hugs Mr. Jenkins. "Thank you, thank you, thank you!"

Mr. Jenkins looks at us. Then he raises his hand

uncomfortably and pats Cassie on the back. She lets him go and walks away. He takes a few steps, and then he stops and turns around. "Since you kids are going to be here, you might as well make yourselves useful. Come with me."

"Yes, sir!" we reply.

"Coming!" adds Cassie.

"Well, come on, then."

We follow Mr. Jenkins into his garage, which is full of precut wood, metal gates, and bars. He must spend a lot of time doing this. I guess he has the time since he is retired. Maybe because he lives alone, he needed a hobby, and he does this. I guess there are worse ways of spending your time. He is a man who has seen some horrible things in his life. He survived the Vietnam War.

"We have to fortify the house."

"We have to do what?" asks Nate.

"We're going to use the boards to cover the windows and doors so that it will be harder for anyone to break in."

"What do you need us to do?"

"Do you see the small precut pieces? They are for the single windows, and the wider ones go to the double windows."

"Yes," we reply.

"I need you to place the wood under each window by size."

"We can do that," says Ethan.

We grab the boards and place them on the ground in front of the windows. Mr. Jenkins comes out of the garage with a drill and a box of screws.

"You know that's not going to work, right," says Eric.

Mr. Jenkins presses the trigger, and the drill spins.

"Holy crap, my phone!" shouts Nate.

He reaches into his pocket and pulls out his phone, frantically pushing on the screen. Nate has an obsession with social media. While I wish I could get on social media right now to get news, I know the internet is down, and the phones are dead, so I leave it alone. Nate's unhealthy obsession with the internet, on the other hand, is coming back to bite him. He is desperate for a lifeline to the world. It's only been a day, and he is already desperate; his fixation on his phone may become a problem if they are not able to fix the power and get the internet back up and running.

"Hey, why is my phone still not working if your drill works?" Nate asks.

"My drill was in a Faraday cage, so the electromagnetic pulse did not fry it."

"Oh!" replies Nate. "What's a Faraday cage?"

"I might as well show you since you're going to be here. Gather around," says Mr. Jenkins. "You too, Cassie."

"Yes, sir!" Cassie says, and she walks into the garage.

"How is your brother?" asks Mr. Jenkins.

"He's sleeping."

"All these years, I planned to survive alone during a disaster. I did not expect to have company, so I do not have enough for the long haul with all you kids, but we'll make do."

"How did you know this would happen?" I ask.

"I didn't, but being in the military taught me always to be prepared. I'm letting you kids stay here, but only because I know some of your parents."

"Thank you, sir," I say.

"We'll do whatever you ask," adds Nate.

Cassie jumps and hugs Mr. Jenkins. "Thank you, thank you!" she exclaims.

"I'm taking a leap of faith with you kids, so do not make me regret it."

"No, sir, I promise you won't regret it! Right, guys?" says Cassie.

"Yes."

"Of course."

"Sure thing."

"Ok. It's time to take the survival pledge," says Mr. Jenkins.

"The survival pledge? What is that?" asks Eric.

"Raise your right hand and repeat after me."

We all raise our right hands and repeat the pledge.

"I, your name, pledge to look after each other and to listen to all my instructions. I promise not to tell anyone else about our survival plans. I vow to keep secret everything I know about this house," says Mr. Jenkins.

He lowers his hand, and we lower ours.

"Congratulations. You're now all members of this survival group." He sticks his hand out and shakes each of ours. "Welcome to the team. Congratulations."

He walks into the house. "All right, you all follow me."

We follow him into the kitchen and then down into his basement. He goes over to a light switch and flips it. To our surprise, the light turns on. We look at each other, shocked. This gives me hope that we won't have to live in the dark forever. If he can get his lights to work, the people who do this for a living can get them working again everywhere. I've taken technology for granted; even things as ubiquitous as electricity and light have their limits. I never imagined a day when I would flip on the light switch, and there would be no power to turn it on.

"We have lights, but we can't let anyone else know that we do. If they find out, they will try to take it from us."

"How did you get the lights to work, Mr. Jenkins?" I ask. "I thought the magnetic pulse thing destroyed technology?"

"I'll explain everything in a minute."

We follow Mr. Jenkins to the corner of the basement, where

we saw him coming out of the floor. He sticks his hand under a rug and lifts up a trap door. This is like something out of a movie; I have never seen anything like this. A basement under the basement! He must have seemed crazy to everyone at the time he built it, but now he looks like a genius.

"This is our final solution."

"What do you mean, final solution?" I ask.

"When all else fails, if the house gets broken into or if the security measures fail, this is where we must make it to for safety."

Mr. Jenkins goes down through the door, climbs downstairs, and turns on the light. "Follow me."

We go downstairs. The first room is small, and it connects to two larger rooms. I call it a small room, but it is large enough to have the landing for the stairs and a large desk, and it serves as the hub for the other two rooms. The room is packed with guns, many of which hang on the wall. It also has electronic equipment, along with what looks like a CB radio on a small table. Under the table, there is a bunch of batteries. The walls of the room are lined with rubber on the inside. The smaller of the other two rooms have lots of canned goods, bags of rice, beans, and barrels of water. The third is a bedroom with bunk beds along its walls.

"This room is a Faraday cage," says Mr. Jenkins. "It's encased in metal on the outside and rubber on the inside. When the EMP went off, the metal on the outside absorbed all the energy while the rubber protected everything inside from it, and that is why we have electricity."

"Aren't the batteries going to run out too at some point?" asks Ethan.

"I had solar panels installed on top of the house. I installed the electronics after the EMP storm in the cool of the night. It has been generating power and charging the batteries since the sun came up this morning. I also have a surplus diesel generator that I finished setting up in the other room right before you kids came over."

We go into the other room with Mr. Jenkins, and there is a generator on the floor with a barrel of fuel next to it. A lot of thought went into building this place to make it survivable. *This guy has thought about everything.*

"How is it so much cooler down here than upstairs?" asks Cassie.

"I just turned on the portable air conditioner. It's going to get cooler. We should probably move your brother down here."

He turns and looks at us. "All of you gather around. These weapons are dangerous and deadly. It is important that you all listen to what I am telling you right now because there will be a time when you may need to use these weapons to defend yourselves and protect each other."

Mr. Jenkins takes an assault rifle off the wall and hands it to me. Before today, I only saw guns on television and on police officers, and now I have a revolver strapped to my back, and I'm holding an assault rifle. What else am I going to have to do before the day ends?

"We have two AK-47s and four AR-15s, and we also have an

SKS. Now, assault rifles are used for long-range defense. The three over there are twelve-gauge shotguns. They are compact, portable, and are good for close confrontations. These four on the table are all 9mm semiautomatic handguns. You use those for short- to medium-range defense."

"I don't believe in violence," says Cassie.

"You may not believe in violence, but the person who is coming to kill you will. From what these boys are telling me, they are already out there. So, you best learn how to defend yourself and protect the group."

"Cassie, we all took the oath, and we promised to protect each other," says Nate. "Learning how to use them is part of what we have to do to stay safe. I know you don't like it, but just listen. It doesn't hurt to learn."

"Now, listen to me carefully," says Mr. Jenkins.

He picks up the AR-15. "The .223 rounds for the AR-15 are in the case over here. The AK-47s and SKS use the 7.62 rounds. The shotguns, on the other hand, use these shells. The four handguns use 9mm rounds, which are over there. Now, the revolver I gave you earlier is a .32, and it uses the rounds over there."

Mr. Jenkins shows us which ammo belongs to each weapon. It is our crash course in weaponry. We learn how to load each of the guns and the right terminologies. It is surreal; yesterday, we were playing football, and today we are learning how to load firearms. I take the revolver from Mr. Jenkins and stare at it. *I am not a killer. I cannot imagine or even entertain the thought of killing someone.* At this point, I realize that Mr.

Jenkins is really expecting us to use these weapons to kill people. This is not how I want to start off life. I don't want the deaths of others on my conscience. There has to be a better way of dealing with this. Maybe he can use his radio to find the police or the Army. I refuse to believe that this is what it has come to.

"Mr. Jenkins, is there a way to find out if the police or military is out there to help on your radio?" I ask.

"The Homeland Security Senate Committee has been talking about the disaster that we would face if there were an EMP attack on the US for years. The government chose not to do anything about it. So, no, the police and Army are not coming because they never prepared for this."

We are truly on our own; the cavalry is not coming. What are we going to do?

Mr. Jenkins puts the rifle in my hands and says, "These here are called magazines. They are also called clips. They are interchangeable between the weapons of the same type so that an AK clip will fit in any AK. Same with the AR or any other weapon. Grab me some .223 rounds."

I reach into the case marked ".223," grab a handful of bullets, and place them on the table. "Is this enough?"

"Yes, this will be fine. Now, this is how you load the ammo into the clip. You take one bullet at a time, and you place it on top of the clip and push down like this. It will fall into place like this."

"Do you need to do anything to stop it from falling out?"

asks Eric.

Mr. Jenkins flips the magazine upside down and shakes it. "Once you put one in, it does not come out until you take it out like this." Mr. Jenkins slides the bullet out of the magazine. "Or you fire it."

"So, the only time the bullet can be fired is when it's in the gun?" asks Cassie.

"Or if it comes in contact with fire," replies Mr. Jenkins. "Now, each of these clips can hold thirty rounds. Take a weapon and grab a handful of bullets, and practice loading it. And be sure not to point it at anyone."

We load ammo into the magazines, one at a time, until they are full. We practice inserting the clips into and removing them from the weapons. Mr. Jenkins takes the AK from me. He squeezes the trigger a few times, but the gun does not fire.

"The weapon is on safety. Even with the bullets, it will not fire until you switch the safety off. You do not aim the gun or turn the safety off unless you intend to shoot. These are very dangerous weapons, and they will kill the person you fire on."

"What about the revolver?" I ask. "It does not have a clip like the others."

"Let me see the revolver."

I take the revolver from behind me and hand it to Mr. Jenkins. He takes it, opens it, and pours the bullets on the table. Then he shows us how to load it.

"This weapon holds six rounds, and it does not have a safety, so be careful with it."

Mr. Jenkins shows us how to load each type of weapon. He also shows us where the safety on each is located and how to safely handle the weapons.

"After you load the bullets into the magazine," he says, "you insert the magazine and turn off the safety. You do it like this on the 9mm."

Mr. Jenkins cocks the gun. "Cocking the weapon loads the bullet into the chamber, and it is now ready to fire. Once the bullet is in the chamber, the only way to get it out is to put the safety on, take the magazine out, and cock it again to eject the bullet. The other way is to fire it."

Mr. Jenkins cocks the gun again, and the bullet pops out.

"These are your sights, and you look through them to line up with your target. Once your target is in sight, you fire."

We continue loading the empty magazines while Mr. Jenkins turns on his radio. He puts on his headset, pulls out a notebook, and begins to listen and write. He does this for a while, so we take our time to learn our way around the guns. We pass around the guns to each other to get a feel for them, practicing everything that we are learning.

"We probably should move your brother down here. It is much cooler," I say.

Mr. Jenkins points to Ethan and Nate. "You come here. Take these shotguns. You load them like this. They hold six rounds, and you can place an extra round in the chamber. Keep it with you at all times."

Nate and Ethan pick up the shotguns. They stare at the weapons and examine them.

"Can you guys help me bring my brother downstairs?" asks Cassie.

CHAPTER FIVE

"It's getting late, and it's cooling down," says Mr. Jenkins. "This is a good time for us to head back outside and finish those windows. We need to fortify this place before any of those thugs out there make their way here."

"Ethan, help Cassie get Jeremy downstairs," I say. "Eric and I will help Mr. Jenkins with the windows."

Mr. Jenkins picks up his shotgun, and we go up the stairs. He closes the bunker door behind us. "You always close this door behind you now, you hear."

"Why did you build this place, Mr. Jenkins?" I ask.

"For situations like this. You never know what's going to happen. People thought I was crazy, but my insanity now gives us a place to be safe and ride this out."

"How did you build it under the house?" asks Nate.

"It took me ten, ten long and hard years to get this built. It's my greatest achievement and our salvation."

"Thank you for sharing it with us," says Cassie.

"There's enough food in here to last me six years. With all you kids, we should be good for ten months."

"Maybe when we finish boarding up the windows, we can go to our houses and bring back whatever supplies we can find," I suggest.

We continue up the stairs and into the kitchen. Nate and Ethan head into the living room to get Jeremy. Mr. Jenkins, Eric, and I go into the garage. It is twilight, and the orange glow is more pronounced in the sky.

Mr. Jenkins opens the garage door. "Now, you boys are going to have to work fast, so you get out there and get a move on and do exactly what I tell you,"

"Yes, sir."

"No problem."

"Now, you boys grab that drill and bring it with you."

Eric picks up the drill, and Mr. Jenkins disappears into the garage.

"What you got there, old man?" someone asks.

I walk into the garage, and Mr. Jenkins cocks his shotgun. It's one of the men that we saw looting earlier. He is pacing menacingly in front of the garage with a pocket knife in his hand.

"You best be leaving now," commands Mr. Jenkins.

The looter grins and steps forward slowly. "Do you know how to use that thing, old man?" he asks.

"You take another step, and you'll find out."

Fear shoots through me. The most violence I have ever seen was on the football field. Sure, we are all tough – we were football players – but when you go on the football field, you expect to go home alive; no one is out to kill you. This is different. These are people trying to kill us, and I don't want to get hurt – or to hurt anyone. I cannot stop my hand from shaking. *This is insane.* The fear grips me, and I don't know what to do. It is as if my mind is frozen, and I can't think. I want to talk and tell the man that he does not have to do this, but my lips are stiff. My heart races, and I tremble.

The fear that I'm feeling has never happened to me before. What am I going to do? This is not happening. It's all a nightmare. Mom is going to walk in any minute now and wake me up. Who am I kidding? This is as real as it gets. What should I do? My thoughts are interrupted by the sound of another man, who appears from the side of the house.

"Better drop that, gramps, or I will have to lay you out," says the second looter as he waves his handgun around.

"I'm not going to say it again. You all best be going now," says Mr. Jenkins.

"Woooooo!" taunts the first looter.

As more of them pour onto the yard, Eric walks into the garage behind Mr. Jenkins. I pull the revolver from my waistband. The gun shakes, and I cannot stop my hand from trembling. *I hope they don't see my fear.*

As soon as the thought crosses my mind, one of the looters speaks up. "What do we have here? If it isn't Courage the Cowardly Dog and his crew of misfits," he teases.

The first and second looters laugh.

"You better put that gun down before you hurt yourself, boy," taunts the first looter, inching closer to us. Mr. Jenkins looks at Eric and me. He fires a shot and hits the first looter. He cocks the shotgun and shoots the second thief, who fires a shot as he falls to the floor. The bullet hits Mr. Jenkins in the chest. Mr. Jenkins grabs where he was hit, drops the shotgun, and falls back against Eric. My hand is still shaking, and I cannot raise the gun to help.

"Now, Courage the Cowardly Dog, put down that gun if you know what's good for you," demands the third looter.

I slowly lower myself to the ground to drop the gun. Eric quickly grabs the shotgun and shoots the third thief. The blast from the shotgun causes the looter to fly backward, out of the garage, and he falls on his back. I have never seen someone killed before, and now four people have been shot in front of me. I lay the gun on the floor and stand up. Mr. Jenkins is still alive, but he is in a lot of pain and is losing a lot of blood.

"What are you doing?" shouts Eric. "Pick up the gun!"

More looters are coming towards us with their weapons. They begin shooting into the garage. Eric fires at them, one shot after another, but they continue to come at us. Eric cocks the gun and continues to fire until the shotgun is empty. A bullet hits the wall next to me, and my hand shakes violently. I drop to the ground as bullets hit Eric everywhere. His lifeless body falls to the ground, and the garage door opens.

Ethan steps into the garage and sees Eric on the floor. "Noooo!" he yells.

He fires an AK-47 at the looters. The sound of the AK is deafening, and it shakes me to the core. Right behind him is Nate with a AR 15. He indiscriminately opens fire at the looters as soon as he steps into the garage. I watch several of the looters fall to the ground. *I can't believe this is happening. I have to help.* I pick up the revolver and aim it at one of the looters. I close my eye, turn my head slightly to the side, and squeeze the trigger. After I fire the first shot, I open my eye and continue shooting at the looters. They scatter and runoff. I keep squeezing the trigger, firing all the rounds, and I continue doing so even after the gun is empty, and all of the looters have run off and disappeared. Ethan keeps screaming, firing until his weapon runs out of bullets. He drops his gun and runs to Eric's side.

"Eric, Eric!" he shouts.

He takes his brother by the hand to check on him. Cassie comes into the garage and runs to Mr. Jenkins. He lies there, bleeding out of the side of his mouth.

"Mr. Jenkins, oh my God, Eric!" shouts Cassie. She kneels

next to Mr. Jenkins. "I need something to put under his head."

I turn and grab a pack of bubble wrap that is in the corner next to me. I gently lift up Mr. Jenkins's head and slide the bubble wrap beneath.

"He's not moving," mumbles Cassie.

"Eric's not breathing!" shouts Ethan. "Help me!"

I snap out of it and run over to Eric.

"His heart is not beating. Let me check his pulse."

His eyes are open, but they are lifeless. I place my hand over his chest. I freeze with my fingers on his neck, realizing that my friend, the toughest of us, is dead. I have to tell his brother that he is dead. How do I do that? I don't want to be the one to tell him. I look at the expression on his face, and I see that he knows that his brother is dead. He knows because he is not trying to revive him. But I still have to tell him to confirm what he already knows. *What the hell, man? How the hell is Eric dead? He was supposed to live forever.* Now for the hard part. I have to look Ethan in the eye and tell him his brother's dead.

Ethan begins to cry, and he pounds on Eric's chest. "Wake up, you. Don't do this to us. Wake up!"

I put my hand on his shoulder, and as I stand there, I suddenly go dead to the world. I cannot hear a sound. It feels as if I'm frozen in time, and I cannot speak or move. I can hear my own heart pounding in my chest. I can hear myself breathing, but I feel nothing, not pain, not the scorching heat, not even the sweat that rolls down my face. I stand there without a thought in my mind. My mind has gone blank. I am just staring at the dead bodies. There are no words to describe the gruesome scene. There is blood everywhere. It's hard to explain how I feel right now because I have no feelings, no thoughts.

"Help me!" shouts Cassie.

Her screaming takes me out of my daze. It's the first thing I've heard after checking Eric's pulse. I turn and look. Nate places his weapon down and comes to Eric's side. There is so much blood on the floor that we cannot tell whose blood it is. I lower myself and sit in a dry spot on the floor, and then I place my hands on both sides of my head and hold it.

What are we going to do? I ask myself. Maybe if I had not been so rattled, I could have done something more. This is all my fault. I was not strong enough to protect us, and Eric and Mr. Jenkins paid for it. I cannot go through this. I cannot lose them like this. I have to be strong. What if they come back? I need to be strong. No, I will be strong for them for us.

"We need to go inside," I say. "They will come back, and we cannot be out here when they do." I rise to my feet.

"I'm not leaving him!" says Ethan.

"Come on, man. We have to go back into the bunker," I say. "That's the safest place to be when they come back."

"We can't leave them out here like this," says Cassie.

"Yeah, man, she's right. We can't leave them out here like this," echoes Nate.

I walk over and grab Mr. Jenkins by the arms. "Give me a hand, and let's put them inside the house."

Cassie rises to her feet. Nate walks over to Mr. Jenkins and grabs him by his legs, and we lift him up and bring him into the house. We carry his body into the kitchen and lay him on the floor.

We go back to the garage, and I place my hand on Ethan's shoulder.

"Ethan, let's move him inside," I say.

"Why, why did this have to happen?" asks Ethan.

"I don't know. I don't know," I reply.

"What am I going to do?" asks Ethan. "What am I going to tell my parents about what happened?"

"We can figure that out later, but the one thing we have to do right now is to get into that bunker. Let's get Eric inside so we can close these doors and get to safety."

Ethan stands up and stares at his brother. I grab Eric's body by the arms, and Nate grabs his legs. Eric is much heavier than Mr. Jenkins, so we struggle to get his body inside. We carry him past Ethan, and we bring him into the house. We lay him in the kitchen, next to Mr. Jenkins. Cassie finds a white sheet that she uses to cover their bodies. I go back into the garage for Ethan. He is standing there, staring at the bloody ground where Eric died. I close the outer door to the garage and lock it. I walk over to Ethan, grab him by the arm, and coach him back inside.

"Come on; we have to go inside."

"He's gone. My brother's gone."

"I know, man, I know, but we need to go inside before they come back."

Ethan finally looks up at me, and we go into the house. We go down into the basement and then into the bunker. I close the bunker door and lock the latch, sealing us in. We all walk into the room with the bunk beds, where Jeremy is sleeping. We sit down, but no one says a word for a while.

I start thinking about everything that just happened. *Why are people acting like monsters? How can people be so cruel and evil? Murderers! Where is the police? Where is the Army? Why is there no one to help us? The world is plunging into chaos. People are dying and becoming savages. I cannot let them hurt anyone else. I have to step up and protect my friends.*

I look at my watch and think about what my grandfather would do. He fought in WWII to protect those who could not defend themselves, and now I have to do the same to protect us.

CHAPTER SIX

We are all shell-shocked. We sit there silently, and we do not know how to comfort each other. It's been a couple of hours since we came down here. One thing is for sure, we are not hot down here. Mr. Jenkins's portable AC is keeping us cool. We are sitting on the bunk beds, and at this point, I can't even think of how we're going to move forward. A big piece of our identity was just taken from us. Eric was funny; he kept us laughing when we were bored. He was the enforcer of the group, and now who will play the role.

The eerie silence breaks when Jeremy opens his eyes and sits up. "Hey, what's going on, guys? What's wrong?"

"Hey," says Cassie. She moves closer to her brother and rubs his hair away from his face. "How do you feel?"

"Better. Where are we?" asks Jeremy. "What is this place?"

"This is Mr. Jenkins's underground bunker."

He sits up and looks at everyone.

"What's wrong? why are you guys crying?"

"Looters came by," replies Cassie. She gets on her feet and stands in front of Jeremy. "They shot Mr. Jenkins and Eric. They are both dead."

Cassie sobs and wraps her arms around Jeremy. She hugs him, and he hugs her.

"What? Eric's dead?"

She releases him and sits back on the bed.

"Wasn't it burning hot a while ago? It feels so much cooler now. What happened to the heat?"

"Mr. Jenkins has a portable air conditioner down here," I say.

"I thought the power was out."

"Mr. Jenkins had a cage, umm, umm," says Cassie.

"A Faraday cage," interrupts Nate.

"Yes, Faraday, a Faraday cage. He had all of his equipment and gear protected from the solar flare. So, he was able to put up his solar panels and have power."

"My shirt is drenched, and it smells horrible. I need to go to the house to get something fresh to wear,"

"No, you can't. The looters are probably still out there, and they will be back because we killed some of them."

"You killed some of them! Why?"

"They came to take our things, and Mr. Jenkins tried to fight them off, and they killed him and Eric. We had no choice. You've been asleep for a long time. Everything has gone to hell out there."

"What things were they trying to take?"

"Come here. Let me show you."

I walk into the entrance of the bunker. I pick up my backpack and take out a T-shirt. I walk over to Jeremy and hand him the shirt.

"You can put this on until you get yourself something that fits better."

Jeremy takes the T-shirt, and he changes out of the wet one. His blisters are all but gone, and he looks so much better than he did earlier. He walks over to the weapons, looks at them, and smiles.

"That's an AK-47! Those are AR-15s!"

Nate and Ethan lift up their heads and look at Jeremy.

"Hey, how do you know all of that?" I ask.

Nate gets up and walks over. "Yeah, how do you know that?" he echoes. "*Call of Duty*, right?"

"They have all of these guns in the game. Plus, they have their stats, like the AK weighs six and a half pounds, and it can shoot up to four hundred meters."

Nate smiles and says, "He knows about the guns. He can show us how they work." He slaps Jeremy on the back.

"Ouch!" says Jeremy. "That hurts."

"Ohh, sorry, man. I got excited and forgot."

"What do you know about these guns?" I ask. "Do you know how to use them?"

"I watched a few tactical training videos that teach about the guns and how to use them, but I've only used a paintball gun. I've never used a real gun."

"Mr. Jenkins gave us a crash course, but I want you to teach me everything you know about these guns, and I mean everything. I'm going to kill each and every one of those responsible for my brother's and my family's deaths," exclaims Ethan. "I'm going to kill whoever is responsible for the solar flare."

"I know you are upset right now, but no one is responsible for the solar flare. It was an act of nature," I said.

"Either way, I want you to teach me everything you know about these weapons."

"And you said playing video gamed was a waste of my time," snickers Jeremy to Cassie.

"That's good, Jeremy," I reply. "Once it's safe enough for us to go outside, you'll have to teach us a thing or two about these guns."

Jeremy looks at the far end of the wall. "Ohhhh! An SKS," he exclaims. He walks over to the gun, picks it up, and admires it with awe. "This one is mine."

When he moves the gun, it knocks over a book that was

covering a flat-screen monitor. I notice the monitor has a keyboard and mouse in front of it on the table. I walk over to investigate. *I wonder why he has a computer. He can't get on the internet. Everything is down.* Chances are he won't have anything useful on it since he doesn't play video games. I guess we have to turn it on to find out what's on it.

"Hey, Mr. Jenkins has a computer," I say.

Everyone gathers around me, anxious to see what's on the computer. I guess everyone is thinking the same thing that I am, that this could be a way to the outside. We could be pleasantly surprised to see the internet working or some app that allows us to talk to others. Having a working computer would at least be a familiar scene and a big win for morale right now. I push the monitor's power button. It turns on and displays a feed from security cameras that must be installed around the house because I can see all the rooms in the house.

"So that's how he knew we were snooping," I say. "Hey, guys, come take a look at this."

Everyone is staring at the monitor like they are watching a captivating movie. That's okay because I am too.

"Mr. Jenkins has cameras wired all over the house, inside and outside. We can see everything that's going on."

"Why do the pictures look like that?" asks Cassie.

"It's dark outside, so the cameras are using infrared," replies Jeremy.

Jeremy is in his element; he is made for this. After years of playing video games and watching videos online, he understands this stuff inside and out. I used to think Jeremy was wasting his time playing paintball. I did go with him once, and I did not enjoy it as much as he did. Now he is putting that experience and his knowledge to work for us. Who would have thought that he would become so valuable to us?

"I wonder what else is in this place," I say.

I look at the CB radio. Lights are flickering on it. I move over towards the radio and turn up the volume knob, and to my surprise, we hear a voice on it. I am not sure what to do about it: should I answer, or should I not? We don't know who that is on the other side; is he a friend of Mr. Jenkins, or is he trying to bait us?

"Blue Eagle, come in Blue Eagle. Blue Eagle report," says a voice over the radio.

"Blue Eagle, what is that?" asks Cassie.

"It's a call sign," replies Jeremy.

The voice is the same one that Mr. Jenkins was talking to when we came downstairs looking for him. I remember the call sign, and I decide he is a friend of Mr. Jenkins. *Maybe he can help us.*

"Wait, I heard Mr. Jenkins say, 'Blue Eagle, over and out,' when we came down to the bunker. I believe he's talking to us, or at least Mr. Jenkins, who is probably Blue Eagle," I say.

Cassie grabs the mic and puts it to her mouth. "Hello! Hello! Is anybody out there?"

The voice is still coming over the radio, asking for Blue Eagle to report.

"I don't think he can hear us," I say.

I look at the radio to see why not. There is a switch labeled talk on the front panel, and I flip it on. "Try it now."

Cassie puts the microphone to her mouth again. "Hello, hello? Can you hear us?"

"Loud and clear, Blue Eagle. Where's Jenkins? He missed the last check-in."

"We had some trouble. Mr. Jenkins was shot by looters. He is dead."

"Jenkins is dead?" asks the man. "He told me you kids were at his house?"

"Yes, yes, we are. We are all here, and we don't know what to do."

"What is your sitrep?"

"What's a sitrep?"

"Your situation report, dear."

"There are five of us. Mr. Jenkins and our friend's brother were both shot and killed. We came back into the bunker and locked it."

"You kids did good by coming into the bunker. Now, you kids stay put. Chances are they are going to come back, so stay where you are. You have enough food and water to last a while. Sorry to hear about Jenkins and your friend's brother. Your call sign for your radio is Blue Eagle. Mine is Bird of Prey. Stay put for now, and I will get back to you kids with further instructions."

I look at the monitor, and I see the looters outside of the house. They are all moving in, taking positions around the house with their weapons in hand. We knew that they would come back, and now here they are. I wonder what they are planning on doing? What are we going to do? I need to tell the others the looters are here.

"Hey, guys, look. The looters are back, and they are surrounding the house."

"What are we going to do?" asks Nate.

"Quick, give me the microphone," I say. "Bird of Prey, this is Blue Eagle. Come in."

"Bird of Prey here. What's going on with you, kids?"

"Mister, the looters are back. They've surrounded the house, and we don't know what to do."

"You kids are in the bunker, and it's locked. You'll be safe there as long as you don't open the door."

"What if they find the bunker door? What do we do then?"

"From what Jenkins tells me, the door is well hidden, and it would take a bulldozer to pry it open. They might go through the house and take a few things, but as long as you kids stay down there and keep quiet, you should be fine."

"What if they do find the door, and they do get it open?"

"Jenkins mentioned that there is a trapdoor that leads to his backyard. If that happens, find the trapdoor, and you can use it to escape. Now, sit tight. Bird of Prey out."

The men surround the house, and then they slowly move in closer, signaling each other to take up positions as they creep forward. They do this for a few minutes, and then they stop, pausing for a minute or two as they decide what to do. They eventually raise their weapons and take aim at the house.

"Everyone, we need to keep quiet," I whisper.

They open fire and shoot at it. The gunfire sounds muffled from inside the bunker. We all huddle around the monitor to watch the action outside. The looters fire their weapons indiscriminately into the house, making sure that if anyone were in the house, they would die. *This is insane!* What are they trying to do? What are they thinking? The looters eventually stop shooting, and they slowly approach the house. They enter and search each of the rooms. There are bullet holes everywhere. Luckily, the cameras are mounted high enough that they were not hit. The looters must be thinking that the cameras are not working because they ignore them, and we watch the whole ordeal. We are all nervous when they enter the basement. They open fire in the basement, spraying it with bullets. The sound of gunfire is slightly louder this time, but it's still muffled where we are in the bunker.

They search the basement but do not find anyone. The men walk past the cameras in the basement and ignore them as well.

"They're going to find us!" clamors Jeremy.

"Shhhh!" says everyone.

They move back upstairs and begin to ransack the house, taking whatever valuables they can carry out. They desecrate the house by relieving themselves in any room they can, and then they leave. We all stand at the monitor, watching until they are gone. We all hope that they left, believing that we have abandoned the house and will not return. They leave the house and go back to the front. The looters stand around their dead buddies outside for a few minutes. The one that looks like he may be the leader spits on the ground and walks off. The other looters follow him, and they leave the property.

I stand there, looking at the monitor, not knowing what to do. We are stuck here and have no choice but to stay put. Going out of the bunker will mean we could possibly die from another confrontation with the looters. For the time being, we will have to stay here. I'm hoping that they don't come back, but it makes sense to stay here, at least for a few days, until things calm down out there. I turn to look at everyone, and they all look defeated. Ethan lost his brother, and we all lost one of our best friends and the man who took us in when no one would.

"That was close," I say. "I think they're all gone now. I believe that we're safe for now. They're not going to be back."

"How do you know that? Did you see the crazed look on their faces?" asks Nate.

"They searched the place and took what they think is valuable. They did not find us, so they probably think we left and are not coming back."

As soon as I finish speaking, the looters appear again on the monitor. This time, they are carrying Molotov cocktails.

"They're back, they're back," says Cassie.

"What are they doing?" asks Nate.

They surround the house on every side.

"They are going to burn down the house. We've got to get out of here," says Nate.

They all light their Molotov cocktails, laughing and shouting as they do. We cannot hear what they are saying because the cameras do not have microphones, but we do see the leader's lips moving. I look at the wall and notice a speaker with two buttons. One says talk, and the other listen. I press the listen button to see if we can hear him.

"You should've just given us what we wanted," says the leader. "I know you're hiding in the woods."

"That's right," says another. "Now, we're going to burn your place to the ground."

They all throw the Molotov cocktails at the house. We watch the monitor as the flames rise all over the house. Some of us begin to panic.

"We've got a get out of here," says Nate.

"Yeah, we need to leave while we have the chance," says Cassie.

"We can't leave," I reply. "The looters are out there watching the house, and besides, the Bird of Prey guy said we would be fine down here."

The looters stay outside, and they watch the blaze as the house burns down, drinking and laughing.

"The trapdoor that Bird of Prey was talking about, we could use that to escape," suggests Nate.

"They're in the backyard. They will see us coming out the door if we try to use it," argues Ethan.

"Why don't we ask the Bird of Prey man what we should do," suggests Cassie.

"How is he going to know what to do?" asks Nate.

"Mr. Jenkins has been preparing for something just like this for a long time," I say. "This is why he has the bunker stocked with food and water. They probably have plans in place for things like this, so if anyone is going to know what to do, it could be him."

I take the microphone and switch it on. "Bird of Prey, come in Bird of Prey. This is Blue Eagle."

"Go ahead, Blue Eagle."

"The looters came back, and they just set the house on fire. We can't escape through the trapdoor yet because they are all over the property. What should we do? Over."

"Are you kids still inside the bunker?"

"Yes, sir, we are."

"The bunker is airtight. The smoke and flames will not get to you. Just don't touch the door. It might get hot. Stay put, and you will be all right."

"Ok, we'll stay down here, then, until the fire's over. Blue Eagle out." I turn to the others. "We need to stay put and ride this out. It should be over once all the materials burn themselves out."

"I hope he's right, or else we're all barbecue," says Nate.

It's not hard to see that everyone is afraid, and so am I. My heart is pounding out of my chest. I know their hearts are pounding out of their chests too. I have never been in this much danger, and neither have they. I always expect Nate to make a joke when things are fine, and from his silence, we are in trouble. I have never seen this type of behavior in the civilized world. What the looters are doing is barbaric and inhumane. What kind of people would do these things to others? The looters look like ordinary people; they don't look like killers! *How do I trust anyone else after this? How can we trust anyone?*

We stand there, staring at each other, listening to the raging fire right above our heads. The looters are still outside, firing their weapons into the house and in the air indiscriminately. Now, because of this ordeal, I know there is no police, and any hopes I have of a government being somewhere out there is gone. It is a tough feeling, a different kind of loneliness. It's a feeling of wanting someone that you can't have. I would give anything for someone in uniform to show up right now, anyone.

We stare at the monitors, watching the house burn. The

looters hang around until the very end. The dry air is burning everything quickly. Eventually, the cameras succumb to the fire, and we lose the video feeds one at a time.

"What happened to the video?" asks Jeremy.

"The fire must have burned through the camera or its wires," I reply, "which means the other cameras are going to go as well."

"That means we're not going to be able to see anything that's happening out there," says Nate.

I pick up the microphone and switch on the radio's talk switch.

"Bird of Prey, this is Blue Eagle."

"Go ahead, Blue Eagle."

"Sir, the fire's burning up the cameras. What should we do?"

"Well, there's nothing you can do about that without putting out the fire, and we know how dangerous it is to go outside right now."

"So, we have to let them burn?"

"That's all you can do right now. You know this means that the solar panels and the wiring are going to burn as well. You probably have plenty of batteries and flashlights, but the radios will stop working eventually. We should probably keep the radio and lights off. Use battery-powered LED flashlights so you can have the battery to use the radio when you really need it."

"Thank you, sir. We will stay put and keep the radio off for now." I turn to the group. "We need to look for the flashlights."

As we search for them, Nate reaches for a box under the table, and he pulls out a battery-operated LED lantern. I reach into a plastic storage container and find a bunch of flashlights inside. "Here they are. I found them," I say.

I reach into the container, take them out, and hand them over to everyone. "Now, let's get all these lights off."

We turn off all the lights. The lantern is powerful enough to illuminate most of the bunker, so we put out the flashlights. With everything that is going on, I did not notice that Ethan returned to the room, but now I see that he is sitting on the bed, staring aimlessly at the walls.

We go into the room and sit down after turning off the lights and radio. I sit next to Ethan, and he slowly turns his head to look at me.

"I'm so sorry, man," I say.

I do not know what else to say to him. We all feel horrible. Eric was Ethan's brother, and he gave his life to save us. I cannot begin to imagine how Ethan feels. I do not have any siblings, but they are twins who came into the world together. I do not know what to say or what words I can use to comfort him. It's a bad situation all around, and there's nothing I can do to make things better. I have a sick feeling in my stomach that will not go away, and looking at Ethan is making it worse.

"I can't believe he's gone. We did everything together. We were born together, and now, just like that, he's gone."

"I'm not going to pretend I know how you feel. Eric was your brother. You are going to feel sad; that's part of the grieving process. It was hard when my grandfather passed, but eventually, as time went on, it got easier. In time, you'll be able to cope with it."

Cassie walks over and sits on the other side of Ethan. She wraps her arms around him and lays her head against his arm, but she does not say a word. We all sit there quietly. It is a somber moment, and no one says a thing.

The fire is raging upstairs, right above our heads. The smell permeates the air all around us. An ominous feeling grips me, and I know the others feel it too. We have never been together and have nothing to say to each other. We are a lively group, always teasing and messing around with one another, but at this time and in the present moment, there is nothing to say. Even though we have nothing to say, though, we understand, and we are there for each other.

As time goes on, I realize we have not turned off the air conditioner. It is still draining the batteries, which now creates a new problem. *If we turn off the air conditioner, the bunker will heat up, and if we don't, we will drain the batteries. What do we do? We are going to need the batteries if we want to use the radio again, and from the way things are going, I know that we are going to need it. I need to say something about it.* There is an array of batteries in the room, and they should last a good while. I let some time go by before bringing them up.

"Hey, guys, we have to turn off the AC. It's draining the

batteries."

"If we turn it off, it's going to get hot in here," says Nate.

"Do we have to?" complains Jeremy.

"Yeah, do we?" adds Cassie.

"Yes, we have to. If we don't, the batteries will drain overnight, and we won't be able to use the radio," I reply.

Nate walks to the AC and stands in front of it. "But this feels so good," he exclaims.

I follow him, and I reach for the switch and turn it off. I look around into the supply room and see bottles of water and food. I turn to Nate and wave him over. "Help me with this."

We take some of the bottles of water and packs of freeze-dried foods, and we distribute them to everyone. We're in a daze trying to process what is happening to us. It is surreal; it feels like we just got a punch in the gut. Ethen is in distress, and everyone else is feeling the pain. The pain is unbearable even for me. I keep replaying the whole thing in my head, over and over. What if I'd reacted differently? What if I hadn't frozen? What if I'd fired the gun? Would that have made a difference in the outcome? Would Mr. Jenkins and Eric still be alive? *Maybe I need to sleep; some sleep would do me good right now.*

I lay back on one of the bottom bunks, and I stare at the top bunk above. *Is this my fault? Why did I not do something? Why did I not fire the gun instead of putting it down? Is Eric's death on me?*

My thoughts are interrupted by Ethen when he walks to the front room and shouts, "I can't take this no more; I need to get out of here!"

I get up and follow him. "You heard Bird of Prey; we need to stay down here for as long as possible to let the initial looting and killing end before we can leave.

"What if our parents made it home and they're looking for us? They're going to think something happened to us. It's been weeks, and we have not heard from them."

"Maybe in a couple of days, we can go out and see if any of them made it home. For now, it's safer if we stay here."

"What about my brother? We need to go out there and bury him. We can't leave them like that," says Ethan.

"We will make burying your brother the first thing we do," I reply. "We all want to help bury your brother and Mr. Jenkins, but it's just not safe right now."

"Safe! Safe! Look around you! We're in a dead stranger's bunker, and my brother's body is lying in the open."

"I don't want anyone else to get hurt."

"Who died and made you boss?" Ethan responds. "Out of my way. I'm not leaving my brother out there like that."

He shoves Nate and me out of the way and climbs the stairs.

"Ethan, wait!" shouts everyone.

We try to stop him from opening the trapdoor, but he continues up the stairs. He grabs hold of the trapdoor to open it.

"Ow!" he shouts.

He quickly removes his hand from the door.

"Are you ok?" asks Cassie.

"I burnt my hand. The door is still hot."

He slowly opens his hand. There is already a blister on his palm.

"The fire might still be burning. It's making the door hot," I say.

"That's probably why it's so hot in here," adds Nate.

"The fire should go out when there's nothing left to burn," I say.

"And once the fire stops, we will all go upstairs and bury your brother and Mr. Jenkins," says Cassie. "Come on, sit down over here."

We reassure Ethan, and he comes back into the room.

"This hurts like hell," he says.

"I saw a medical kit in the storage area earlier while I was looking around, and it has burn spray in it," says Jeremy.

He gets up and walks into the storage area. He comes back with the burn spray.

Cassie takes it and walks over to Ethan. "Give me your hand!"

Ethan slowly opens his hand. Cassie takes it and administers the burn spray. "How is that?"

"It feels much better. Thank you."

"What were you thinking?"

"I don't know what I was thinking."

"You were thinking about your brother. It's natural, and I understand. Under normal circumstances, dealing with it is difficult, but these are not a normal circumstance, so we have to be very careful and mindful."

"I'm sorry, guys. I didn't mean to snap like that. I don't even know what I was thinking."

"Don't even worry about it, man," I say. "Just don't do that again. We don't have any doctors around, and it could've been worse."

I can understand Ethan acting irrationally; he is in mourning. He really wants to bury his brother, but he needs to think about his safety right now and how, if he goes outside, he may get us killed too. I lie on the bunk and sigh.

Cassie comes over and sits at the edge of my bed. "Are you ok?" she asks.

"I just need to rest for a little while. I feel a headache coming on."

I lie there and close my eyes. My mind is racing, thinking about everything that is happening. Along with the grief, it's apparent that I am not going to get any sleep. I try to meditate, which works for a little while, but then the thoughts and grief overwhelm me again. I cannot get any relief from the thought that is haunting me. It feels like my mind is working against me; it seems like it wants to keep the horror of the day at the forefront. I have to do something to shake these feelings and stop these thoughts so I can sleep.

I look at my watch, and four hours have passed. I sit up and look around me. By now, everyone is lying down. They are still awake, but no one says a word. I get up and take a bottle of water to quench my thirst. I take the water bottle back to the bed with me, and I lie down.

I wake up the next morning feeling the same. The little bit of sleep did not make the feelings go away. My mouth feels like someone sucked all the moisture out of it. I reach for my bottle of water, and I drink. Everyone else is awake, but they just lie there. It is hot, so we lay there and let the day go by, and yet I find the eerie silence comforting.

The next day is more of the same, and this goes on for days as we cope with our new life. We want to move on, but being stuck in the bunker is a constant reminder of where we are and what we are faced with.

CHAPTER SEVEN

The temperature in the shelter has risen to an uncomfortable level. I roll over to my back and slowly open my eyes. I stare at the top bunk above me with no thoughts on my mind. Amidst the chaos, for a brief moment, I have found peace. I look at my watch. *This can't be*, I think. *It is twelve thirty-three p.m. I slept most of the day away. I guess it's not a bad thing since there is nothing to do anyway.* We've been in this bunker for almost two weeks, bored out of our minds. We've been unable to sleep longer with the heat, and the stress of Eric's death has made it nearly impossible. Last night was the first time we all were able to sleep, and it was welcome.

I lie there and continue staring at the bunk bed. Out of nowhere, my mind is filled with images of Eric and Mr. Jenkins, and now I cannot stop thinking about them. *I need some water.* I prop myself up onto my elbows and look around. Everyone besides Jeremy is still asleep. He has stacked a couple of boxes into a table and is playing a game of connect four by himself. The makeshift table is where we spend most of our time down here. We found some games Mr. Jenkins stashed away in the pantry, and those plus the ones we got our first day here are helping us. I guess he kept them around for when he finally had to come into the bunker for survival. It's odd, though; he had board games no one to survive with. I guess this is why he took us in; after all, who wants to live through the apocalypse alone? I can't imagine anyone being stuck in this heat by themselves. They would probably go crazy. If we had not come across the games, we would have died of boredom.

Turning myself, I sit up and place my feet firmly on the floor. I reach for the water bottle that is next to the bed, open it, and begin drinking. Jeremy looks over at me with a half-smile, which immediately disappears from his face. He pours out the pieces of his game and starts a new one. I get up and slowly walk over to him, drinking my water. I finish the bottle and toss it into a trashcan in the corner of the room.

"Hey, what's up?"

"Nothing, just waiting for you guys to wake up," he says. "I've been awake for a while."

Jeremy came down with something and has been sick. He has been sleeping for almost the whole week. I guess all the time in bed made him restless. As I stand there talking to him, Cassie wakes up. She slowly sits and looks our way. I reach for a bottle of water out of the case next to Jeremy, open the bottle, walk over, and hand it to her.

"Hey, sleepyhead."

She rubs her eyes and asks, "What time is it?"

I look down at my watch. "Twelve forty p.m."

Cassie takes the bottle of water out of my hand. She slowly sips the water, and I sit down next to her.

"It's so hot. This heat is unbearable," she complains.

"I'm just glad we were able to sleep in so late. We won't have to be miserable all day long."

I take off my T-shirt, and it is soaked in sweat.

"That's so unfair. You get to take off your shirts to cool off, and I can't."

Ethan and Nate begin to wake up. They sit up on their beds and then rise to their feet.

"Man, what time is it?" asks Nate.

"Twelve forty p.m., and it feels like a thousand degrees," says Cassie.

"Jeremy, could you get them a couple of water bottles, man?" I ask.

Jeremy leans over the case of water next to him and tosses a water bottle to Nate and one to Ethan.

"What do we do now?" asks Nate.

"Now we wait like we've been doing. It's the only thing we can do," I say. "We have food and water, and we found some games for us to pass the time. We will have to wait here until it's safe enough to go outside."

"We've been down here for almost three weeks; how much longer do we have to wait?" asks Nate.

As the day goes by, we spend our time playing with the board games. We try keeping busy to take our mind off what's going on and to pass the time, but times seem to move ever so slowly, and our days drag on forever. The hours seem to last days, and the minutes feel like hours. We play one game after the next, trying to forget what is happening outside and all around us.

I feel sorry for Cassie; we all have our shirts off to keep us cool, but she does not want to take hers off. I cannot blame her. I guess if I was her, I might not want to take it off either. We did manage to find a bunch of hand towels in the storage area that we soaked, and we use them to keep us cool. Cassie and I wear our towels around our necks, and the others hang them over their heads.

We stacked some boxes together to form a table in between the bunk beds that we use to play the board games. It is as hot as a sauna in the bunker. We are drinking gallons upon gallons of water to keep cool; it is a good thing that Mr. Jenkins has a toilet for us to use. If it were not for the misery of this heat, the bunker would have been a good place to sit out the end of the world. *My gosh, the end of the world, is precisely what this is.*

CHAPTER EIGHT

The heat has been fierce for the past month that we've been in the bunker. It must have reached its peak, as now it is subsiding. It is only cooler by a few degrees, though, so even though it's cooled down some, it's still hot. We decide not to leave the bunker because we just do not want to chance the looters finding us again. We are all bored out of our minds. You can only play these board games for so long before you lose interest, and we reached that point a week ago. And to make matters worse, we still seem to be unable to fall asleep most nights. On the upside, we have been sleeping most of the mornings away. We've been eating freeze-dried steaks and the other food that Mr. Jenkins has down here. It has been a long month, and we have no idea what is going on in the outside world. I want to power up the radio and check in with Bird of Prey to see what he can tell us about what has been going on, but I have not sat at the table with the radio much. I guess it is because I do not want to make myself depressed with a constant reminder of the outside world.

One morning, I walk over to the equipment room, and I notice something that I did not pay attention to before. Under the table is a small electric generator underneath a box. I can't believe I did not pay attention to it before. Mr. Jenkins said he had a generator, and it still did not register. I saw the barrel of gasoline in the supply room, but it did not dawn on me, nor did I remember that Mr. Jenkins had said he'd had one. I pull the box off the generator. It looks like it is already wired to the bunker. I push the start button, and the light on the charging mechanism for the batteries turns on, which means the batteries are charging. The sound of the generator gets everyone's attention. They are all looking at me as they approach the room. I run past them to the portable air conditioner and switch it on. Once it turns on, the questions start.

"What are you doing?"

"I thought we needed to save the batteries. Won't the AC drain them?"

"What are you doing, bro?"

"The heat has finally driven, Sir. Lancelot insane."

The air conditioner is cranking away, and the air is blowing out of it. Cassie rushes over, and she stands in front of me. She lifts her shirt slightly to let the air under it.

"Oh my God, this feels good!" she exclaims.

"I forgot that Mr. Jenkins said he had a backup generator. I just realized that it's been here under the table the whole time."

"You mean we could've had AC the entire time we've been here," said Nate.

"That is crazy. We've been burning down here for a whole month. I can't believe it," said Ethan.

We all gather around the AC to feel the air, which keeps getting colder and colder. Everyone is smiling and laughing. Ethan is the only one not laughing, but he does join us in front of the air conditioner. It's going to take a while for the heat to dissipate, but at least we will not have to suffer it anymore. The constant perspiration and the drinking of the gallons of water are over. Finally, there will be some relief from the misery. Everyone's been on edge, wanting to leave the bunker. Now that we have the air conditioner, it should be easier to convince everyone to stay here, since it's safer.

Maybe in a few days, we can go to our houses to see if there is anything we can bring back to make us more comfortable. I miss my pillow. Maybe we can check on our parents and see if they made it home. Bird of Prey has been telling us to stay put. He said a lot of people are rioting and looting. We are safer in the bunker than in our own homes. We have not spoken to him for over a week, though, and now that we have power, we will be able to contact the outside world more often. We can go to our houses now and get our favorite DVDs and play them on Mr. Jenkins's computer. We will be able to do something other than play board games. The air from the AC is getting cooler. Tonight is going to be a good night; we will be able to sleep well.

We eventually sit at the edge of the bunks closest to the AC, except for Cassie, who stands in front of it.

"Are you going to share any of the air, Cassie?" asks Jeremy.

"I watched you guys walking around shirtless for a month, and now it's my turn to cool off."

"I can feel it cooling down in here already," says Nate.

Cassie flips her hair over and leans forward to cool it off. She eventually sighs, walks to the bunk bed, and sits next to Jeremy.

There's such a happy feeling that night. We are able to get a full night's sleep. We are finally comfortable, and we are enjoying the AC.

When I wake up the next day, the generator is off. I know that it must have run out of gas, so I take some gas from one of the barrels, fill the generator, and turn it on again. We did not lose power to the air conditioner even though the generator was off because Mr. Jinkens's system runs off the batteries when there is no power.

Mr. Jenkins has a small electric stove, and we can use it now to boil water to hydrate the food that we've been eating. I find a pot, and I run an extension cord to the generator. I boil some water and add it to the freeze-dried eggs and rehydrate them. It tastes much better than what we've been eating for the past month. The others begin waking up. Nate comes into the storage room.

"What are you cooking?" he asks.

"Check it out. No more dry food," I reply.

I open a pack of eggs and pour water into it. Then I stick a spoon in it and hand it to Nate. "Try this."

Nate takes the pack and puts a spoonful in his mouth.

"Bro! this taste like eggs."

"I know, right!"

The others wake up, and we all eat breakfast and sit down to plan our day. We decide to take the day and just relax; everyone is happy to eat something that is not dry.

After breakfast, Cassie gives me a long hug and tells me, "Thank you for finding the generator." It feels as odd as the day Nate hit me, and thoughts of her beauty run through my head, but I just shrug it off.

We are all grateful for this reprieve, as we were thinking that we were doomed to the heat. Our spirits are up. We play board games and begin planning for tomorrow when we will leave the bunker to go to our homes. We decide not to call Bird of Prey today; instead, we will call him tomorrow before we exit the bunker. We stay up for most of the night, playing cards and board games. We all pass out and fall asleep one after the other. Cassie sits next to me on my bunk bed, and we both lean back against the wall and talk.

The next morning, I wake up to see that both Cassie and I went to sleep on my bunk bed. She is lying on my chest. I touch her arm, and she feels so soft. My thoughts confuse me. *She smells too good and feels so soft.* I do not know how to handle the thoughts, so I tap her to wake her up. She opens her eyes and looks up at me. We stare at each other briefly, and then I shrug it off and hop out of bed. Everyone else is already awake and eating in the storage room. I walk in and fix myself something to eat. I take a spoonful, and then I notice Cassie staring at me from the other room. I smile at her and then look at my watch. It is after twelve pm.

"We have to call Bird of Prey to find out if things have calmed down," I say.

I walk to the other room, past Cassie, to the cage. I sit down and turn on the radio. Everyone gathers around me. The radio is on, and I flip the talk switch on.

"Hello! This is Blue Eagle. Come in, Bird of Prey."

There is no immediate answer. We all wait with bated breath for a reply, but nothing comes through.

"Are you sure it's working?" asks Nate.

"Yes, it's on, and everything is exactly as it was before. It should be working," I reply.

"Maybe something happened to him, like what happened to us," says Cassie.

"I hope not," I reply. "Right now, he's our only access to the outside world."

"Well, keep trying," continues Cassie.

"Hello, Bird of Prey. This is Blue Eagle. Come in. Bird of Prey, this is Blue Eagle. Come in," I say into the microphone.

I repeat myself over and over again for what seems like

forever, even though it's only a few minutes.

"Maybe something did happen to him," echoes Jeremy.

"No, that can't be," I say. "We need as much help as we can get, and right now, he's all we have, so no, I refuse to believe that he's—"

As I'm speaking, I'm interrupted by Bird of Prey, who comes on the radio.

"This is Blue Eagle," I answer. "Come in, Bird of Prey. This is Blue Eagle. Over."

"Oh, thank my lucky stars you kids are ok. I've been trying to get to you kids for over a week."

"We shut down everything like you said, including the radio, so the battery wouldn't die."

"Well, I wish you kids had checked in sooner so I could have given you an update on the situation."

"What's going on?"

"Well, with the power being out and all, some of the nuclear power plants are going into meltdown, and you're near the Gravel Neck facility. I'm getting reports that it is going critical."

"What does that mean?"

"That means you have to get the heck out of Dodge before the meltdown. It's going to irradiate everything in a fifty-mile radius, which includes the area you're in right now. You have to leave the bunker and seek shelter elsewhere, outside the fallout radius."

"What should we do?"

"Well, pack as much food and water as you can carry, take some weapons and ammunition, and head northwest, away from the plant."

"Northwest to where?"

"Right now, where doesn't matter. You just need to get out of there. Your best bet is to get at least twenty miles northwest, well over the ten miles you need to get out of the fallout radius. But I wouldn't stop there; I would keep going."

"How do we get in touch with you again if we leave the radio behind?"

"My frequency is 2511, and you have my call sign. If you find another radio, let me know if you made it out ok."

"Are you up north?"

"No, I'm in the Midwest, but you need to hurry up. You have anywhere from six to twenty-four hours before this thing goes critical. Go, go, go! Bird of Prey out."

We are all quiet and in shock. We stare at each other without saying a word. In just over a month, the world has been devastated. We thought we had shelter in this bunker to keep us safe from the evil people and to protect us from the elements, but we were wrong. The safety and security we felt down here was just a pipe dream. We have to leave the safety of this bunker, and who knows what awaits us out there. In just a day, we've already seen how people in our neighborhood have become savages, killing indiscriminately, killing without care or remorse. Now we have to head into the heart of the madness, the heart of this burning hell. We just got the air conditioner to work. We just started to cool down. We don't know if we will ever find air conditioning again. Where are we going to live, where will we sleep? There are so many unknowns that I can't possibly think about all of them right now. *We need to go.*

"We need to pack up and get out of here," I say.

"Jeremy and I did not bring any bags with us," says Cassie. "We need to go back to our house and get our bags to pack."

"There are some camping bags in the supply room. I saw them when I found the games," says Jeremy.

"We're going to need to pack as much as we can because we may not get another chance to have food and water for a while once we're on the road," I say.

"We're going to need a change of clothes," adds Cassie.

"Nate doesn't have anything either," I reply. "We can stop by one of the stores in the mall and grab some clothes on our way out of town."

"What about the looters?" asks Ethan.

"It's been three weeks. They've probably moved on already," I reply.

"And if they have not, we shoot first and ask questions later," adds Ethan.

I look up at him.

"Why can't we stop at each of our houses and grab anything that's important to us? This may be our last chance to," continues Ethan.

"Fine," I say. "We'll make quick stops for us to get anything we want to keep, but make sure it's light, and it's able to fit in your bag."

We each grab a backpack and go into the supply room, where we start to pack food, water, and anything else we might need.

"Hey, there are a bunch of sleeping bags in the corner, under the camping bags. We should take some of them too," suggests Jeremy.

"You're right," agrees Nate. "We may have to camp out."

"We should each take one because we never know when we're going to need them," I add.

"Hey, there are more camping bags here," says Jeremy.

"They're bigger than the backpacks and can hold more. We can use them instead."

We each take a camping bag and begin to pack.

"Come on," I say. "Take as much as you can carry without overexerting yourselves."

Mr. Jenkins has a lot of supplies, I think, as I pack. *He was preparing, and he was ready for an extended stay in the bunker. It was as if he knew something like this might happen, that the end of the world, this burning, was coming. He has plenty of freeze-dried food and water and camping and sleeping bags. He also has a lot of snacks to nibble on. This is the perfect place for us to hole up until things calm down, but if we stay, we can never leave again. We will run out of supplies eventually, and the nuclear fallout will make it impossible for us to leave without dying. Just look at all this food. We have all the comforts of home here: a bed to sleep in and water to drink and bathe with.*

We will need to take only the essentials, things that we will need to survive out there. We are not even sure what it is we need to survive, but he has a little bit of everything. I wish we could all stay here and ride this out. What are we going to do? How will we survive out there? Where is my father? I wonder as I look at my watch, rubbing clean the glass with my thumb. *He always knew what to do and had all the answers. I could really use his help right now.*

Look at them. Look at me. We are not prepared for this. A month ago, life was perfect, and now we have to worry about people who are trying to kill us and take what we have. We are forced to carry guns to protect ourselves. Oh my God, I shot someone. At the thought, I drop the package of freeze-dried food I am holding. Terror and dread fall over me as I stand there, thinking about what I have done. *How did it come to this? I was supposed to play college ball. It was not supposed to happen this way. Get a grip, Lance. My friends could die if I am weak. No hesitation. I hesitated, and Eric paid the ultimate price. If I do not protect the rest of the group, his death is meaningless. Eric was so young, and he died too soon. Both he and Ethan had the potential to make it all the way to the pros.*

I will never taste my mother's Key lime pie or her lemonade again. I could use some of her lemonade right now. My mom was the best; she used to make me hot chocolate all the time. I can still remember how she always made a marshmallow face in my cup. I know Cassie and Nate would love to have some too right now. They are like the brother and sister I never had. They love my mother's pie. My dad and I have not been getting along lately. He was putting a lot of pressure on me for school so I could get a scholarship. He loves to hike and go camping, and he's had survival training; he would know what we need to make it out there.

Oh my God, we're all orphans! My seventeenth birthday is in two months, and my parents will not be there to celebrate with me. They will not be there to see me off to college, and now I probably will never go. The world will never be the same. The blue sky is gone, and the heat is unbearable. There is a foul smell in the air, and it's so horrible that you can taste it. We all know what it is. After the first time we discussed it, we haven't mentioned it again. I guess it's too painful to talk about right now. It is a reminder of all the people that we lost.

We have to venture into the world. We were hoping to stay here, hoping to find safety here, a safety that Mr. Jenkins and Eric gave their lives for. We suffered all this loss for nothing. Both Eric and Mr. Jenkins are dead. They gave up their lives for this place. We could have found some solace in being here. We were coping with the understanding that they'd sacrificed their lives so we could be here and that their sacrifice was not in vain. It makes it that much harder to leave this place, knowing that their deaths were meaningless. But they weren't pointless; they died so that we could survive, and we must survive. So much for being captain of the football team! None of that matters now; nothing we did matters. The only thing that matters is that we must survive. We have to make it, and we have to protect each other because we're all that we've got. We need to get out of here. If what Bird of Prey told us is true, we're in a lot of danger as long as we are here. So, we have to get out of here. I don't want to go. I must go.

CHAPTER NINE

Cassie breaks my concentration by tapping me on the shoulder. "Why aren't you packing?" she asks.

I look down at my watch. Fifteen minutes have gone by, and my bag is still empty. I have not collected anything to bring with me on this journey. If we make a mistake and do not take the right provisions, we will not get a chance to come back here. They are just packing anything they can get their hands-on, and I need to stop them and organize this effort. If I don't take charge and help them figure this out, we might have no food or water, only candy bars.

"Hey, guys. We need to make sure that whatever we're taking are things we're going to need. We need to make sure that we have food and water and have room for ammo and weapons."

"Dude, I'm already packed," says Nate.

"What do you have in there?" I ask.

Nate hands the bag over to me, and I pour its contents onto the small table in the supply room.

"Hey, what are you doing?" he asks.

The bag is full of food; he did not pack any water or ammo.

"You only packed food. What are you going to drink? The

human body can survive a month without food, but can only survive three days without water."

"In this heat, I doubt you'll survive a day without water," adds Cassie.

"We have to plan this right. We can't just go out there without the right supplies because we won't survive if we haphazardly throw things together. We each need to carry enough food and water to last at least a week. We're going to have to ration so we won't run out too quickly."

I scan the room, looking at the different types of foods that we have. Mr. Jenkins has freeze-dried meat, vegetables, corn, breakfast, and desserts. The packs are tiny, but when you add water to them, they expand, and one package can become a full meal.

"If we have to walk in the heat, we will need to keep up our energy. We need to pack as much protein as possible. Put as much as you can fit in the bag," I suggest.

I take the freeze-dried foods and pass them around to everyone. "We should pack at least seven breakfast, lunch, and dinner packages. That's enough food for a week."

Nate interrupts. "And take as much of the candy as you can carry."

"Those candy bars are going to melt as soon as we get outside," says Ethan.

"Well, I'm going to eat as much as I can now," Nate replies, and he shoves a candy bar into his mouth.

We continue packing our bags, filling them up with food and water bottles. We are packing more water than food because we will use more water. I'm hoping there is a place out here where we can resupply. If there isn't, we will not last more than a week. As we pack, I notice a set of pots, and it dawns on me that we will need to heat up water to pour into the bags of food. We might need it to boil drinking water if we do not find a clean water source. We have to take some of these pots with us. If we happen to find fresh eggs or meat, we will need the pots and pans to cook them anyway. Some fresh eggs sound good right about now. I've been eating this dry food for so long that I've forgotten what fresh food tastes like. The idea of fresh food is like a distant memory, a mirage that you can't taste or swallow. Now the only thing I can do is hope for a freshly cooked meal. *I need to tell them to pack a couple of pots.*

"Hey, guys, we will need to take a couple of these small pots so that we can boil water for the food. Make sure you pack one."

"Well, what are we going to use for fire?" asks Nate.

I scan the room until I see some bottles of rubbing alcohol. I walk over and grab one.

"Here. We each need to carry one of these. We can use it as fuel to start a fire."

I continue scanning the room, and I see matchboxes stacked underneath the table. I walk over to them. We should have checked the bunker thoroughly, but we were just concerned about food and water. After a month of being here, we still don't know what all is in it. We would have been able to pack quicker if we'd known where everything is. I pick up a box of matches.

"I'll take one of those."

I pass out the boxes of matches, one to each of them. When I move the matches, I expose a box hidden behind them. The box becomes loose and pops open, and it is filled with silver and gold coins neatly packed inside individual plastic cases. I stare at the coins in awe. I had never seen gold coins before, though my grandfather did have silver coins when I was younger. My father stored them in a safety deposit box at the bank after my grandfather died. There is a lot of gold and silver in the box. *We should probably take them with us. Mr. Jenkins would probably not want us to leave them behind since no one will be coming back here for the next ten thousand years.*

"Hey, guys, take a look at these." I place the box on the table. They all walk over to the table and stare into the box.

Jeremy reaches into it. "Cool, gold coins!"

"We all should take some of these with us. We don't know if we'll need money out there. If we need to buy something, we might be able to use these to get it."

"Mr. Jenkins was prepared for anything, wasn't he?" says Jeremy.

We take the coins out of the cases and place them on the table. We count a total of two hundred and twenty silver coins and one hundred gold coins. There is also a certificate in the box that has the value of each of the coins. Each of the silver coins is worth twenty-eight dollars. The gold coins are valued at sixteen hundred dollars each.

"Oh my God, Mr. Jenkins is rich," I say. "According to this, gold is worth $160,000. We're going to have to be very careful out there so that people don't find out we have this much gold, or they will try to steal it."

"Yeah," replies Nate, "we probably should not keep it all in one place. We should put some in our pockets and some in our bags."

We divvy up the coins five ways, putting some of the coins in our pockets and the rest in our bags like Nate suggested. We fill up the camping bags that we found with food and water. The sleeping bags we roll up neatly and attach to the bottoms of the camping bags. I look at my watch again, and it has been almost an hour since we last spoke to Bird of Prey. We need to leave now.

"Hey, guys, we need to leave now, or we will not make it out the fallout zone before the meltdown. We need to choose a weapon and pack ammo for it."

"We can't bring guns outside. The police will arrest us," says Jeremy.

"What police? There are no police. There's no Army, no Air Force, no Marines. There's nothing, nothing," Ethan complains as he snatches an AR-15 off the wall.

Ethan's grief has turned into anger. He is angry at the world; he lost his brother and his best friend in one day. The same disaster took away his parents, and his heart is hardened. I don't know how to address his anger, and it may be a problem, but then again, in this chaos, it may become an asset. It has been a little over a month, and I can't find anything to say or do to help him deal with the grief. For now, I will let him vent before I say anything.

"He's right," I say. "Things are wild out there. We have to be able to protect ourselves."

I put my hand on Ethan's shoulder. "We're going to look out for each other. We're going to make it."

"In that case, I'll take this one," exclaims Jeremy as he picks up the SKS. I take an AK-47.

"You have to carry extra clips with you. We can use the vests over there to put ammunition," says Jeremy.

From under the table, he pulls out a crate filled with clips for the weapons, and he distributes them. "We have to load them now, so they will be ready when we need them," he continues.

Jeremy seems to be in his element. He knows everything about the weapons and how they work. We all listen to him with our full attention as he tells us about our weapons. It has been over a month since we last touched them, but Jeremy has been messing with them every day. He takes the time to explain to us how to use cover so that we have protection when we are being attacked, and he shows us how to use the scopes mounted on the weapons. We are all impressed with Jeremy, and for the first time, I do not hear Cassie telling him to be quiet while speaking. She seems happy that he is contributing to the group. We fill our bags with ammo, and we each take a rifle and a handgun. Mr. Jenkins also has holsters for the handguns, and Cassie grabs the one that straps to her leg. She tries to strap it on, but she can't get it to fit properly.

"Let me help you out with that," I say.

I get on a knee in front of her, loosen the strap, and then fasten it around her legs.

"See, it's not so bad. You just loosen the straps, and it fits perfectly." I look up at her, and she gazes back at me intently. She has never looked at me like this before. It makes me feel a little uncomfortable, so I look back down. I finish strapping the holster on her, and I get up from the floor. I take a holster, snap it to my belt, and place the revolver Mr. Jenkins gave me into it. We finish packing, and I go into the other room. Nate is next to the candy, stuffing a plastic bag.

"Are you sure you can carry all of that?" I ask.

"You're going to be glad I took these when you need a snack."

"We have to go!" I shout.

We gather in the storage room.

"We have to get out of here, but we will need to be sure that it is safe to go out of the trapdoor," I explain.

"I can take point and be the first to go out," says Jeremy. "I'll check and make sure it's safe before anyone else follows."

"No! No way. I will not allow it," scolds Cassie.

"Why not? I spent a lot of time doing things like this at

paintball. I know more about this stuff than any of you, and besides, I'm the smallest and the least likely to be seen."

"I will not let you do it. Mom left me in charge, and I said no."

After Jeremy's close call, Cassie is worried that he might get hurt. It sounds like she is protecting herself from having to feel that way again. Jeremy is right; he is good at this, and we need him now. Cassie has to realize by now we all have to grow up and do things that we would not normally do.

I walk over and place my hand on Cassie's shoulder. "Cassie, I know you're scared, but he's right. He is the smallest out of us and the least likely to be seen."

"He's my brother, and I said no."

"Cassie, I know how you feel," says Ethan, "because I just lost my brother, but Lance is right. Jeremy's better equipped than any of us to go out and see what's going on."

"But I don't want anything to happen to him. I would not be able to take it."

Jeremy moves closer to Cassie and takes her by the arm.

"I can do this. I feel like I have been training for this all my life. I'm just doing some recon. I promise I'll be back."

Cassie grabs Jeremy and hugs him. "You better be, or you're in big trouble."

I walk over to the small trapdoor, which is situated in the back of the supply room. I open the door, and a blast of hot air rushes past me. Jeremy walks past Cassie, Nate, and

Ethan. He leans forward and starts to go through the door.

I stop him by grabbing his shoulder. "Hey, you be careful out there, ok. I want you back here in one piece. Your sister will break me into pieces if you aren't."

Jeremy looks at me and nods his head. He climbs into a small crawl space that stretches for about fifteen yards.

"Now we follow him and wait at the exit for his signal," I say.

I lean over and go into the crawl space after Jeremy. Everyone else follows behind me. When Jeremy reaches the ladder, he takes the bag off and throws the rifle over his shoulder. He climbs the ladder and swings the door open. He sticks his head out of the door, and he looks around. He continues climbing out until he disappears out of the hole.

We all stand around, waiting for him to come back with the all-clear. The anxiety is unnerving, but you can clearly see it on Cassie's face. I look down at my watch, and I notice my hand is shaking. *I have to get myself together.* I hold my hands together, and the shaking stops. Holding the shaking hand, though, is not a solution because, eventually, I have to let it go, and then what? Everyone is going to notice it, but I am not going to let it stop me. I have to make it stop. *Maybe if I take a couple of deep breaths, I will calm down, and it will stop.*

"What's taking so long?" complains Cassie.

"He's okay," I reply. "He's just making sure everything is ok before we go out."

As I speak, Jeremy's head appears above the opening. "You can come out. Everything's fine."

"Are you sure?" I ask.

"Yes, I checked all around the house. It's all clear. There's no one out here."

I take my rifle and hand it up to Jeremy, followed by my bag and then his bag. I grab the ladder with my right hand, place my right foot on it, and then I turn to the others.

"You can hand me your stuff once I get up there."

I climb the ladder and reach outside. I jump out of the mouth of the trapdoor to find the same weird and ominous orange glow in the sky. I look up and quickly place my hand over my eyes to protect it from the blazing sun. The glare is intense. It has been over a month since I last saw the sky. I guess I was hoping that the blue would be there. I suppose it means that our world is changing, and it may be a permanent change. This is going to take some time to get used to. I do not like it at all. I wonder what has changed in the atmosphere to make it orange and what it means for us. Since we are out here now, we will have to figure it out.

"What's wrong with the sky?" asks Jeremy.

"I don't know."

The first of the guns are handed up to us, followed by the rest of the bags. I grab them out of the hole and pass them to Jeremy. Nate's head pokes out of the hole, and he climbs out and joins us.

Cassie sticks out her hand. "A little help."

I take her by the hand, and she climbs out and stands at the mouth of the hole, which is about two feet off the ground.

"Don't let me fall."

"I've got you. Just jump."

She jumps into my arms, and I catch her against my chest. Her face lands on the side of my neck. She pulls away slowly, and I let her down softly to the ground. Then Ethan comes out of the hole. We pick up our weapons and strap on our bags. We look around as we decide which way we should go. The house was burnt to the grown. A once beautiful home is now utterly destroyed. To my shock, the bikes are still in the back; they were not damaged by the fire. They are leaning on the only part of the house still standing, about four feet of wall. I guess the looters were so drunk with rage that they did not pay attention to the bikes. This is good because we need them now. Walking in this heat would not allow us to get to safety.

"Hey, the bikes are still here. They didn't take the bikes," says Nate.

"We will stop at each of our homes to get what we need," I instruct the others. "We will have to move fast. We cannot be out here too long. Each of us will have no more than five minutes to get what we need."

"Hey, how do we know which way to go to get away from the fallout?" asks Nate.

"Good question. We don't have a GPS," adds Ethan.

"I saw an atlas in the basement of my house when we were there," I say. "We can use it to find our way. We'll head to my house first, and then we'll do Ethan and Cassie on our way out."

"Hey, what about you, Nate? You don't need anything from your house?" asks Jeremy.

"My house burned down," replies Nate.

"Come on, let's get out of here," I say.

"Eric's bike is still here," says Nate.

"Don't touch it. Leave it where it is," demand Ethan.

"Hey, wait. I don't have a bike," says Jeremy.

"Ok, change of plans," I say. "We go to Cassie's house first so we can get her and Jeremy's bikes. We'll be a lot faster if they get their bikes first."

"I'll take point," says Jeremy.

"Be careful," says Cassie.

Jeremy takes off to the side of the house, to the end of the bushes, and he peeps around the trees. We all pick up our bikes and proceed behind him. He turns around, and he signals us to move forward. Jeremy cocks his gun and proceeds to walk down the street. He gets to the end of the road and signals us to follow. We turn the corner, and I immediately notice several corpses lying in front of a house. It appears that they have been shot, and their homes looted. To my amazement, Jeremy just keeps going. The devastation outside is much worse than when we first went to Mr. Jenkins's house. There are many more bodies on the street than before. We suck it up and continue walking. We reach

Cassie and Jeremy's house, and we dismount the bikes. We search around the house to make sure it's safe, and then we take up positions outside.

"Ok, you guys have five minutes, so make it count," I say.

Cassie and Jeremy drop their bags and rifles on the ground, and they run into the house while we stand guard outside.

"Nate, Ethan, we need to keep a lookout."

They both nod their heads. We get the bikes and lay them alongside our bags. Nate and Ethan walk to either side of the front of the house to keep an eye out for anyone approaching. I look at my watch, and it is two p.m. *I hope the sun goes down soon*, I think. *It is going to be a long and brutal walk out of here because of this heat. Once we're out of the fallout zone, we should probably travel at night so that we can keep from dehydrated.*

The garage door opens, and Jeremy steps out, rolling out their bikes. The front door opens. Cassie comes out with some fresh clothes on and with a few pairs of jeans and some T-shirts. They both go to their bags and stuff them with their clothing.

"Go and close the garage door," says Cassie.

"It doesn't matter," replies Jeremy. "We're never coming back here anyway."

Frustrated, Cassie walks into the garage. She pulls the door down and comes out through the front door.

"We should be able to move faster since we are all on bikes now. Jeremy, why don't you take point," I say.

We all climb onto our bikes. Jeremy goes to the front of the pack. He gets to the corner, and he slows down. He looks around the corner and signals us to move forward. He does this around every corner until we get to my house. We dismount our bikes in front of my house.

"Jeremy, Ethan, and Cassie watch our backs. Nate, come with me."

Nate and I walk into the house. We make our way upstairs and into my bedroom. I head straight to my dresser, open the drawers, and lay my clothes on the bed. "Grab what you need, man."

"Are you sure? I don't want to…"

"Don't worry about it, man. If you don't take them, they're just going to stay here and go to waste."

We each grab a few pairs of jeans and T's, and we head out. I stop at the door and stare back into the room.

"Let's go, Lance!"

I walk out of the room and go down the stairs. We get downstairs, and Nate walks straight to the door.

"I'll be right out," I say. "I have to get the map."

Nate opens the door and walks out of the house. I stand there momentarily, looking around. *I cannot believe that I will never be able to come back to this house. I've lived here all my life. I've never been away from here for more than two weeks, and now I will never come back here. I still can't believe that this is happening. This is a nightmare, a nightmare that you can't wake up from because you're already awake, and you're praying that you can go back to sleep to forget for a while.*

I go down to the basement and pick up the box of pictures. I take the pictures out of the box, along with my father's map books. We drove to Florida for vacation when I was eleven, and my dad made me his navigator. He taught me how to read the maps. After that trip, my mother bought him a GPS system. My father hated using GPS. Looking back now, I'm thankful I learned how to read these maps because now we will need to know how to use them. I open the book and flip through a few pages.

I walk up the stairs and grab my jeans and T-shirt. As I pick up my clothes, I notice my mom's pen and pad on the counter. I set everything down, walk over, and grab the pen. I write a note to my mother and father that reads, "Mom and Dad, in case you make it here, I'm ok. My friends and I are heading northwest out of town to get away from the nuclear reactor, which is going critical. I love both of you very much." I signed my name at the bottom and added, "P.S. Dad, I have Grandad's watch."

I take another long look at the house before walking to the table. I pick up my things and leave. I look back into the house one last time and then close the door.

"Five minutes, bro. We are on the clock," says Nate as I step out the door.

"I had to get the map book. We will need it to find our way around."

We mount our bikes. Jeremy heads to the front and takes the

lead as we head to Ethan's house. It's a few blocks from mine, so we take one last chance to look around. The neighborhood is devastated. The smell of smoke and the corpses of the dead fill the air, even a month later. As we ride around, the eerie feeling that I felt out here the first day comes back. It feels like danger is right around the corner. Along the way, we take in the sight of the burning homes and some of those that were looted.

We get to Ethan's house, and I automatically take point and go on the lookout. Nate and Jeremy join me, and eventually, Cassie walks to the side of the house to look around back. I leave Jeremy and Nate in the front, walk to my bike, and go into my bag. I retrieve the maps, turning the page to our state, Virginia, then to the county, and then to our township. I look at the map, and I determine where we are located. I begin plotting a route to the highway that we can take to get out of town. I need to find the shortest route out of the city. We have twenty miles to make up on bikes. This would be easy if not for the heat, but now it will be an arduous journey, and any distance I can remove to make it a shorter ride will be worth it. I plot the route we will take; it's longer than twenty miles because it's not a straight shot. As I stand there, figuring out the best way, Ethan walks out of his house and closes the door.

"He's back!" I shout.

They all come over, and I set the map book on top of my bag.

"Ok, we can take this road straight to the highway, and we can ride the highway out of town," I say.

"And where is it that we're going to go?" asks Ethan.

"Anywhere but here," replies Cassie.

"You know, all of the big cities on the East Coast have nuclear power plants," says Nate. "Maybe our best bet is to head northwest like Bird of Prey said, into Pennsylvania."

"He's right," says Ethan. "We should be heading away from the East Coast."

"Bird of Prey said to head northwest. I think that's where we should be going," I add.

"Northwest it is, towards Pennsylvania," says Ethan.

"We need to get on Route 50, to I-81," I tell them. "That will take us to I-68, which should take us away from here. Let's head out."

CHAPTER TEN

We make it safely out of the neighborhood and onto the main road. As soon as we got onto the road, we notice that there are dozens of cars whose windows have been smashed or shot out. There are bodies of people who succumbed to the heat inside some of the vehicles. The further we go, the more devastation we see. It's not until we get to a clearing with a view of the entire neighborhood that we are able to understand the gravity of the destruction. Smoke is still streaming out of homes. The trees are on fire because the leaves dried out from the heat. Survivors are walking about, looking for aid, but there is no help. I want to stop and help, but I know we are on a tight schedule. We have to get out of town, and we have to get to safety.

It's like a war zone out here, I think. The area does not look recognizable. How can we just walk away and leave all these people here to die? We need to say something because I would want someone to say something to me. At least if I say something, they will have a fighting chance.

"Hey, guys, I think we need to tell everyone that the fallout is going to head this way."

"Are you sure that's a good idea?" asks Cassie.

"Would you want someone to tell you if there was danger approaching?"

"You saw how they acted when they killed my brother. Imagine when they find out that they're all going to die."

"How will we live with ourselves if we don't tell them, knowing that all these people could have a chance to make it out but will die?"

I stop my bike and spin it around. I face the crowd and place my hands around my mouth. "Hey, everybody, the Gravel Neck nuclear power plant is going critical. We're all in the fallout zone. You have to get at least ten miles from here to be in the safe zone from the fallout!"

Two men are going from vehicle to vehicle, taking out whatever they can find. They stop and look at me.

"Hey, kid, what did you say?" asks one of the men.

"The nuclear power plant, it's going critical, and we're in the fallout radius. We have to get at least ten miles north of here not to get caught in the fallout."

The men slowly walk towards us. The people who were walking around stop what they are doing and begin walking towards us as well. One of the men pulls out his weapon, and as quickly as he draws it, Jeremy and Ethan draw their rifles and point them at the two men. We just came out of the bunker, it's been less than thirty minutes since we've been out, and already we're facing a conflict.

"Give us those bikes and whatever you got in those packs," says the other man.

I look back at Ethan and Jeremy, and then I look at the two men. I can feel the tension all around, a sense of danger filling the air, an ominous feeling all around. I need to defuse the situation and take control. I need these two to calm down; we don't need a repeat of Mr. Jenkins's garage. The sad thing is that these people have been out here for over a month, trying to survive. Everything they've been through has hardened them. They are on edge, so we need to be careful about how we handle the situation.

"Calm down! There's no need for all of this! I didn't have to tell you a thing. We could have just ridden past and let you die, but we stopped to save your lives. There's no need for this hostility."

"Yeah, but you did tell us. Now, give us those bikes before I take you out of your misery!"

He raises his gun at me, but before the man can finish speaking, gunfire erupts. The man with the gun is shot several times, and he falls to the ground. Before the first hits the ground, the other man is shot as well. The crowd disperses, screaming as they run—my jaw drops in shock. I turn around to see smoke coming out of the barrel of Ethan's gun. Ethan killed the men without giving me a chance to talk them down. What is wrong with him? Did watching Eric's death turned him into a killer? He's changed. I don't know what he is thinking; before Eric's passing, he wouldn't have hurt a fly.

"Why did you do that?" I shout.

"Because he was going to kill you, you fool."

"You didn't know that. We were just talking."

"Mr. Jenkins talked with the looters, and both he and my brother are dead. No more talking. I'm not going to let anyone else die."

He becomes very emotional. I walk over to him, and I take the gun from his hand and hug him.

"It's all right, man. I know, bro, I know."

I get back on my bike, and I turn around to look at the men. The people are still running away and hiding from us. I see the same fear in the eyes of the people that I saw in our eyes when the looters attacked us. Then it dawns on me that to those people, we are the looters. Even though we were defending ourselves, we killed, and that was enough to create fear in their hearts.

We quietly peddle our way down the street. We ride through the carnage without saying a word, taking in the solemn sights. The occasional scream can also be heard as we ride down the street. I am not happy that Ethan shot the men, but in a way, he is right. The look in their eyes was something I have seen before. I came face to face with it when the looters shot Eric and Mr. Jenkins. I did not recognize it standing there then, but now I can see they were out for blood.

The heat is unbearable. We have only gone a few miles, and I am exhausted. Looking at everyone else, they all look exhausted too. I ride up to the middle of the pack.

"Hey, guys, I think it's about time for us to take a rest. I'm exhausted."

"You ain't lying about that," says Nate. "This is the type of heat that even people from Africa won't survive, and I'm black."

Ethan cracks a slight smile, Cassie chuckles, and Jeremy laughs.

"Wow! I don't think I've ever heard you tell a funny joke," I say.

Everyone laughs. We pull over to the far side of the road, take off our camping bags, and reach for our water. I crack open the bottle and slowly sip on the water. It's the best water that I've ever tasted. I'm very thirsty, and it feels good hitting the back of my throat. It has been over a month since the solar flare, and the heat is down significantly, but it is still unbearably hot. The water is warm, but that does not stop us from enjoying it, and it does not stop each of us from finishing the whole bottle.

"Hey, Ethan, you did good back there," says Nate.

"He saved our lives. I thought they were going to kill us," exclaims Cassie.

"But just don't kill everyone we run into," I complain.

We look at each other, and then we chuckle.

"Hey, if we have to do it again, I got your back," adds Jeremy.

I finish my water and toss the bottle aside. I reach into my bag and pull out the map. I go to the page for our area and locate where we are.

"We have another six miles to go before we get to Route 50. We need to get a move on; there's no telling when the plant will go critical."

I close the book and place it into the mouth of my bag. I stand up, grab my bag, and hoist it onto my back. Everyone else gets up and straps on their bags. I pick up my rifle and throw it over my shoulders. We all climb on our bikes and ride down the street in a single file. I can't believe how dry the leaves on the trees are and how brown the grass is. This burning didn't just kill the people, but it killed the plants too. Everything is either dead or dying. We've been on the road for a while now, and what should have been a short, ten-mile bike ride has turned out to be an all-day event. Pedaling too fast would quickly exhaust us, so we haven't been able to get out of Dodge as fast as we wanted to. We have to take it easy, have to ride slow and stop often.

We must have gone at least nine miles since our last stop and are almost at the ten-mile mark, with a few hundred feet to go, moving at a steady pace, when suddenly Cassie's bike begins to fall behind.

"Hey, wait," she calls.

"What's wrong," I ask. I turn around and ride back to her. "Hey, what's up?"

"I don't know. This stupid bike won't move."

I inspect Cassie's bike, and I notice she has a flat rear tire.

"There's the problem."

"What? What is it?"

"You got a flat."

"Damn it!"

Nate walks over. "Hey, what's going on, guys?"

"Cassie's got a flat."

Jeremy and Ethan make their way over. "She's got a flat, man," Nate says.

Everyone looks disappointed. I can understand the sentiment because it seems like someone has it out for us. We thought we would ride our way out of town, but now it looks like we will be walking it. We've come so close, and now this happens to us.

"What are we going to do?" asks Cassie.

"We need to fix the flat," says Jeremy. "We need to find a supercenter. They should have what we need to fix the flat or a new bike."

"There's a supercenter not too far from here," I say. "We can probably walk there in five minutes."

We all hop off our bikes, change direction, and head towards the supercenter. It's a grueling march, and the backpacks feel like they weigh a ton. It makes us exhausted, and we have to rehydrate ourselves regularly. Keeping hydrated also means that we have to get rid of the water we are drinking, so we have to stop often to relieve ourselves. It is a crazy paradox that only a balance temperature will get rid of.

Hey, I have to take a leak," says Ethan.

"Me too," says Nate.

"I have to go too," I reply. "Let's pull to the side of the road, and we can go in the woods."

"I'm not peeing in the bushes," says Cassie.

"If you can wait till we get to the supercenter, you can use the bathroom there," I tell her.

We pull to the side of the road and head to the edge of the woods. We leave Cassie with the bikes and bags, but we take our rifles with us. After taking care of business, we come out of the woods, grab our bikes, and continue walking. We hear gunfire in the distance, and we turn back and look in the direction it's coming from. It persists for a while, but we ignore it and keep walking to the store.

"There it is," says Cassie.

"Yeah, I can see it," adds Jeremy.

We finally reach the shopping center. I look at my watch, and it says four p.m. We have some daylight left, enough to make it out of town before it turns dark so we can find somewhere to rest for the night. As we get near the parking lot, we smell that awful odor in the air again. Inside the parking lot are some dead corpses sitting in their vehicles. It is a painful and uncomfortable sight to look at. These people have been dead for weeks; they died because they had no shelter from the initial flare.

We walk through the parking lot, searching for potential danger as we go, and then we enter the supercenter. The store looks like it has been raided; the supplies are gone off the shelves, and even the soda and juice aisles are empty. It appears that people were taking any type of beverage they could to quench the thirst. We walk around the store, looking for the materials we need to fix the bike. Then we head to the back of the store, going through aisle after empty aisle.

"Oh, the bathroom," exclaims Cassie. She drops her bag

and runs into the restroom.

"Nate, go with her and stand outside the door. Make sure she's safe," I direct.

"Jeremy's her brother. Have him look after her."

"Do you know how to fix a patch?"

Nate lays his bag down. He grabs his rifle and walks towards the restroom. We continue walking to the back to the sporting goods section.

When we get there, we find that it is still stocked with bikes.

"I guess people were not thinking about riding out of town," I say. "Finally, something's going our way."

"We can just get a new bike for Cassie. We don't have to waste time fixing the old one," replies Jeremy.

"Hey, guys, we're in luck," I say. "Look at all these bikes."

"Wow!" exclaims Jeremy. "I only have one thing in mind: an upgrade."

"Hey, we're not here to steal anything."

"Stealing?" replies Ethan. "Look around you."

"We don't have to steal it," says Jeremy. "We have gold, remember."

"Fine," I say, "we'll use the gold to pay for whatever we take."

"Great idea, Lance. Why don't we go pay the invisible cashier?" snickers Ethan.

"We are not thieves. I've never stolen a thing in my life, and I'm not about to start now," I say.

Just then, Nate walks over towards us.

"You're supposed to be watching her."

"Man, she's taking too long."

"Come help us with these bikes."

"Hey, we can all get new bikes," says Nate

"Yes, that's what I just said," replies Jeremy.

"You can take whatever you want, but we're paying for whatever we take," I say.

"Dude, there's nobody here to pay, bro," says Nate.

"Yeah, that's what I said," adds Ethan.

"It doesn't matter," I say. "We are not thieves, so we pay

for what we take. Now, give me a hand with this bike."

Jeremy disappears into the next aisle. While he's gone, we take down enough bikes for all of us. Jeremy comes from the next aisle with boxes of inner tubes, along with two air pumps.

"I found some inner tubes to take with us in case one of us gets a flat again," he explains.

As we're talking, Cassie comes down the aisle. She is followed by two girls, one of whom looks about our age and another who looks about nine or ten years old. The older girl has long brown hair. She wears braces, but they do not take away from her beautiful smile, and her gorgeous figure overshadows any noticeable flaws. She looks like the perfect girl next door. We all stop what we are doing and watch as they come down the aisle towards us.

"Hey, guys!" says Cassie. "This is Taylor and her little sister, Emma."

"Hi!" we all respond.

"They're going to come with us," continues Cassie.

We all look at each other and then look back at Cassie.

"Um, Cassie, can we talk to you for a minute?" I ask.

"Wait right here. I'll be right back," Cassie tells the girls as we walk away.

We turn into an empty aisle and form a circle.

"What are you doing? What do you mean they're coming with us?" I ask.

"Where did they come from?" asks Ethan.

"They were on their way to their aunt's house and stopped here for a few things to take with them when the solar flare hit. They've been here ever since. They were with their mother, shopping. There were a lot of people in the store when they first got here. Some of them died, and they put their bodies in the freezer. Their mother died too."

"We don't know anything about them," complains Ethan.

"Well, she's kind of cute," whispers Nate.

"You know what's about to happen! We can't leave them here to die!" scolds Cassie.

"We don't have time to sit around and debate this," I

respond. I turn around and walk down the aisle.

"Then, I'm staying. You guys can go on without me!" shouts Cassie. "Jeremy, you're staying with me!"

"You can't be serious," I say.

"We're staying where?" asks Jeremy.

"I've never been more serious in my life! I'm not leaving them here to die. I've already told them what's going to happen, and they want to come with us. Either they go with us, or I stay."

I turn around and walk back to Cassie.

"Lance, we probably should take them with us," says Nate. "They seem harmless, and if we leave them here, they are going to die, and besides, they haven't tried to kill us."

"Fine, we'll take them with us," I say, "but if they try anything—"

"They won't," interrupts Cassie.

We go back to the bike aisle, where Taylor and Emma are waiting. The two of them are walking up and down the aisle, looking at the bikes. They stop when they hear us coming, and they turn to face us.

Cassie walks over to them, places her arm around the younger one, and introduces them again. "Guys, this is Emma and her sister, Taylor," she says.

Nate's face is filled with a smile that I've never seen before. He walks over to Taylor and introduces himself. "Hi, I'm Nate." He takes her hand and kisses the back of it. "It's my pleasure to make your acquaintance."

Nate is so stricken that he does not notice when she rolls her eyes and pulls her hand from his.

"And these are my friends, Lance, Ethan, and Jeremy," adds Nate.

"Hi," says Taylor. She moves in closer to us and smiles. "Thank you for taking us with you. Cassie told us about the fallout. We really appreciate it."

"We were getting some new bikes to ride out of here. Can you and your sister ride?" I ask.

"I know how to speak for myself," says Emma. "I'm eleven,

not slow, and yes, I can ride a bike."

"Emma!" scolds Taylor.

"Oh, she told you, man," laughs Nate.

"Jeremy, could you get two more bikes for them?" I ask.

"You're going to need a backpack to carry provisions," says Cassie.

"Hey, while I'm here," says Nate, elated, "I can get some clothing of my own instead of wearing yours."

We disperse into the aisles, looking for things that we need. There's a shelf in the sporting goods aisle that is full of binoculars, and I grab two pairs of the most expensive ones. There are also ropes, along with camping and sleeping bags. I grab two of the camping bags and two sleeping bags.

Nate walks into the aisle. He walks over to me and grabs one of the bags. "Are you changing your bag?" he asks.

"No, this is for Taylor and her sister."

"Good idea. I'll give it to them."

He takes the bags out of my hand and walks off to the other aisle. "Taylor," he shouts.

I follow him into the bicycle aisle. He walks up to Taylor and hands her the bags. "I found these in the other aisle and thought you and your sister could use them to carry your things."

Taylor leans her head slightly to the side and takes the bags from him. "Thank you."

As she walks away, Nate walks over to me, smiling. I look at him and shake my head.

Jeremy comes back to the aisle, and I hand him one of the binoculars.

"Cool, man, where did you find these?"

"I found them down the next aisle. I thought you could use one since you're the official scout."

"Scout!" He smiles and shakes his head.

Everyone begins to regroup in the bicycle aisle. Taylor comes back with clothes for her and her sister, along with a jewelry box, and she packs her bags.

"Too bad there's no more food and water," I say. "We have

to share what we have with them."

Taylor looks up at me. "We have food and water."

"You do!" says Cassie.

"Yes, when people started coming in and taking the food, we stashed away some water bottles in a broom closet, along with some food."

"Well, you're going to need some of that food and water for your bags," I say, "but don't overdo it. You don't want them to be too heavy to carry."

Taylor gets up and heads to the back of the store. Nate follows her. "I'll give you a hand with that," he says.

They disappear into the broom closet. Nate comes back into the aisle with two cases of bottled water. Cassie follows behind him with bags of chips and other snack foods.

"That's it? Is that all you have?" I ask.

"It was a madhouse in here. People were fighting and pushing each other. We're lucky we have this," replies Taylor.

"That's ok," says Nate. "We have enough to share with you, don't we, guys?"

We finish packing our bags until there's no more room left. There is some water bottles leftover on the floor.

"Guys, drink up," I say. "We will need to hydrate before we head back out there."

We drink as much of the extra water as we can.

Jeremy takes a child's trailer and attaches it to his bike.

"What are you doing?" asks Cassie.

"We can carry more things if we use the trailer," he says.

"Great idea, man," says Nate.

"Grab whatever extras we need and put them in the trailer," I direct.

We fill the trailer with the water and the snacks that Taylor had. We also place inner tubes and air pumps for the bike in the trailer. We strap on our backpacks, and we pick up our weapons. Then we all walk towards the door. On my way out of the store, I realize I've almost forgotten something.

"Hold on, guys. I forgot to pay for the things that we have."

"Pay! Who are you going to pay? There's no one here to

pay," says Taylor.

I reach into my pocket and take out two gold coins. I walk to Taylor and show them to her. "We are not thieves," I say. "We pay for what we take."

I walk over to the cash register and lay two pieces of gold on it. Then I walk back to the group.

"We have to get out of here now," I tell them. "If the nuclear plant goes off, we'll be in the blast radius. We need to get a few more miles north in the next hour or so to be in the safer zone. Now, we have enough gold to last us a while. Wherever we go, even if there's no one to take money from us" – I wave a gold coin around – "we pay for what we use. We are not thieves."

We walk out of the store and into the parking lot.

CHAPTER ELEVEN

The road out of town is a long and exhausting one. We leave the supercenter, and after a long walk, we finally make it past the ten-mile mark. A sense of relief overtakes us. We are finally safe, at least from the fallout.

"I think we're here," I say, "but we should probably keep going a little further to be on the safe side."

"I agree," echoes Ethan. "We need to get further away from the fallout zone."

We keep riding well into the evening. Nate rides alongside Taylor and her sister. *I have not seen a smile on his face since the morning the Burning began. He is chatting up Taylor, but I don't think she is into him at all. I don't think I can tell him she's not interested. I probably should tell him, but he looks so happy. He is my best friend; I have to tell him! No, I can't mess it up for him. I'll tell him later. I'll let him enjoy it while it lasts.*

We make it to a police station not too far from the city limits. There are some police cars outside. We stop to get a view of the station.

"Hey, we need to stop at the police station to see if there is anyone there," I suggest.

"It looks deserted," says Cassie.

"Well, let's check it out anyway, just in case."

"Hey, wait," commands Nate as he rolls up and grabs my arm. "I don't know if it's a good idea for us to go in there with these guns."

"Yeah, I think you're right about that one."

"We can stash them in between those cars over there," suggests Ethan.

"Yeah, let's do that," I say.

We move into the parking lot and offload our backpacks and weapons between the cars. At this point, I remember the looters and the people who are trying to take everything from us.

"We can't all go inside," I say. "Some of us have to stay out here to watch the bags."

"I'll stay," Ethan says.

"I'll stay with him," Jeremy adds.

The rest of us offload our bags and weapons, and we head inside. We walk up the stairs and into the station. As we enter, immediately to our left, we see a man handcuffed to a bench. He died from solar radiation. Some of the ceiling tiles were dislodged and have fallen onto the floor. Fluorescent lights are hanging from the ceiling, slightly swaying back and forth. There is a counter towards the right side of the entrance that has three bullet holes in the wall behind it.

We walk by the front desk and go through a set of double doors, where there is an open area with a bunch of desks and offices along the inside of the outer wall. In one of the offices, there is a man with a suit on, sitting in his chair, with his face and arms laid out on the table. We walk closer to him, and we can clearly see that he also suffered from solar radiation. His gun and badge are clearly visible on the side of his belt. We are so busy looking at the scene that we do not notice Emma is hiding her face behind her sister.

"I think she's scared," I say. I lean over so that I'm eye-level with Emma. "It's ok. We're all scared. You can wait outside if you want."

"Yeah, I think you're right. I'll take her outside," Taylor says. She takes Emma by the hand and walks out of the station.

We continue down the room to an opening that leads to a locker room. Cassie is in front, and she enters the locker room before us. She screams.

I step into the locker room, and she plants her face into my chest. I look around the room, and there are seven or eight police officers who were overwhelmed and died from solar radiation. Cassie runs out of the locker room just as Nate enters.

"Come on, man. It doesn't look like we're going to find much help here," he says.

I stand there, looking at the men. Nate turns around to leave the room.

"Wait!"

"There's nothing here, man."

"Their vests. We can use their bulletproof vests."

"What?"

"If Eric and Mr. Jenkins had been wearing vests, they might have survived our encounter with the looters."

"Yeah, I guess so."

"Give me a hand getting the vests off of them."

It's really a creepy sight, but we both suck it up and take the vests off the officers.

Cassie, who seems to have mustered up some courage, walks back into the room. "What are you guys doing?"

"Here, hold on to these," Nate says. He hands her some vests.

"Why are you taking off their clothes?"

"We're not taken off their clothes. These are bulletproof vests, and we need them."

"Why are you taking them off the dead ones? There's a room full of them over there."

Nate and I look at each other and drop the vests that we are holding. We stand up and look at Cassie, and she points at the door. "This way."

We follow her down the hallway and into a second locker room, where there are all types of bulletproof vests and weapons.

We take the vests and sling them over our shoulders. Nate grabs a shotgun, along with an AR-15 and other SWAT gear.

I take a couple of handguns, and I turn to Cassie and Nate. "We should probably get out of here. There's nothing here for us. All the cops are gone. We're on our own."

As we leave the room, we see a holding cell down the hall, in an adjacent room. I notice a hand on the floor, protruding from inside the cell. The fingers are moving.

I turn and tap Nate on the shoulder. "Hey, wait. There's someone alive in the cell."

I rush over to the cell and toss the vest and guns to the floor. There are about five people in the cell. All of them appear to be dead except for the one. Empty bottles of water and food wrappers litter the floor.

"We can help him."

"Do you think that's a good idea?"

"He's in jail," says Cassie. "He must've done something. What if he's a killer or rapist or something?"

"What if he's in here for an unpaid parking ticket? Do you want him to die in here?" I ask. "Come and help me find the keys to the cell so we can help him out."

We go to the front to look for the keys to the cell. We move from desk to desk, opening each of the drawers as we go. Nate disappears into the front entrance and comes back with a set of keys.

"I found them."

We rush to the back to open the cell. We try one key after another until we find the right key for the cell.

I open the cell, and we walk in. I slowly turn the man over. He is severely dehydrated, and his lips are cracked.

"There's a break room in the back. It has plenty of water," Cassie says, and she takes off to the back.

I lift his head and hold him up. Cassie returns with several bottles of water.

"We need to sit him up against the wall. Grab his other arm," I say.

Nate takes his other arm, and we lift him and prop him up against the wall.

Cassie hands me a bottle of water. "Here you go."

I take the bottle, open it, and put it to the man's mouth. "Here's some water. It's ok. We're going to get you the help you need."

"Pour one over his head," says Nate. He takes a bottle, cracks it open, and pours it over the man's head. The man slowly drinks the water, and life begins to return to his eyes. He finishes drinking and tries to talk. His mouth is still dry, so he can only mumble, and we can't understand what he is trying to tell us.

"What did he say?" asks Nate.

"I don't know, man," I reply.

Cassie comes closer to him and places her ears near his mouth. "I think he's saying, 'more.'" She opens the last bottle and puts it on his lips, and he drinks it.

"You're going to be fine."

While we attend to the man, we hear a voice down the hall. "Guys, where are you?" calls Taylor.

"We're back here," says Nate.

As they were waiting outside for us, they must have begun to worry about us, wondering why we were taking so long. She comes to the back and sees us giving the man water.

"What are you guys doing? Who is that?"

"We don't know," I say. "We found him here, and he needed our help. He needs to drink a lot more water so he can recover."

"What are we going to do? We can't leave him here, and we have to get out of here," says Nate.

"We can't leave him here to die," says Cassie.

"We can't take him with us," I reply.

"Why don't we stay here for the night," suggests Taylor. "There's no one here. It looks like it has not been looted, probably because it's a police station."

"We can stay here and head out early in the morning before it starts to get hot," adds Cassie.

"She does have a point," agrees Nate. "We do need to find somewhere to rest for the night, and a police station is probably as safe as we can get."

"Let's get our things and bring them inside," I say.

"We'll be right back, ok?" Cassie says to the man.

As we walk to the front, I see the body in the office and remember that Emma was afraid. "Hey, guys, hold on a second."

I go into the office, drag the corpses to a corner, and place them out of sight.

"What are you doing?" asks Cassie.

"Emma was in here earlier, and she was afraid of the bodies. I'm moving them out of sight. There is a door in the back of the break room. We probably should use that to bring everyone inside. I'll go to the back, and you knock on the door when you're ready to come in. Don't forget to bring my things with you."

Cassie goes to the back of the building, and Nate, Taylor, and I walk out of the front entrance. Ethan, Jeremy, and Emma are standing outside, with the bikes leaning against the cars.

As we walk down the steps, Nate turns to Taylor. "Hey, um, I got this for you." He reaches for an AR-15 that's strapped to his bag and hands it to her. "I'll show you how to shoot it."

Taylor stops, and she cocks the gun. She takes aim and shoots a gasoline can that's sitting on top of one of the police cars. "You mean like this?"

I chuckle.

"Holy crap, where did you learn how to shoot like that?" asks Nate.

"The aunt that we were on our way to see has a farm in

North Carolina. Every year, we spend a few weeks there during the summer."

She throws the weapon over her shoulder and walks away, seemingly annoyed at Nate. He is so smitten by her that he is oblivious to her lack of interest in him.

We pick up our things and go to the back of the police station. As usual, Jeremy takes point, looking around the corner and making sure that there is no one lurking and waiting for us. He signals us to come around, and we go to the door. I bang on it, and Cassie pushes it open. We go inside and head straight into the break area.

By this time, it is dusk. The light that was piercing through the window is all but gone. I go into my bag, take out a lantern, and set it on the countertop. We take the sleeping bags and lay them out in the break room. Jeremy finds food and water in one of the break room cabinets. We take the plastic cups that are on the counter to drink from, and we pick through the food that's on the counter to find something that's still edible. Then we all sit down and quietly eat.

Jeremy gets up and rumbles through the cabinets. He finds a jar of peanut butter and some jelly. He grabs a plastic knife and makes himself a sandwich.

"Don't eat that. That bread is stale," says Cassie.

He bites into the sandwich. "It tastes fine." He walks over to his sleeping bag and plants himself on it. "I don't see anyone making any more bread. What are we going to do when we run out of food?" he continues.

"As long as we keep finding empty places like this one, we can eat and have shelter," says Ethan.

"Eventually, even places like this are going to run out of food," says Nate.

"We'll cross that bridge when we get there," I reply.

"I don't know if you've noticed," says Nate, "but all the trees are dried out. The leaves are falling. The solar flare killed the trees, and that means that no new food is growing out here. We're going to have to figure out how we can stash some food for us to have."

"Remember how scared Nate was when he thought he hurt Lance?" interrupts Jeremy.

"Scared? I wasn't scared. I was concerned about his safety since I hit him so hard, but I wasn't scared."

"What are you guys talking about?" asks Ethan.

"The day that the Burning began," I reply.

"The burning, what is that?" asks Cassie.

"The Burning!" I say, looking around the room. "You know, everything got burned, the Burning!"

"Aw, I get it, the Burning," says Nate.

"So, we're naming the cataclysmic event now?" asks Cassie.

"I don't know, I like it," says Taylor.

"I like it too," adds Nate.

"So, anyway," I continue, "we were playing touch football outside when Nate decided to tackle me and knocked the wind out of me."

"He didn't just tackle you. He knocked you out. You were out cold, man," exclaims Jeremy.

"Which is why I was concerned for his safety," says Nate.

"What did you do that for?" asks Ethan.

"It's a good thing it happened because we took him into the house, and it saved us from being exposed to the Burning," replies Nate.

This is the first time since Eric was killed that I've seen Ethan engaging in conversation. He might have even smiled a little. He lost his brother – not just his brother, but also his identical twin, with him since birth – and he is taking it hard.

"Hey, how did you guys survive the heat," I ask.

"We were in the house. All the lights went out, and the video game too. I thought it was a blackout until we opened the door to go outside, and the unbearable heat hit us. It was a good thing that we had a few bags of ice in our deep freezer that we were able to use to keep ourselves cool. When we finally came out of the house, we bumped into you guys. We didn't know what had happened."

"We spent a couple of days stuck in Lance's basement," says Nate. "The heat was unbearable. I thought I was going to die."

"Yeah, worst two days of my life," I say.

"You're not kidding. The heat was horrible," agrees Cassie.

"Oh, it wasn't bad because of the heat. It was bad because I was stuck with you guys for two days," I say with a laugh.

For the first time in a month, I see smiles on the faces of my friends.

Nate turns and looks at Taylor. "Hey, what about you, Taylor. What's your story?"

"My mom, my sister, and I were on our way to visit my aunt in North Carolina. We spend time there every summer helping her out on the farm. We stopped for Emma to use the bathroom at the supercenter and to get something to drink. That's when... What did you call it again?" asks Taylor.

"The Burning," I say.

"Right, that's when the Burning began. It got scorching hot, so some of the employees had everyone go to the back and into a freezer. It kept us cool for a while, but eventually, it started warming up in the freezer, too, although not as warm as it was outside. Eventually, the next morning, people started getting sick. They grew these boils all over their bodies. My mother got sick too, and by the third day, people began to die. That's when we left the freezer and came to the front of the store. We used the freezer for the bodies of the dead, and by day four, Mom died. After that, the people who were still alive took what they could and left the store. Other people came into the store and took the water and food. We did not know what was going on, and we did not know what to do. We stashed some food and water in one of the broom closets and hid in the bathroom."

"It was really scary," says Emma. "People were fighting for water and food. I thought they were going to kill us."

She begins to sob, and Taylor places her arm around her to comfort her. "It's going to be ok. We're going be fine."

"I miss Mommy. I hate this stupid Burning. It took Mommy away, and I will never see her again."

"Look, we met all these people who are helping us!"

Nate looks at Emma. He gets up, walks over, and sits next to her. "Hey, it's going to be ok. The Burning took away our mothers and fathers too. It changed all of our lives. I know we are not the family you want, but right now, we have each other, a new family. Right, guys?"

"Yes, that's right," says Taylor. "We have a new family now, and besides, Mom would want us to move on, especially with what's going on."

We've all had a bad few weeks, and we are all exhausted and beat. No matter how much we comfort each other, I can see it on all their faces. This is a nightmare that they will not have the luxury of waking up from, and what's worse, it has just begun. We are a new family, forced together by an extraordinary circumstance, forced together by the end of the world, by the Burning. We have to survive. We will need to stick together and protect each other to do it. My thoughts are interrupted by a moan from the man in the cell.

"What the hell was that?" asks Ethan.

"There's a prisoner in one of the cells," explains Cassie. "He's still alive. We gave him some water and tried to help him. It sounds like he's getting better. I'll get him some more."

"Wait, you don't even know who this guy is. Why should we risk our lives to help him? He could be just like the people who killed my brother."

"We can't let him die," replies Cassie. "He's not one of the people who hurt your brother, and besides, he hasn't done anything to try to hurt us."

She gets up and grabs two bottles of water.

"Hold on. I'll go with you," I say. I get up and follow her to the cell.

The man is awake. "More water," he mumbles.

Cassie opens the bottle of water and passes it to me. I crouch down in front of him and put the bottle to his mouth. Enough of his strength has returned that he is able to take the bottle out of my hand and drink.

"What is your name?" I ask.

"Hector."

He finishes the first bottle. "Can I have some more, please?"

Cassie waves another bottle of water in front of him. "Not until you tell us why they have you locked up in here."

"I'll tell you everything. Let me have some more water."

Hector is Latino, but he barely has an accent. His body is covered in tattoos. Judging by his physique, he must work out five days a week. Cassie opens the bottle and hands it to him. He drinks most of the water, and then Cassie takes the bottle from him.

"Easy," I say.

He sits up against the wall and gets comfortable. His throat is still dry, but he starts to talk.

"They picked me up on some bogus charge," says Hector as he pauses to swallow. "All I know is that it got really hot," he says, and then he pauses again. "They were giving us water for a while, but they stopped." Another pause. "A week ago and left these bottles and food you see on the floor for us. We rationed the food and water the best we could, but we ran out. Eventually, they all begin to die until I was the only one left. They never told us what happened."

Hector reaches for the water bottle. Cassie hands it to him, and he finishes drinking it.

I kneel down next to him. "There was a massive solar flare that hit the Earth. It burned up the atmosphere. A lot of people died from the heat and the solar radiation that came with it. It also created an electromagnetic pulse that caused electricity and all technology to stop working. Cars, TVs, cell phones, radios, nothing works."

"So, what's going on out there?"

"We told you what happened," says Cassie. "Now, you come clean about why they arrested you and locked you in here before we close you back in and stop giving you water."

"Ok, ok, calm down. What's wrong with her?"

"You have to understand there's chaos out there, and one of our friends was killed by looters. We need to be cautious. She's only trying to protect the group."

"I already told you. I'm Hector."

"That's your name, but who are you?"

"Does it matter who I am? You saved my life when you didn't have to. Why should I harm you?"

Cassie and I look at each other, and we both know that he cannot be part of our family. He is hiding something, but I understand his reluctance to tell us why he is here. He is a criminal, after all, and he probably thinks it will make a difference in how we treat him if we knew. Knowing what he did won't make a difference, though, because we were not going to let him die. That is not who we are.

"Help me to the bench."

I move the body that was on the bench to the floor, and then Cassie and I help him over to the bench.

"I can hear more people in the back, so I'll stay here, but do me a favor, though. Could you move these guys from in here for me? They're not much for conversation."

Cassie and I grab the bodies by the ankles, and one by one, we drag them out of the cells and into the locker room with the dead officers. I walk to the break room, get water and food, and bring it over to the cell.

"Here, eat up so you can regain your strength. I got you some extra water too."

"Thank you."

I turn to leave the cell, with Cassie in tow.

"Hey, I told you my name, but you haven't told me yours."

"Sorry! I'm Cassie, and that's Lance."

"Well, Cassie and Lance, thank you for saving my life."

We leave the cell and return to the break room.

CHAPTER TWELVE

I slowly wake up to the smell of eggs. I am confused at first, thinking the past month might have been all a dream. It smells like my mother is making breakfast. I close my eyes so the moment will last. On the weekends, every Sunday, my mom makes breakfast. The only time she ever misses making it is when she has the flu. It is a tradition that I become accustomed to. I miss her so much right now, and I wish I could just hold her and tell her I love her, right. I know that our weekend breakfast is a thing of the past, a time that is gone and that I will never get back. *I wonder where the smell is coming from,* I think. I lie there, smelling the food until the reality of the heat brings me back to my senses.

I open my eyes, turn my head, and look at Cassie, who is lying across from me. While the notion of my mother making breakfast is wishful thinking, the smell of the food is real. I hear the sound of a spoon scraping over a pot. I sit up and see Hector standing over the stove, pouring what looks like eggs from one pan to another. The other pan is piled with cooked eggs. I stretch my arms and wipe my eyes. Hector looks over at me.

"Good morning. I couldn't sleep. Cooking helps me relax."

I get off my sleeping bag and walk towards Hector in the kitchen area.

"How did you get the fire going? I thought the gas was out."

"Check it out." He points to a propane tank on the floor next to the stove. "And I found some powdered eggs."

"They have a propane backup! Nice!"

I walk to the table, pull out a chair, and sit down. Hector walks over and sets the eggs and bacon on the table. It is a strange sight, seeing a man like Hector cooking. His lips are cracked, and his skin is still dry from the damage that the heat did to him. *He is fortunate that we came along and found him when we did, or else he would have died. Looking at him now, he seems like an ok guy. I wonder what he did?* There is an aroma coming from the oven. It smells like bread.

"Are you baking something?"

"The cops had a lot of dry food, including flower and dehydrated meat. I am baking some bread and biscuits," says Hector. "Eat up. With all this food I found, I thought we might as well have a fiesta."

The others begin to wake up. They are probably as confused as I am at the smell, waking up to the scent of bacon and eggs. It is a pleasant surprise.

"There are some plates in the cabinet right there."

I walk to the cabinet, grab a stack of paper plates, and set them on the table. I take one of the plates and fill it up with eggs and bacon.

"Oh my God, what is that smell?" asks Cassie.

One by one, everyone wakes up, smelling, and commenting on the eggs and bacon.

"Is that food I smell?"

"Who cooked?"

"That smells so good?"

Nate is the first to the table. He sits next to me and grabs a plate.

"Damn, you cooked all this? Thanks, man."

"Come on, vatos. The food is getting cold. Eat up."

'Who the hell are you?" asks Ethan.

Everyone is up now, and we all sit around the table. Ethan is staring at Hector.

"Guys, this is Hector," I say. "He was the one in the cell. He made us this breakfast."

The ovens timer dings. Hector takes out pans of bread and biscuits. He finishes cooking the meal, and he takes a seat at the head of the table. We fill our plates, passing the eggs bacon around.

"Thanks, Hector."

"Yeah, we appreciate it."

"How did you get the stove working? I thought the gas was out?" asks Nate.

"They have propane, and you kids ask too many questions."

"I don't care how you did it," continues Nate. "I'm just glad you did."

"Yes, thank you, Hector," says Cassie.

We eat the eggs as if it's the first time tasting them. There are smiles all around the table. *In our darkest hour,* I think, *we are able to come together as one, over a meal, to enjoy each other's company once more. If we can come together and do this, then all is not lost. There is hope that the world we knew can continue.* We eat and drink to our hearts' content. The food gives us a sense of community that we have not felt since the Burning began.

I look at my watch, and it is nine a.m. I notice that the temperature has dropped significantly again for this time of day. We've now gone from an average of 115 to what feels like one hundred degrees. *I guess I should be grateful that it is cooling down, but with all this death and destruction, how can I?* I did not say anything to anyone about the temperature.

We sit at the table for over an hour, and I do not want to upset the sense of normalcy they are feeling. We are finally doing something that is familiar. For the first time in a month, we are not thinking about struggling for our lives. Instead, we are all sitting around the table, talking, and enjoying a meal.

"You kids have been out there for the past month?"

"Well, after the second day," I say, "We stayed in a bunker that our neighbor Mr. Jenkins had. Ethan's brother, Eric, was killed by looters, along with Mr. Jenkins. We hid in Mr. Jenkins's bunker for a few weeks, but we had to leave to get out of the fallout zone of the nuclear power plant near us. It went critical," I say.

"Are you saying the nuclear power plants are going critical

and dropping radiation in this area?"

"This area is out of the fallout zone, but there are nuclear power plants all up and down the East Coast, so the further west we go, the safer it will be."

"Hey, maybe we can just stay here for a while since it's out of the fallout zone. We have food and water," suggests Cassie.

"I don't know if that's a good idea," I reply. "We're still dangerously close to the nuclear power plants, so we should keep moving."

"And how do you kids know all of this?"

"Mr. Jenkins's bunker had a ham radio. We used it to talk to a man who talks to other people who had radios across the country," says Nate.

"I thought you said all technology stopped working. How did the radio work?"

"Mr. Jenkins has a Faraday cage that protects the radio and other technology from the EMP. He was a prepper," answers Jeremy.

"A prepper, what is that?"

"A prepper is someone who prepares for disasters like this by storing food and other supplies so they can have them for emergencies," says Jeremy.

"So, why didn't you stay there?"

"We only had three months of supplies for all of us," I say. "Once they ran out, we would have had to come outside, and the radiation would have killed us. That's why we had to leave."

"That's a shame, vatos. It sounds like a good place for you to be right now."

"I know this seems like a good place for us to hole up, but we don't want to be this close to nuclear fallout, so we have to keep heading west. We'll head northwest into Pennsylvania."

"How about we stay put for a couple of days before heading out into this mess again?" asks Cassie.

"This might seem like a safe place for now," I answer, "but the same way we found it, others can find it too. I think the safest thing to do is to keep moving."

"What about the rest of us? What if we don't want to go?" asks Taylor.

"Why don't we put it to a vote?" suggests Cassie.

"Guys," says Ethan, "as Lance said, there could be others who will come and try to take this place from us. And what if the rest of the cops come back?"

I looked at Nate to see if he will back me up, but he is focused on Taylor. His eyes move whichever way Taylor moves. At this point, I think Nate will vote the way she does to get on her good side. I cannot rely on Nate to understand the danger of us staying here.

"All in favor of staying, raise your hand," says Taylor.

Everyone raises their hand except for Ethan and me.

"Hey, why does he get to vote?" asks Ethan.

Hector has his hand up along with everyone else. He puts his hand down and looks at Ethan. "Come on, man. I made breakfast. I think I earned a vote with the group. Besides, it doesn't matter how you vote. I'm staying either way."

"So, it's settled. We're staying," says Taylor.

"Why should we do anything she says? We barely know her," complains Ethan.

"Hey, you leave her alone!" shouts Emma. "My sister knows what she's doing, and she's smart."

"I have to agree with Taylor on this one. No one has come in here. They probably think the cops are still here," says Nate. "Like she said, we have a roof over our heads and food to eat."

I turn to Cassie and look at her. She seems conflicted as to what we should do. She probably feels safe and is content with staying. After all, it was less than an hour after leaving the bunker that Ethan had to kill the men. Under those conditions, anyplace we can lock ourselves in is worth it to her and the others. The danger here is that others will come here for help, just like we did. What if more looters are looking to settle a score with the cops? If they come in here looking for them, we're the ones who will have to face them, and it did not go well the first time we did that.

"I know what you said about not being safe and all, but you know, it's worse out there, and right now, there's no one here to bother us," Cassie finally says.

"Fine, we stay," I reply. "But we need to secure this place and figure out how we will get out of here in case we are attacked. We should make sure our things are packed in case we have to make a quick getaway."

Hector leans back in his seat and turns to me. "So, you're the leader. I can use a man like you. Why don't you stick around and work for me?"

"Work for you?"

"My people are all over this area. With the cops gone, I'm going to run the show."

"The only thing I'm doing is getting my friends to safety. We're heading northwest, and you should probably head west as far as you can to get away from any fallout."

As we speak, everyone begins getting up to pack the sleeping bags and belongings. I get up and do the same. I roll up my sleeping bag and attach it to my backpack. We need to be prepared just in case we have to leave in a rush. We close the locker room door, but the stench of death seeps into the room. I open the windows in the hopes that it will air out the room. They all must be desperate for safety if they are willing to bear the stench to stay here.

"Nate, Ethan, come with me. We have to secure the door in the front office."

Nate and Ethan walk to the front with me. There is a door in the main office that leads to the front entrance, the same one we used yesterday when we came in here. I look around, thinking of a way to block the door closed and prevent anyone from getting in. We have to stop anyone from just walking in to give us time to get away if we need to. I look around, but the only thing I can see that might be useful are the desks. There are desks all over the large room. Some are made of wood, and others are made of metal. I walk over to a metal desk and grab one side with both hands.

"Hey, give me a hand with this. We can use them to block the entrance."

"Yeah, we can stack them, maybe put a couple of rows to make it hard to move," suggests Ethan.

We grab the desks and move them into position, creating two rows. We stack the desks, one on top of the other, in each row.

As I grab the third desk, I see the folder on top of it. The name on it says, "Hector Nunez." I open the folder, and on the first page are mugshots of Hector. I quickly peruse the file. According to his file, Hector was the head of a local street gang that was involved in drug trafficking, racketeering, holdups, and murder. Hector was being held for the killing of a rival gang leader. That is the last thing I want to hear. It's not good news for us; this is probably why he did not want to tell us what he was arrested for. *We are in danger with every second we spend around this guy. I need to tell the others, and we need to get out of here.*

"Hey, guys, come and take a look at this."

Ethan and Eric come over to me. I flip through the file and show them Hector's rap sheet. We go through it page by page, in shock, and we do not know what to say about it. As we review the record, I feel a hand on my shoulder. The hand startles me, and I jump. I turn around, and it is Hector. We are all startled at his presence, especially since we are going through his file.

"Now, you vatos shouldn't be going through a man's private business. What are we going to do about this?"

"Look, man, we didn't see anything," says Nate.

"Yeah, we didn't see anything," I repeat.

"Give me the file."

I close the folder and hand it to him.

"Now, let's keep this between us. The girls, they don't need to know about this, right?"

"No problem. We'll just keep it between us," I say.

"Good man! I really appreciate you vatos not saying anything. You don't want to give them the wrong impression of me, do you?"

"No, you seem like a swell guy," I say.

"And you made us breakfast," adds Nate.

"I made you breakfast, so we're friends, right?" asks Hector.

"Yes."

"Of course."

"Sure, we are."

"As a friend, I'm asking to keep it between us. I don't want Cassie sticking me back in the cell to die."

We chuckle.

"She probably would, too," says Nate.

"So, you vatos understand. Good!"

Hector takes the file folder from me and walks away. We stare at each other until he disappears into the back. All three of us put our hands on the desk and lean over it. We look at each other, and we know this is bad.

"What should we do?" asks Nate.

I lift the desk, and they pick it up with me.

"Nothing right now," I say. "We don't want him to get suspicious. For now, we just play along, and we'll get out of here in the morning."

We move the last desks and finish stacking them.

"Should we tell the rest of them?" asks Nate.

"No, we don't want them acting suspiciously. He'll figure out we told them. For now, we just play along."

Now that we know who Hector is, I think it makes sense why he asked me to work for him. We need to be careful with him because he is a dangerous person. I need to think of a way to get us away from him, but for now, I need to act natural, as if nothing is wrong.

After moving the desks, we head back to the break room and sit at the table. We grab some water and begin drinking.

Moments later, Hector walks into the room wearing a bulletproof vest and holding a shotgun. All of a sudden, he looks very menacing. I don't know if it's all in my head because we just saw his rap sheet or if the feeling is real. Either way, I'm feeling uncomfortable around him.

"Hey, I tell you, these cops have everything. I mean, look at this bad boy."

He cocks the shotgun and smiles a sinister smile, the type you only see on a villain in the movies. Jeremy comes out of the SWAT locker and into the break room. He is wearing a helmet and has a bunch of others in his arms.

"Hey, guys, look at what I found."

Emma looks at Jeremy and shakes her head. "You silly."

"These protect you from getting shot in the head. We should all take one."

"That's not a bad idea, you know. It's extra protection," I say.

The days go by until, one day, we are going through the case files in the cabinet to pass the time, reading one file after another. It is hot, but last night, it was cold. We had just gotten the generator at the bunker working and had a working air conditioner when we left. I did not think I would say this when we were stuck there, but I miss that place.

Hector disappears through an office door. He is gone for a long while, and I begin to get concerned about what he is doing.

"Hey, have any of you seen Hector?" I ask.

"Not since he went through that door," answers Cassie.

"I'll be back."

"Where are you going?" she asks.

"To check on Hector and see what he is up to."

I leave everyone behind and walk into the back room. It is large, with shelves that go from the floor to the ceiling. The shelves are filled with bins and boxes. I walk down one of the aisles, looking at the boxes as I go along. I realize that they are evidence boxes. This room must be the evidence locker, where the police put things that they seize when they arrest people. There are all types of evidence in these boxes. I slide one of the boxes slightly off the shelf and inside is a bloody knife inside of a Ziploc bag. After seeing the knife, my curiosity gets the best of me. I began looking in the boxes, reaching up as far as I can and pulling them off the shelves. It is an intriguing experience. I learn that there are objects that can kill that I never considered before.

Finally, I stop looking at the boxes and walk down the aisle. As I turn the corner, I see Hector taking things out of the boxes and piling them up in a corner. He is collecting all manner of paraphernalia, pills, and other illegal substances. He also has many valuable things in the pile. The world is falling apart, and there are no police officers and no authorities. Men like Hector will stand to profit the most in the chaos. It is not a surprise to see him stealing the evidence since his rap sheet that said he was the leader of a street gang and that he was wanted for a possible murder. I clumsily knock over a folder off the shelf, which disturbs Hector.

"Hey, give me a hand with these boxes," asks Hector.

"I'm not going to help you steal evidence."

"What evidence, man? Do you see any cops and judges around here, man?"

"When they rebuild the government, they might need some of this evidence for trial."

"Wake up, man. This is over. The cops are dead. This is a new reality, the way to survive. I was going to share it with you. I mean, it's only fair, but since you don't want it, I think I'm going to keep it all for myself."

"I don't want to be part of it, and I'm not going to help you with it."

I look at my watch, and it is well past six o'clock in the evening. The time has gone by faster today; we had the files to keep our minds occupied.

Hector looks at my wrist and sees that I have a working watch. He walks closer to me with a smile on his face. "How did you get your watch to work?"

"This watch is my grandfather's. He left it for my dad after he passed away. It doesn't use a battery. It has a mechanical movement."

"Help me look through these boxes for a watch like that. One of these boxes must have a good watch."

Hector grabs a box and tosses it to me, and I catch it.

"Hector, I already told you. I'm not going to help you steal."

"Do you know how valuable a working watch is going to be out here?"

"I'm going upfront. I need something to drink, and besides, it's probably time for us to figure out what we're going to eat."

"I'll make you guys some burgers. We have meat in the freezer. I know it's going bad, but it will do. The deep freezer kept them cool enough to survive."

I leave the evidence room and head back to the central area to rejoin everyone else. They are all in the break room. I can hear their voices coming from the back. I enter the break room, and they are all sitting around the table, playing a board game.

"Grab a seat, man. We were waiting for you," says Nate.

"Where's Hector?" asks Cassie.

"He's in the evidence locker, stealing whatever he can."

I walk to the table, pull out a seat, and sit down.

"He said there's meat in the freezer, and he's going to make burgers."

"Good, I'm starving," says Nate.

"Yeah, me too," adds Jeremy.

They continue playing while I drink my water. Ethan gets up from the table and walks over to one of the cabinets. He grabs a bag of chips and walks back with two paper plates. He pours the chips onto the plates at either end of the table for us to share. Hector walks into the room with about twenty or so wristwatches on both of his arms, from his wrists going up to his forearms.

"Look what I found from a heist!" he says.

"Oh, can I have one?" asks Jeremy.

"Yeah, me too," adds Nate.

"Those are probably the watches from that jewelry store heist," comments Cassie.

"Well, they're all mine now! Here you go, vatos."

He tosses a watch to Jeremy and one to Nate. He has a bag on his shoulder. He takes off all but one of the watches, and he places them into the bag. He walks over to the cabinet in the corner and opens it. He takes out packs of beef patties and raises them in the air.

"These were dehydrated and freeze-dried. They are still good, so tonight, we eat like kings."

I push my chair back, and I stand up. I don't want Hector to gain influence, especially with the others, because they don't know about his criminal past.

"Let us give you a hand with that," I say.

"I got this. I used to work at a place called Pinky Burgers. We had the best burgers in town. Tell you what, you can get the buns ready when the burgers are done."

"How are we going to eat burgers without buns?" I ask.

"Look in the oven," say Hector.

I open the oven and see buns in a pan. He made them when he cooked in the morning. Taylor gets up from the table. "I'll get the buns, Lance. You can sit down. I do need to contribute something."

She goes to the oven and takes out the buns. Hector goes into the cabinet, grabs a couple of pans, and sets them on the stove. Taylor takes out the hamburger buns and sets them on the table. Hector lights the stove and tosses the meat into the pans. He pours water on the meat to hydrate it.

"This is how we did it back in the day." He adds salt and pepper to the meat.

Taylor has a strange look on her face. She sniffs the air and walks over towards the meat. "Is that the meat I smell?"

"The meat is good. I'm going to cook it really well."

"I'm not going to eat that. It smells horrible."

"You better take your time and enjoy it. If that solar radiation killed all the people, it probably killed all the animals too. This may be the last burger you ever have."

"He might be right," I say, "and besides, if he cooks it well enough, it should be fine."

Taylor sets a couple of buns on a plate that she's laid out on the counter.

It is amazing how playing the game takes our focus and our minds off what is going on outside, I think. *I know I wanted to leave, but I am glad that we stayed for the night. For now, we are safe, relatively speaking, of course. I am not sure about Hector, but so far, he has not done anything to hurt us, and he is grateful to be alive. Although he deserves the benefit of the doubt, discovering his past makes it very hard to trust him.*

The smell of the burgers that Hector is cooking makes our mouths watery. Hector was not kidding: he is making those burgers faster than anyone I've ever seen.

He grabs the pan, takes the burgers out of it, and places them on the buns. "Eat up."

We grab the plates and distribute the food. Ethan is frantically looking through the cabinets.

"What's up, Ethan?" I ask.

"Ketchup, I need ketchup."

He opens a cabinet, and he finds a bottle of ketchup. He walks to the table and plasters his burger with it.

"What are you doing, man?" I ask.

"If this is my last burger, I'm going to make sure I enjoy it."

He closes the bun and bites into the burger. Ketchup falls from either side of the burger and hits the plate.

"How does it taste?" asks Taylor.

Ethan's mouth is full, so when he mumbles, we cannot understand what he is saying. He looks like he is enjoying the burger. Taylor, though, is reluctant to bite into hers. I put ketchup on mine and take a bite.

"That's pretty good."

I take another bite. Taylor puts some ketchup on her burger, and then she reluctantly puts it to her mouth and takes a bite. She nods her head slightly in approval and continues eating.

We are enjoying the food so much that we do not notice that Hector disappeared. *He's probably in the evidence locker again.* We sit around the table, playing and talking. The time flies quickly, but we stay up well into the night. At one point, I look over at the corner, and Emma is already lying in her sleeping bag. She looks over at me, and I smile at her. She smiles back at me and turns over in her bag.

"I'm going to turn in. All of those burgers made me sleepy," says Ethan.

"Yeah, me too," says Nate.

"Taylor," calls out Emma.

Taylor turns around and looks at her sister.

"I need the words," Emma continues.

"You told Dad more than a year ago that you didn't need the words anymore."

"I can't sleep. Can you say the words to me, please?"

"What are the words?" asks Cassie.

"My dad used to tuck her in at night, and he would say things like 'don't let the bed bugs bite' and 'have sweet dreams about candy and ice cream' to her."

"That sounds sweet."

"Annoying is more like it."

Taylor takes out her sleeping bag. She lays the bag next to Emma's bag and sits on it. Taylor gently strokes Emma's hair and speaks softly in her ear. I cannot make out everything she is whispering into her sister's ear, but I do hear her say something about having sweet dreams about cupcakes. Moments later, she finishes, and Emma falls asleep. *That was nice of her to help her sister that way.* The thought makes me wish that I had a brother or a sister. *Taylor and Cassie don't know how lucky they are.* I turn and look at Ethan and wonder what is going through his mind. He's just lost his brother, and he is probably not in a good place right now after watching the interaction between Taylor and Emma.

We grab our sleeping bags and lay them in our spots. It has already cooled down tonight. In fact, it is very cool. Until tonight, it has been hot since the Burning began; last night was cooler than usual, but nothing like tonight. We will need to lie in our sleeping bags because of the cold. Hector comes back out of the room with two bags in his hand.

"What you got there?" I ask.

"Nothing much, just a little souvenir."

He grabs a chair from the table and sits down. He leans back, places his feet on the table, and closes his eyes. I turn down the light level of the lantern. I do not know how long it takes, but eventually, I fall asleep.

CHAPTER THIRTEEN

I wake up in the middle of the night, blinded by the moonlight, which is piercing through the window. There's a full moon out, and it is the brightest I have ever seen. I roll over on my back and look at my watch. It is one-thirty in the morning, but I do not feel a bit tired. I guess not doing any physical activity, and the temperature cooling down overnight has raised my energy level. As I lie there, I begin to wonder why it is so cold at night. It's August, and a few days ago, it was too hot to even breathe. I wonder if anyone else is awake. I prop myself up on my right elbow and glance around. They are all asleep. I guess I am the only one who cannot sleep.

As I lie back down, I notice that Hector is not in his seat. Trusting him is difficult to do since I know what kind of a person he is. *He's probably in the evidence locker, stealing again,* I think. *It might be a good idea to go see what he is up to back there.*

I sit up, and that is when I notice that his bags are gone. I get up on my feet, take the lantern off the table, and head down the hall to the evidence locker. I open the door and enter the room.

"Hector!"

The room is completely dark, too dark for anyone, not even Hector, to see in. I walk through the aisles, looking for him, but he is nowhere to be found. Hector has taken his belongings in the middle of the night and left. As I head back to the break room, I notice that he left behind a pile of things that he put together in a corner. *Maybe Hector's coming back*, I think. *If he does return, he might return with members of his gang if they are still alive. Who knows what they are going to do when they do get here? We need to get out of here before he does return! I have to wake up the others.*

I rush back to the break room. I lay the lantern on the floor next to Nate, and I shake him until he wakes up. "Hey, Nate, wake up! Nate, wake up!"

Nate slowly turns on his back and rubs his eyes. He gazes at me and places his hand on my arm. "Come on, man. What time is it?"

"Hector disappeared while we were sleeping, and he may be rounding up members of his gang to come back for the rest of the stuff."

Nate quickly pops out of the sleeping bag, and he sits up. "We need to get out of here."

He turns to Ethan and shakes him. I walk over to Cassie and wake her up. Taylor wakes up from the commotion.

"What's going on?" asks Taylor.

"It's the middle of the night. Why are you waking us up?" asks Cassie.

Nate wakes Jeremy and Emma up. They are all wondering why we are waking them, and I have to tell them why they are being woken in the middle of one of the few comfortable nights they've had since the Burning.

"Hector disappeared," I tell them, "and he may be coming back, and we should leave before he does."

Cassie cocks her head to the side. She looks at me disapprovingly and begins to lie back down.

"I'm going back to sleep," she says.

I walk and stand over her. "You don't know who Hector really is. He is the leader of a street gang, and he was in here for suspicion of murder."

"What?" she shouts. "And you didn't tell us?"

"He literally threatened us if we said anything," Nate explains. "He caught us looking at his file and said not to say anything."

"We did not say anything because we were afraid that your reaction might tip him off that we told you," I add. "We decided to wait because we thought we would be leaving soon. Now we need to get out of here before he comes back."

"He seemed like a nice guy," says Cassie.

"He cooked for us," says Taylor.

"Are you sure you didn't make a mistake?" asks Cassie.

"Yes! He is a criminal who is wanted for murder. So, let's get out while we can."

We pack as quickly as we can, taking whatever we can carry. I take the stack of bulletproof vests and hand one to each of them.

"We need to wear these out there."

As we put on the vests, Emma is just looking at hers. She does not know what to do with it. Nate, who's constantly been trying to get close to Taylor, apparently thinks he can impress her by helping Emma. He walks over and offers to help her put the vest on.

"Emma, do you need some help with that?"

As soon as she hands it to him, Taylor takes it out of his hands. "I got it. Come here, Emma."

The poor guy can't win. He's fallen for her, head over heels, but she doesn't even notice him, or she avoids him whenever possible.

We frantically finish packing and strap on our bags, and as we get ready to leave, Jeremy puts on his helmet. He looks ridiculous because the helmet swallows his head. Jeremy picks up another helmet, walks over to Emma, and places it on her head. He snaps the straps under her cheeks and walks away. Emma is blushing. They have not spoken to each other much since they met, but they are both smiling, and she seems happy to have his help. Maybe Nate could learn a thing or two from him. We take the rest of the helmets and divide them among us.

I did not want to stay at the police station the first night, but it provided us with food and shelter. The time has come for us to leave it behind. I can't help but think, *If we had not found that file on Hector, would we be leaving now? Would I be concerned with him leaving in the middle of the night? It is funny how a little bit of information can change your whole perspective.*

I take out the map book, walk to the table, and set the book in front of the lantern. We all stare at the map, deciding the best route for us to head out of town. We need to find some shelter, but the map is a street map; it's only useful for plotting a route.

"We are near the highway, so we should continue along the same route until we get to it. The highway should take us further away from the East Coast and away from the nuclear plants that are experiencing the meltdowns," I say.

I plot out the route, and to my amazement, they all agree without any objection. I find it somewhat strange since they were all giving different ideas on how to do things earlier. *The only reason I can think for why they agree now is that I warned them not to stay at the police station, and now we have to get away from a crazed killer, a man with a gang of thugs who are probably on their way here right now. What has the world become? It feels like only the scum of the earth survived. Now we are out in the world, just us against the world, with no one we can trust. I long for the days when you could meet someone and establish some level of trust right away. I will have to be more careful with whom I trust.*

After putting the lantern and atlas away, I reach into my pocket and put four pieces of gold on the table. I take out a flashlight, open the door, and we leave the police station. I step outside, and the first thing I feel is a rush of cold air all over my body. We have not been outside for more than a day, and during that time, the temperature has dropped significantly at night. Unfortunately, we are not dressed for the temperature we encounter. We are in T-shirts and jeans. We can probably walk out here for a while, but eventually, our bodies will feel the chill. I don't care, though; I love it. It beats the heat we've been suffering under for over a month, and I know the others feel like I do. *Look at them. They are all happy and all smiles.*

As they follow me into the parking lot, they begin commenting on the temperature.

"It's chilly out," says Cassie.

"It feels good. I prefer this to the heat," I say.

"We're going to need some sweaters," suggests Taylor.

"We're going to have to find a store to get something warm to wear," adds Cassie.

"There are still plenty of clothes left in the store Emma and I were in."

Remembering that we told the people we encountered outside the neighborhood to leave the area, I do not want to turn back and go to the supercenter. If that crowd listened to us, the supercenter might be where they are holing up right now. I don't think it's a good idea to move backward.

"It's probably safer for us to keep going," I reply. "We should be able to find a mall near the highway. It's safer for us to keep moving forward rather than turning back."

We make our way through the parking lot on our bikes and ride out onto the street. The moonlight is intense. The whole street is illuminated by the moon, and the light allows us to navigate without flashlights. I look up, and I see the sky is littered with stars. The brightness of the moon makes it look like twilight when there is enough light that you don't need your headlights to drive. There are so many stars; I've never seen that many before. They are clustered together across the whole sky. *I wonder why the moon is so bright that we can see so many more stars?*

"Taylor, look at all the stars," says Emma.

"I know, and look at the moon. I wonder why it's so clear?" replies Taylor.

"It's probably because the solar flare burned the atmosphere away. That's probably why it's hot in the day, and now it's getting cold at night," says Nate.

"So, you are not just a dumb jock," says Cassie.

We all laugh. Taylor glances at Nate, but she quickly looks away when he notices. I can tell she is impressed with his answer. Maybe she's playing hard to get. *Maybe not.*

It is eerily quiet. The smell of smoke and the stench of rotting flesh fills the air. The further we ride away from town, the less intense the smell becomes. We ride for forty minutes and travel about eight miles by my estimation. We are able to ride much faster than we did in the daytime; the cool of the night keeps us from exhaustion. We don't need to make frequent stops to drink and relieve ourselves.

"Look, there are some stores over there," says Nate.

There is a strip mall not too far from where we are.

"Good catch, Nate. It's not too far. Let's go," I suggest.

We ride the short distance to the shopping mall and pull into the parking lot. We ride through the lot until we reach a sporting goods store. It is nighttime, so we are spared the nauseating and gruesome scene in the parking lot.

"I'm sure we can find something in here," I comment.

We lay our bikes in front of the store and walk to the front door. We are so used to it automatically opening that we stand there, waiting for it to slide open.

"There's no power. The doors won't open," laughs Ethan.

"We should be able to push it open," I say.

Ethan pushes the doors, and they swing open. "After you."

We walk past him and enter the store. I turn on the flashlight, pointing it in different sections of the store as I walk around. The bright moonlight helps illuminates the store.

"Do you see anything?" asks Cassie.

"We need to get to the outdoor section," I respond.

"Over there," says Jeremy.

I aim the flashlight in the direction he's pointing, and we see a section with sweatshirts and jackets. We go over and find it is stocked with coats and other outdoor gear.

"This is it. Grab what you need," I say.

I set the flashlight on top of a rack. Then I walk around, feeling the fabric of the coats.

"What do you think about this one?" asks Taylor.

"I like it," answers Cassie.

I look through the coats and find a red one in my size. I put it on to see if it is a good fit. I look at myself in the mirror and think that it looks good on me.

Jeremy walks over, wearing a green fatigue jacket. He stops and puts on a green fatigue hat. "What do you think?"

He smiles and spins around to show off the jacket. I look down at my brightly colored jacket, and all of a sudden, my choice no longer makes sense. We have to be inconspicuous, and wearing brightly colored jackets will cause us to stand out like a green hat with an orange bill. I can't believe the little guy has the right ideas on this stuff. From now on, I will follow his lead on the survival stuff. I'm not reliable when it comes to those decisions. I hope Cassie is proud of him.

"Guys, Jeremy has the right idea," I say. "We can't wear these noticeable colors. We have to keep a low profile, and bright colors will not help."

"But I like this one," complains Cassie.

"Do you want to be cute, or do you want to be safe?" I ask.

"I like mine too," adds Taylor.

"Walking through the woods with pink on is not much of a camouflage," says Ethan.

"Fine, but you owe me a jacket," Cassie replies.

After talking it over, Jeremy takes us to the rack with the fatigues. There are a few colors to choose from. I try a green one on, but I settle on black. We each select a jacket, and we try them on to make sure they fit. We take hats to match our coats, along with some hooded sweaters. We look like a ragtag band of raiders, but we are ready to conquer the new reality and the elements. We cannot stay in the store too long, though, because, just then, I notice a group of people going into one of the stores across from us. I don't want to take the chance.

"Hey, we have to go."

"Why? I'm not done," replies Cassie.

"Look at the store across from us, people."

It's a group consisting of two women and two men, but it is enough to make us alarmed. I'm uneasy right now. I've never been nervous around people, but this situation has me on edge. Everyone is out for themselves and will kill anyone who gets in their way. It's kill or be killed, and I don't want Ethan to kill anyone else.

"It's probably best that we leave because we don't know what their intentions are."

We put on our jackets and head back outside. Ethan and I go out the door first and safeguard our belongings. We are warm and ready to take on the road out of Virginia. We hop on our bikes and head out of the strip mall. I realize that I did not pay for any of the things we have. *I can't leave without paying for this stuff.*

"Hold on a second," I say. I go back inside, reach into my pocket, and pull out a gold coin. I set it on the cash register and head back outside.

We get back on the road and continue towards our

destination. I start thinking about my reaction to the other people, and then it dawns on me that we are headed into the unknown. Yes, we are leaving behind the desolation and the nuclear radiation that will kill us painfully, but we are also leaving the relative safety and knowledge of our neighborhoods, our home, going into uncharted territory.

An ominous and dreadful feeling washes over me as the realization of the situation sinks in. *We are on a quest into the unknown. What will we find on the other side? Will there be safety, or are we heading towards disaster? We will have to be careful. If what we have seen in our own neighborhood is an indication of what lies ahead, we need to stick together as one and trust no one. Look at them. I wonder if any of them have thought about this. I wonder if they have thought of the dangers that are lurking and waiting ahead of us.*

It all feels surreal. I cannot shake my sense of dread, a fear of the unknown.

"Why is it so cold?" asks Emma.

"It's the middle of summer, and we're wearing coats," says Nate.

"I heard what you said earlier, Nate, but this is not adding up," adds Ethan.

I begin to wonder how the temperature went from being a hot box to freezing cold at night. Maybe Nate is right. Maybe the atmosphere is gone. After all, look how clear the sky is. *That doesn't make sense either. If we don't have an atmosphere, why aren't we dead?*

We continue riding for a while until we pass a "Welcome to

Pennsylvania" sign. A feeling of relief comes over me. We made it out of the danger zone, and now we can rest a little easier.

"We're here," says an elated Ethan.

"Let's stop over there," I suggest.

We pull to the side of the road because I want us to figure out what we should do next.

"Why are we stopping?" asks Ethan.

"We just passed the Pennsylvania border, so we're safe for now from the radiation," I say. "We need to decide if we are going to ride on further or if we should find a spot to camp out for the rest of the night."

"I don't think we should stay on the border," says Taylor. "We need to find a good place for us to camp."

We ride for a bit longer until we come across what looks like a heavily wooded area. It seems like a good place for us to camp for the night, so I tell the others to pull over.

"Hey, I think we can hide and sleep for the rest of the night here," I suggest.

"That's actually a good area for us to camp. It's heavily wooded and will hide us well," comments Taylor.

We ride our bikes through the woods as far as we can and go the rest of the way on foot. Eventually, we find a nice flat area with a few trees to provide some shade in the daytime.

"What do you guys think about here," I ask.

"This is perfect," answers Taylor.

We lean our bikes against the trees, roll out our sleeping bags, and set up camp.

"Taking the sleeping bags along was a great idea, and I don't think we would be able to survive out here without them," comments Taylor.

"It's cold out here," I say. "The temperature must be about forty or forty-five degrees. The sleeping bags alone will not keep us warm through the night."

"I agree. We're going to need a fire," adds Taylor.

"We need to gather firewood to start a fire, and we only have another three or so hours of night left," I say.

We walk around, collecting whatever sticks we can find. The wood is dry from the heat. I take a few sticks, pour some rubbing alcohol over them, and start the fire. Everyone piles whatever sticks they gathered next to the fire. We move our sleeping bags and form a circle around the fire. We've stacked enough wood to last us a few hours until the sun comes out and warms things up. We are all tired from the long ride and our abrupt escape from the police station. We turn in and do not waste any time falling asleep.

CHAPTER FOURTEEN

It is early in the morning. The sunlight is intense, and we can already feel the heat. I sit up to look around me. Taylor and Emma are missing. I wake up Nate. Cassie and Ethan are already awake, lying in their sleeping bags.

"Taylor and Emma are missing. Did they tell any of you where they were going?" I ask.

"They probably went to do girl stuff," answers Cassie. "They'll be back shortly."

I am concerned about them being out there by themselves. They did not tell any of us where they were going, and if something happens, we will not know where to find them. I get up and look into the woods to see if I can find them, but I do not get even a glimpse of them.

"Stop worrying," says Cassie, snickering. "I'm sure she didn't say anything because girls don't broadcast to a group of guys when they are going to the bathroom."

"She didn't even tell you. She could have," I respond.

I walk back to my sleeping bag and sit down. I pick up my backpack and rifle through it. I don't know what I'm looking for, but I need something to do, and it gives me something to take my mind off things. I rumble through my bag until my hand feels the pictures of my family I took from my basement. I slowly retrieve them, and there is a picture of my dad on top. I stare at it for a brief moment, and then I move on to the next picture. My parents' wedding picture is behind my dad's photo. My friends and I take a lot of pictures on our phones, and now all of those memories are gone. I think I am starting to understand how Nate feels. I watch him as he sits on his bag, holding onto his cell phone with the hope it will magically start working again. We depended on technology, and now not having it has made our misery that much more. *I'm going stir crazy; I can't believe how much time we spent online, whether it was texting or posting on social media, and now I'm feeling the need to communicate to find out what's going on around the world. Now, these pictures are all I have to pass the time.*

As I gaze at my parents' wedding picture, I become deaf to the world. It's not that I cannot hear, but the sounds around me are drowned out as if I am in a pool of water. I feel like I am the only one left in the world. I do not feel the wind against my face, and I hear no noise. My mind goes silent. My heart fills with deep sorrow and sadness. The grief overwhelms me, and I cannot contain myself. I realize that I cannot lose control in front of everyone and I must remain strong. I get up and walk into the woods.

I walk through the trees, staring at the picture, and a drop of water falls on the face of my watch. I look through the tree branches at the sky, which is a hazy orange color, but there is not a cloud in sight. The numbness goes away, the feeling comes back to my face, and I begin to hear again. I feel the wetness on my cheek. I take my hand and wipe my face. Tears fall from my eyes, and I am overwhelmed with emotions. It is making sick to my stomach, and I don't know what to do to make it stop. It feels like my insides are being ripped into two. I want this feeling to stop. I want it to go away. I want to go home and be with my parents. Instead, I'm stuck out here, stuck with a broken heart. How do I fix it? What do I do to fix it?

I hear Nate's voice behind me, calling my name. "Lance, are you ok, man?"

I quickly dry my face and wipe away the tears. I neatly stack the pictures, place them into my back pocket, and turn to Nate. "Hey, I just stepped away for some air."

Nate knows me well enough to realize that something is wrong.

"You know if you need to talk, I'm here for you."

"I'm ok. I'll be right there."

Nate heads back, and I stand there, motionless, with a heavy heart, as I watch him disappear into the trees. Now that my senses are back, I notice the horrible smell in the air again. The air all around smells foul, but this is a distinct odor. I look down at the ground, and then I look around me. The ground is littered with dead birds and other animals. They must have died from the heat and radiation poison. It's a very eerie sight, which quickly becomes uncomfortable to look at.

I turn around and return to the camp. I come out of the tree line to see that everyone, including Taylor and Emma, is sitting around in a circle, eating breakfast and talking. I join everyone, and I arrange my sleeping bag to sit down. Ethan is in the middle of speaking, expressing concern about what we should do next.

"We need to find a house or somewhere we can stay. We can stay out here for a few more days, but we will need a permanent home."

"We can't just take somebody's house," says Cassie.

"If we find a house that is empty, with no one in it, we need to keep it for us."

"Ethan is right," adds Nate. "We are safe at the moment, but we can't stay out here."

"We have no idea what's going on in this town," replies Cassie. "We barely made it out of the fallout area and into the safe zone. We don't know anything about this place, its layout, nor the people. We should not be taking their homes."

I have lots of thoughts on the matter but do not say anything to the group. I want to hear their opinions first. I do not want to make it look like I'm pushing all of my ideas on them.

"I agree that we should find a place for us to stay. Being outside in the elements is not safe, especially with this weather," says Taylor. "But we should stay put until we can find an area that is safe enough for us to stay."

"What do you think, Lance?" asks Nate as he looks around at everyone for approval of the question.

"I agree with Taylor," I reply. "It's far too dangerous for us to keep going until we know what is out there. We should scout the area before moving in."

"We need to do something," says Ethan. "We can't live out here."

"We'd probably be better off with somewhere to lay our heads at night," says Nate.

I reach into my bag and pull out a bottle of water. I take a couple of sips while I ponder our dilemma. They all stare at me with bated breath, waiting for my response. My silence and their stares became awkward.

They are expecting me to have the answer to all of their problems. Even though no one is saying it, somehow, I became the de facto leader. I'm no leader. I'm just a kid trying to save his and his friends' lives from this disaster. I don't want them to look at me this way. I already screwed up with Eric and Mr. Jenkins. What if I screw up again? What if someone else dies because of me? I can't go through that again. I can't live with the thought of my decision causing harm to someone else. I can only do my part to help the group, but I should not be expected to be responsible for them.

My thoughts are interrupted by Cassie, who shouts, "Lance!"

"We are safer here than we would be anywhere else in this town for now. Until we learn what kind of people live here and find a permanent dwelling, it will be best for us to stay out here for a while," I finally say.

"What happens when we run out of food?" asks Cassie.

"And water?" adds Ethan.

I do not want the dissent to become paralyzing to the point where we cannot function, so I need to think of a way to satisfy everyone enough so we can move forward. We can't sit here and fight with each other about what to do. We should be scouting the place to find somewhere to live and food and water to drink. A few days have passed since leaving the police station, and everyone is getting restless and tired of being out in the elements, so I quickly devise a plan to help us resupply, which will also keep everyone's minds occupied.

"A few of us can stay at the campsite while the rest of us scout the area for supplies and a possible place to stay," I say. "Ethan and Jeremy, you two can come with me on a supply run."

Cassie immediately objects to the plan. "That's not fair. I don't want to be left behind. I want to go too."

"We can't all go. Some of us have to remain behind to watch the camp."

"Why don't we draw straws to figure out who goes and who stays?" suggests Taylor.

"Good idea," I say.

"That sounds fair," replies Cassie.

Everyone agrees that it will be a fair way to determine who goes and who stays. It will also allow everyone to take turns on these supply runs so no one will complain. I pick up a few dry twigs and break them down: four long ones for those going out scouting and three short ones for those staying behind. I put all seven sticks into my hand and walk over to the group.

"To make it fair, I will pull the last one."

They each pick a stick. Jeremy and Ethan both pull long sticks, and Cassie and Nate pull short sticks. Emma pulls a short stick. Taylor is the last one to pull, and I open my hand to reveal a long stick. Cassie is very disappointed that she cannot go. We have to be fair, though, and pulling the sticks was the best way to do that.

Cassie pulls Taylor to the side, and they have a private conversation. The four of us pick up our bags and empty them out to make room for whatever supplies we are going to return with. We strap on our bags and make our way towards the tree line to our bikes. We go into the woods and then walk towards the street.

"How are we going to find our way back to the camp?" asks Jeremy.

Ethan pulls a machete from his bag that he took from the bunker. He strikes a tree at eye level and cuts some bark off of it.

"See, breadcrumbs," he says. "We mark every fifth or sixth tree so we can have a path to follow on our way back."

We continue walking through the woods, marking the trees as we go along. We must have been at least a quarter-mile off the road. We keep going until we reach the tree line.

"Slow down!" I shout to the others before they leave the cover of the trees. "We need to check and make sure it's safe."

We scan the area, but we do not see anyone in either direction. Ethan cuts into the last tree to mark the entrance into the woods. Then we walk out onto the road and climb onto our bikes. I look at my watch and see that it is about a quarter past ten. It's still early in the day, and we can get a lot done out here. The boredom creeps in when you are out here for days, and this cure is just what the doctor ordered. Cassie really wanted to get out of these woods, but so did everyone else. I realize we just decided to come out here without a plan. Not having a plan is not a good idea out here.

"We should ride west, away from the fallout," I say. "We need to stay as far as we can from it."

We start riding down the road, away from the woods, heading west. We ride quietly, observing the area as we go. We do not say much to each other on this ride. I do not know if it is the heat that causes the long period of silence we've had lately or if we just do not have anything to say. I know I have plenty to say; I just don't know where to start. Do we talk about our homes, our parents, the internet? I have to say something to get us talking again; the silence is killing me. Maybe if we pull over and get a drink, I can break the ice and start a conversation with them.

"How about we take a quick break for a drink?"

"I thought you would never ask," Ethan exclaims.

"Yes, I could use a drink," says Taylor.

We stop in the middle of the road, near a bunch of cars, and take a drink of water. The cars that are on the highway are like the ones in the parking lots, with the dead in and outside of them. When their cars stopped working, they either suffocated or died of radiation poison. Either way, it must have been a horrible way to die.

"We've ridden for at least ten minutes and haven't seen anything out here. We probably should take the next exit," I suggest.

We drink our water, and then we ride for another fifteen minutes until we reach a small strip mall at the next exit. When we enter the parking lot, we see that the same gruesome scene from the highway is everywhere. There are bodies of people who succumbed to radiation poisoning and heat lying in the parking lot. It is a sight and a smell that is becoming all too familiar. Ethan vomits at the sight of a mother leaning out of the back seat of a car, clutching her child. They are both dead. It is the same story everywhere: people's cars stopped working after the EMP, and they could not get to safety. Many died this way, and children and infants were no exceptions.

"Are you ok, man?" I ask.

"I'm good."

"Have some water."

Ethan takes a sip of water, and we continue through the parking lot. Most of the stores are clothing and thrift stores. They will not have the food and water that we need. I open the door to a thrift store and look around inside. It has been partially looted, but there are still plenty of things to pick through.

"Looks like people have been coming to these stores for supplies," I say.

"You would think that since they've been looting, the stores would be empty," comments Taylor.

"It's probably because so many people died. There aren't that many people to steal," I respond.

"I don't think we're going to find anything here."

"You may be right. We should keep going."

We ride out of the parking lot and continue on for another thirty minutes. We spend time exploring the road. There are a few neighborhoods nearby. However, we do not go into any of them, though they seem to be quiet.

We come to another area with a strip mall, which has a supermarket. We pull into the parking lot, and again, we're faced with the same horrific scene. You would think that I would be used to seeing the dead everywhere by now, but that's not the case. I cringe at the sight of it every time, wishing that it was just a dream. I desperately want to pinch myself, so I can wake up from this never-ending nightmare. I know if I do, I will only bruise myself, adding to my suffering.

I continue on, but I cannot help but wonder if my mother and father died the same way. I wonder if they are lying on the side of the road somewhere, with no one to bury them and no one to care. These people died without dignity, and there is no government to organize and collect the bodies. There are no family members, no friends to eulogize them, no memorial services, no funeral processions. Worst of all is that they may have no one left to remember them.

This is the worst tragedy that humankind has ever faced. It is the destruction of our society and of our entire way of life. So much death, and not one shot was fired. So many fires, so much devastation, and not one single bomb were dropped. Nature did in minutes what some of the most powerful countries in the world could not do in years. The Burning all but annihilated life on earth, but we can't stop and help right now; we have to keep moving.

We continue riding through the parking lot, and as we get closer to the supermarket, we see two men struggling with another man for his bag. We stop at the entrance and stare at them for a moment. My mind begins racing. *Is this what the world has become? Is this how we should expect people to behave? Without any law enforcement, people have become very dangerous and destructive. I would like to help, but we cannot get involved in every skirmish. We would put ourselves in too much danger, and if we do, we will make a lot of enemies very fast.*

Before I can finish my thought, Ethan fires a shot into the air. The men stop and look at us. Ethan has left us no choice but to draw our weapons. When the two men see our weapons, they let go of the bag and run off. The man picks up his bag and takes off in the other direction.

"Warn us next time before you do something like that!" I complain.

"Warn you? Those are the same type of people that killed my brother, so no, I will not let them do the same thing to someone else."

"We can't get involved in other people's problems. We have our own problems to worry about."

"Look around you. Do you see the police, the Army? It's up

to us to help. If we don't stop them, who will?"

Ethan grabs me by the shirt, and I grab his wrist. *He is angry. I guess the anger from the loss of Eric is still inside him. He needs an outlet, and if I have to be his outlet, so be it. I need to get him thinking straight again. He needs to understand that we cannot be the police. It is not something we can handle. I need to make him understand.*

"If you weren't so scared, maybe my brother would still be alive right now! I'm not going to cower like you did and cause innocent people to die."

Taylor grabs Ethan by the arm, and he lets go of my shirt. She steps in between us. "You don't have to worry about anyone hurting you. You're doing a good job of it yourselves!"

"What do you want from me?" I ask Ethan.

"I want you to be the same fearless captain you were on the football field out here and not, not this, whatever you've become."

He walks away. I stand there for a moment, thinking about what he has said. He's shaken me to the core. I have long been upset at myself for not doing more to prevent Eric's and Mr. Jenkins's deaths, but now I know I could have done more, and Ethan knows it too. Taylor rubs my arm.

"Are you ok?" she asks.

"I'm fine."

"He's grieving; he didn't mean what he said. Give him time. Your relationship will get better."

We continue on until we enter the supermarket. To our surprise, the entire store is intact. Hardly anything has been removed from the premises. It is odd that the two men were after that man's bag with this many resources available for the taking. I don't have the time to stand around thinking about that right now, though; we have to find the supplies that we came for.

Taylor disappears into one of the aisles. I follow her, and she is filling her bag with feminine products. I do not want to embarrass her, so I walk away. *This must be why Cassie wanted to come. She was probably giving Taylor a shopping list back in the woods when they were whispering.* I walk into the snack aisle and see Jeremy gathering cookies and chips. Ethan is in the beverage aisle getting water bottles and soda. There is a lot of tension between us right now, so I avoid him and leave the aisle. *I know Ethen is angry, but there is no need for him to behave this way. His behavior is creating tension in the group, and we don't need that right now.*

I continue walking through the supermarket, looking for anything we can use out in the woods. I open my bag and fill it up with peanut butter, jelly, crackers, and other essentials. I look through the perishable goods, but they are all destroyed. The cheese is hard, and the lunch meats are spoiled; there is no hope of saving any of them. At this point, I realize our best bet is to get canned goods. I walk through the store, telling everyone to fit as many canned goods as they are able to carry into their packs.

"Jeremy, we can put some of this stuff into the hitch on your bike," I ask. "Hey, everyone, let's put some of this stuff into Jeremy's hitch."

We walk down the canned goods aisles, and we all begin selecting our favorites. It occurs to me that the only way we will be eating meat again is if it's canned. I grabbed canned sardines, tuna, salmon, and chicken. I bring them outside and dump them into the hitch. We also take other essentials like canned beans and soup products. We pack our bags and head out of the store.

"Is there anything else any of you think we may need?" I ask.

"I have everything I came for," says Taylor.

"I know. We need a can opener to open the cans," says Jeremy.

"I got it," replies Ethan, and he leaves to go and find one.

"Anything else?" I ask.

Ethan comes back to the front with two can openers and some knives and utensils. On our way towards the front of the store, we pass the registers. I reach into my pocket for the coins, and this time, I set a silver coin on top of the register. We did not take as much as from the other stores, so a gold coin seems like overkill.

Jeremy retakes point and looks outside the door. The area is empty, so we make our way outside and climb on our bikes. We ride out of the parking lot, onto the highway, and head eastward, towards the camp.

"Keep an eye out. Those two guys might've taken off, but that doesn't mean they did not hang around and watch us," I warn.

The heat is unbearable, and the heavier bags make for a slow ride back. We expend more energy getting back to camp than we did going to the supermarket. We do stop a few times to drink. Finally, we reach the entrance to our base camp. We stayed vigilant the whole ride back and did not see anyone following us. That is the one thing I'm going the hate the most about the apocalypse: having to watch my back all the time. It's a good thing we have friends to help us do it.

"We're here," says Ethan.

The marked tree is visible from a distance. We reach the edge of the trees and dismount our bikes. We take our bikes, walk into the tree line, and disappear into the woods. As we walk, I realize we depend solely on the tree markings to find our way back to the camp. If Eric had not put those markings there, there is no way we would have been able to find our way back. I also notice something very odd. There are no birds, insects, or other animals running around.

"Have you guys noticed that there are no birds in the trees?"

"You're right. I have not seen one bird or any insects," answers Ethan.

"There are no crickets at night either," adds Taylor.

"If all the animals and insects died, then the ecosystem will be out of balance," I say. "The rest of the animals that did survive will eventually die out, including us."

We reach the edge of the tree line and see our camp. Cassie and Emma are sitting down, talking. Nate picks up his rifle as we near the camp; presumably, he heard us walking through the trees. He looks toward the tree line and sees us, and then he places the rifle back down next to him. They all come to meet us at the edge of the trees.

Nate goes straight to Taylor. "I can help you with that."

"I can handle it," Taylor replies, brushing him off, and he stands there, looking dissed.

I put my bag against his chest. "You can take mine."

We walk back into the campground and begin to set up for dinner. It is well into the night by the time we finish eating. We sit around the fire, talking for a while. I look over at Nate, and he is holding his cell phone, staring aimlessly into the black screen. He hasn't said much the whole night; he's either been watching Taylor or his phone. I can't imagine what he's going through right now. The two things he desires most in this world are Taylor and his phone, and he can't have either of them. I do understand about the phone, though, because I wish I had mine right now.

"Do you have five bars on that thing?" I ask.

"Yeah, I'm online right now, watching eight-second videos."

"I get it, man. I wish I had mine too."

"I know. Mine is in my bag, and I'm just praying for it to start working again," adds Taylor.

"I miss playing *Minecraft*," says Emma.

"I miss *Call of Duty*," says Jeremy.

"We going to have to build our society and eventually get

things working again," I say.

We talk late into the night until Emma falls asleep. By this time, we're all exhausted from the heat.

"I'm going to turn in," says Taylor.

Since we are all tired, we all decide it is time to go to sleep.

"Me too."

"I'm beat."

"Good night."

I add more wood to the fire and climb into my sleeping bag. For the next couple of weeks, we do the same routine, going out scouting and bringing back supplies to the camp. By the fourth day, we decide to move to a new location farther down the road. We figure it is wise to move our site every five days or so, not get too comfortable and make ourselves vulnerable. It has been over two weeks, and the days are blending into each other. The tension between Ethan and I is not making it easy to bear. I thought things were going to get better with Ethan, but it is a rollercoaster ride. His mood changes as often as night and day. I do not know how to handle him anymore, and he is becoming a problem, not just for me but for the group.

We're out on another scouting mission right now for more supplies. The supplies from our previous run lasted almost the whole week we've been at this location. For the past month, we've been moving around, setting up camp in different places each week. Today, we are running low on supplies, and we need to head out to get some more.

Nate continues his quest for Taylor's heart; the entire bike ride today, he is talking up a storm. I guess love does make you a fool.

We stop our bikes when we see a group of people down the road attacking a man.

"Pull to the side of the road," I say.

We quickly do so, hiding from their view.

"What are they doing?" asks Taylor.

"I don't know," I answer.

"We should do something," says Ethan.

I pull out my binoculars and look at what is going on. They are just kids around our age. They are all wearing green armbands. The man gets on his knees, and he appears to be begging for his life.

"They're going to kill him," says Ethan, "we need to do something."

"There are more of them than us," I say. "I want everyone to make it back to camp. We are not losing any more people."

"We're on bikes; we can at least distract them so he can get away."

As we discuss it, we hear several gunshots. We turn and look, and the man falls on his face. Ethan looks at me, angrily. They drag a woman out. She is screaming and fighting them off.

218

"Screw this!" says Ethan. He cocks his weapon and steps out of the shadows.

"Ethan, wait!" I whisper.

He looks at me disapprovingly; he aims his weapon in the air and fires five or six rounds. The kids turn around and look in our direction. They draw their weapons and aim them at us. Getting their attention is enough to allow the woman to get away. She runs down the street as they walk towards us.

"Come on, let's go!" I command.

We hop on our bikes and ride for dear life in the other direction. They give chase, firing several shots towards us. We quickly move out of their sight and range into safety.

"You could have gotten one of us killed," I say.

"We are all alive, and the woman is alive," replies Ethan. "The man might have lived if you weren't…"

I ride past him, pull up in front of him, and stop my bike. He quickly stops and turns so as not to plow into me.

"What the hell's your problem," he asks.

"No, what's your problem? You're being reckless with our lives. One of us might have gotten killed back there, and you don't even care."

"And because of you, someone did get killed!"

"His death is not on us; it's on them."

"You can tell yourself whatever you have to, to feel better! If you weren't such coward—"

Nate steps in between us. "What are you guys doing? We are boys, and we should be getting closer in this hellhole, not trying to tear each other apart." Nate grabs my arm. "He's what, the same kid who ran around the kiddie pool with you when you were six?"

Nate releases my arm, and he points back and forth at both of us. "You two fix this, or don't bother coming back to camp."

He gets onto his bike and looks at us. "Come on, Taylor."

Surprisingly, Taylor seems impressed with his take-charge attitude. She looks at us, and then she follows him down the road. We stand there quietly, and we watch them ride down the road. I look down at the ground and lightly kick a pebble. *Nate is right; we cannot keep going like this. The situation may blow up at the wrong time. We have to fix this.*

I turn and look at him. "Look, I get it. I choked on the winning play of the big game. It's something I must live with for the rest of my life, something I think about every day, man. If and when we need to fight, I will fight for us, but I am not going to risk any of our lives if we don't have to. And if you don't understand that, then you are not the kid I ran around the kiddie pool with."

I put up my hand for him to shake. "So, what is it going to be?"

Ethan looks at my hand for a moment, and then he puts out his hand and shakes it. I pull him in for a hug.

"Let's just put this group first, ok?"

We get on our bikes and ride down the road.

For the next month and a half, we keep running into the green armband gang. We have to change our campsite more frequently so they won't catch up with us. We do not know who the kids with the green armbands are, but there are a lot of them. It seems like they are everywhere. Wherever we go, there they are. We try to avoid them as much as possible. We do not want to get into a confrontation with them; they always outnumber us. The green armband gang is a group that we will eventually have to deal with.

In the meantime, the situation between Ethan and me has improved some, but it is still tense. I think his improvement is mostly because of his fear of the group rejecting him and not his willingness to let go. However, Ethan is more cooperative with me.

We have been out here in the woods for more than three months, but we still do not have a place to call home. We've gone out and scouted many areas that looked suitable to live in. The problem is that wherever we go, we run into the green armband gang, but we manage to avoid them. For now, we stay in the woods, and tonight, we sit by the fire, and we laugh and talk. I don't know what tomorrow will bring, but whatever it is, we will face it head-on. We may need to move out of Pennsylvania. That is a discussion I can bring up in the morning. We are not going to be able to avoid the green armband gang forever.

CHAPTER FIFTEEN

"Ouch!" I say.

I'm awakened by a pounding on my side. It feels like someone kicking me. It does not hurt, but they're kicking me hard enough to get my attention. My first thought is *Nate is going to get it*. I turn and open my eyes to the sight of a rifle barrel in my face. I glance at the barrel, and then I look up to see who is holding it. The first thing I notice is the slight breeze blowing her blonde hair across her face. She moves the hair from her face. A few strands are blowing over her lips. She is the most beautiful girl I have ever seen. Her skin is fair, and she stands about five feet, six inches tall. The only problem is she has a gun in my face.

"Oh, shit!"

"Get up!"

I look around the campsite and see about eight or nine others with their guns pointed at the rest of the group. They are all wearing green armbands. This is the day that I feared, the day that the green armband gang caught up with us. I thought we were cautious and that they would not find our campsite. Now here they are, all over our campsite. *I wonder what they are going to do to us?*

"I said, get up!" shouts the girl.

"Ok."

"Get up, on your feet!" the others shout.

"Hold on, we have to unzip these stupid bags," says Cassie.

We get out of our sleeping bags. They've already collected our guns while we slept. I count ten of them. They overtook us while we slept, and there is nothing we can do. At this point, our only option is to cooperate and hope they don't shoot us like they do other people. I slowly get out of my sleeping bag to give myself time to think, but I don't see a way out of this. We are outnumbered and outgunned. *Damn. They have us.* She shoves the barrel of a rifle into my back – not violently, but very gently, which makes me believe that she might not want to hurt us.

"Move!"

"Look, you can have whatever you want. Just take what you want and be on your way."

One of them walks over to me as I'm speaking, and he gets in my face. "What I want is for you to shut your mouth and start moving."

"Everything we have in the world is in our bags," I say. "If you're taking us somewhere, could we at least take our bags with us?"

"We've got your bags," says the blonde. "Just come with us, and I promise you that no one is going to get hurt. We don't want to hurt you."

I turn around and look at everyone, and I nod to them, signaling that it is ok to go. They could have just killed us in our sleep, but they did not. What choice do we have? If we don't go with them, they might just start shooting. They pick up our bags and make us form a single line, and then we begin walking out of the woods. They lead us to the opposite side of the woods from where we first entered the trail.

"Where are you taking us?" asks Nate.

"Just do what we say. No one will get hurt, and you will find out," says the leader.

The blonde quickens her pace and catches up with me. She lowers her weapon and looks at me.

"Hi! I'm Kirsten," she says.

I look at her.

"Don't be afraid. Everything is going to be okay. I promise."

"Your promises aren't exactly comforting right now."

"We are not going to hurt you as long as you don't try to get away."

"So, why are you doing this?"

"We have a place called the Sanctuary."

"The Sanctuary?"

"It's where we're taking you. We just don't trust you yet, so we have to be cautious."

"Tell me, Kirsten, why should we trust you when you're taking us hostage?"

The leader turns around and walks back to Kirsten. "You

need to learn how to follow orders and keep your mouth shut, and as far as what is going to happen to them, that's for Tyler to decide."

"Tyler, who is Tyler?" I ask.

"You'll find out soon enough!" says the leader.

Kirsten puts her head down and walks away from me. We continue walking the trail for what seems to be a very long time until we make it out of the woods and onto a street.

"I'm thirsty!" complains Emma.

"I said to keep your mouths shut," repeats the leader.

"We've been walking for a long time, and it's burning hot out here," I say.

"John!" shouts Kirsten.

The leader stops and turns around.

"What is it now?" he asks.

"He's right, you know. She's just a kid, and besides, I'm thirsty too."

"Take five, everybody," John says.

They sit us on the side of the road, and they hand each of us a bottle of water. They also have water to drink, and we sit down for the next ten minutes. I guess they don't want us dead for this Tyler guy since they are letting us drink. *Every time we run into them, they are always killing someone. What's different about us? Why are they not killing us?*

225

"Break time is over. Everybody up!" commands John.

"No!" shouts Cassie.

John turns and looks at Cassie. He quickly walks towards her.

"We're not going anywhere until you tell us what this is all about!" she demands.

"You get up and move, or I will shoot you!" replies John.

Kirsten looks over at me, and then she walks over to John.

"Let me handle this, John."

She walks over to me and lays her rifle beside her.

"The place that we are going to is a safe place with food, water, and a bed to lay your head-on. We just need to speak to our leader, Tyler, to see if you can stay there."

"Why are you doing all this? Why not just invite us? If you'd have just asked us, we would have come with you."

"I've only been with them for over a month. We tried asking others, and they came in and created problems, so now we need to take more precautions."

We all look at each other, unsure whether to trust her or not. She does seem to be the more reasonable of the group.

"Look, I know this is not the best way for us to introduce ourselves, but you've been out there, and you've seen how people are. I promise I will not let anything happen to any of you."

After she tells us this, we decide to go forward. We all get up and begin walking down the road with them. The Sanctuary's guards are all kids around our ages except for John, who looks a little older.

We walk quite a way, and it is well into the afternoon when we reach the place they call the Sanctuary. It is a gated community with two large metal doors at the front entrance. There are young people all around, patrolling the gates. They open the metal gates and allow us in. At the front of the community is a clubhouse. The front of the clubhouse has a wooden structure that looks like a gallows. There is an eerie feeling, an ominous sense of uneasiness around the place. I sense that the rest of the group feels the same way because they all looked as disturbed as I am. Everyone at the Sanctuary wears the same green armband. The neighborhood seems like somewhere you would want to live before the Burning. The grass is dry, and so are the hedges. You can see that this place was once beautiful, from the design to the choice of plants. The people who lived in this neighborhood must have been wealthy.

Those who live here now have added to the original wall to make it higher. You can see where the old wall ends, and the new one begins from the difference in brick colors. They take us into a house that is not too far from the entrance. The house is empty, and there is a room situated in the back, where they put us. The room is large enough for a twin bed on one side and a couch and plenty of chairs on the other. Kirsten and John walk into the room with us.

"Wait here," says Kirsten.

"What are we waiting for?" asks Cassie.

"Tyler," replies John.

He walks out, and Kirsten closes the door.

"I don't trust these people," hisses Cassie.

"I don't trust them either," adds Taylor.

"I have to agree with them," says Ethan.

They are right not to trust these people. I do not trust them either. I am getting a weird vibe about the place, but we are here, and it's probably worth hearing what their leader, Tyler, has to say. My biggest concern right now is the man they killed when Ethan intervened to save the woman. *What kind of people are they? Did the man do something, or did they kill him for fun? They already had him under control; there was no real reason to kill him. Maybe that was just a rogue group misbehaving, or it could be what they do. In either case, we will have to make a decision: do we leave or do we stay? I need to tell the others what I think. We have to discuss our options before we meet this Tyler.*

"If Kirsten's right and they are offering us a chance to start over, with shelter, food, and safety, we need to give it some serious thought before we reject it," I say.

"That John guy creeps me out," complains Cassie.

"Me too," adds Emma.

"I say we figure out a way out of here. These are the same green armband freaks we've been avoiding, and now you want us to hear them out? We've survived by ourselves for almost four months. We don't need them," says Ethen.

"I think we should try to survive on our own. I don't like this place," insists Taylor.

"They took our bags and all our guns. We can't leave until we get them back," I respond.

"What if they want to kill us?" asks Jeremy.

"They would have killed us in our sleep if that's what they wanted to do," I reply. "They kept us alive and brought us this far. I don't think they would do that just to kill us."

"I say we make a break for it," suggests Ethan. "I saw them drop our bags and guns in the other room."

"They have a couple of guards behind the door," warns Taylor. "There is no way we will be able to get to our bags and guns before they get to us."

"Let's speak with this Tyler, and if we don't like what he has to say, we leave," I suggest.

Everyone agrees that this will be the plan. If we do not like the situation, we will get our guns and our belongings and leave. We will fight our way out if we need to, but we will first look for an escape route that does not require us to put ourselves or anyone else in danger. We will only fight if we are left with no other choice. I don't think it will come to a gunfight, but just in case it does, we will be ready.

"There were a lot of guards at the front gate. How do you propose we make our escape?" asks Nate.

"It looks like guards are walking the perimeter of the wall as well," I add.

"There are also some patrolling the streets," says Cassie.

"Maybe fighting our way out is not the best option," I reply.

"I agree. There are too many of them and too few of us," says Nate.

"If we don't like what this Tyler has to say, we'll just tell them that we don't want to stay and leave," suggests Taylor.

"So far, they have not hurt us, and they gave us water when we needed it," I say. "I am hopeful that this works out, but we've been out there, and we know that this situation has people acting like animals. We would probably have taken the same precautions they have, so let's not rule out staying yet."

"Ok, but if we stay, we must be careful, and we should only trust each other. No one else outside this group should know our plans," pleads Cassie.

We have a plan, which will only be put in place if we don't like what's going on, and we don't feel safe. Right now, Kirsten has been the only one who seems genuinely concerned about us. We need to talk to her to find out some more about this place.

"I understand we all have concerns, but Kirsten is not like the others," I say. "She seems genuine,"

"Are you saying it because you think she is or because she's had her claws in you since the camp?" asks Cassie.

"I think he's got the hots for her," snorts Jeremy.

"That has nothing to do with it, and no, I do not have the hots for her," I scold. "I just get the sense that she might be someone who can help us in the future."

We spend most of the day stuck in the room. The time seems
to pass by very slowly. We have not eaten all day, and we are
thirsty due to the heat. We knock on the door several times,
but the two sentries at the door just tell us they cannot do
anything until Tyler speaks with us. It is well into the evening
when the door opens, and John walks into the room and says,
"Let's go."

"Where are we going?" I ask.

"To meet Tyler."

We follow John out of the house and onto the street. We
begin walking back towards the clubhouse. As we walk, we all
take notice of our surroundings, making mental notes of the
layout and security. The community seems to be made up
entirely of children and teenagers. Some look like they are in
their twenties. They make a spectacle of us, staring at us from
the time we come out of the house until we are out of their
view – and then we are stared at by others. The staring makes
me uncomfortable. I feel like a caged animal that is being
paraded in the carnival. I wish they would stop looking at us.
I wonder why I don't see a smile on any of their faces. You
would think they would be happy to have this place. We
arrive in front of the clubhouse. The gallows structure that
we noticed earlier appears to have been completed. It has
ropes hanging from each of the three beams, which are
situated on top of a platform. This makes us very nervous.
We look at each other, and we stare back at the structure. *Are
they planning on hanging us? What kind of people are they?*

"What's up with that?" asks Nate, pointing towards the
gallows with his head.

"I guess we're about to find out," I reply.

We enter the clubhouse. It is lavishly decorated with beautiful furniture. In the main area, there are couches, and John tells us to have a seat. Across from us, two men are sitting at a desk outside of an office. John walks over to the desk and speaks to the men. One of them gets up, knocks on the door, and walks into the office. Moments later, he comes out and talks to John, and John walks over to the area where we sit.

"Tyler will see you now."

We all get up, and John points to me. "Just you."

I turn around and reassure everyone, and then I walk towards Tyler's office. One of the two men at the desk gets up. He opens the door and lets me in.

There is a man sitting behind a large desk in the office. He appears to be in his late twenties. He is wearing Army fatigues, and his rank says, "Captain." The name on the uniform says, "Tyler."

As I walk into the office, he stands up from behind the desk. He smiles and waves for me to come forward.

"Come in. Have a seat."

I slowly step into the room, looking around the office as I walk towards the chair. He must have selected the very best to decorate his office. The office has statues of knights and beautiful pictures, but the one that catches my eye is the painting of the French Revolution, of Liberty leading the people. *The French must have thought the world was ending, too, with all the killing that was going on around them.* Tyler stands up and sticks out his hand to shake.

"I'm Captain Tyler."

I stick my hand out, and we shake hands.

"I'm Lance."

I sit down on one of the two chairs opposite Tyler.

He grabs a pitcher of water and pours a glass.

"Water?"

"Yes, please."

He pours a glass and slides it across the desk to me. I pick it up and begin drinking.

"As I said, I'm Captain Tyler, and I'm in charge of this place."

I stop drinking and set the glass down in front of me.

"What is this place?"

"Getting there. My best guess is we were hit by a massive solar flare that took out our technology and gave us a massive dose of radiation."

He slides his chair back and gets up from his seat. He continues talking as he paces back and forth with his hands behind his back.

"A lot of people succumbed to the radiation, many of whom fell ill and died in great agony. I don't have to tell you that. I'm sure you had to live through it."

"Yes, we saw many sick people on our way out of town. One of our friends was also sick too, but he's better now."

"We lost a lot of people. I saw the chaos around me, and my military training kicked in. I wanted to help people. I wanted to help everyone, and that's when I saw this tragedy was an opportunity for a do-over. So, I recruited guys like John, and we secured this place. We call it the Sanctuary. It's a place where young people like yourself can come for safety. Here, you have a place to stay where you can eat in peace and feel safe. The only thing we ask of anyone who lives here is to contribute in some way."

He stops speaking, looks at me briefly, smiles, and then he continues pacing.

"As you might've noticed, we have some people patrolling the gates. They are crucial to the safety of this place, and without safety, there is no cohesion. To build this cohesion, we need the participation and cooperation of all the members of the Sanctuary. We have some who are on water duty, making sure that our water supply is adequate. We have those that manage our food; their job is to go and find stashes of food wherever they can to supply this place for years to come."

Tyler stops pacing and looks at me. He walks towards the large window behind his desk and calls me over.

"Come, join me."

I get up, walk over towards the window, and stand next to him.

"Look, look over there."

Tyler points to a structure that is under construction in a large field connected to the Sanctuary. The field is a large one and has a lot of people tending to animals and plants.

"Do you see that? That's going to be a greenhouse. It's going to be temperature controlled. We will be able to grow food outside, even with the heat, for the next hundred years. So, you see, Lance, young people like you and your group are what we need to make this place strong. Once we've built up Sanctuary and fortified all our facilities, we can go out and recruit more and increase our numbers."

"What do you mean to increase your numbers?"

"You see, Lance, there is danger on the horizon. There is a war coming, and we have to purge ourselves of that danger to prevent the war. All we have are each other and our ingenuity. By purging ourselves of the old ways that haven't worked for us, we'll be strong enough to survive the coming onslaught."

"So, what do you want from me?"

"Lance, we are at a crossroads in history. We have a chance to change the path that we've been on, to purge ourselves of lies, prejudices, and inequalities that we inherited over the centuries. It's all up to us to reach out and remake the world as we see fit, to right all the wrongs that have been committed over the centuries. Do you want to be part of that change, Lance? Do you want a world that is safe for you and your friends? We can have a secure future."

I look at Tyler but do not quite know how to answer the question, mainly because I'm not sure what he is talking about. *Tyler is rambling on about a coming war, but none of it makes sense. The military has been destroyed, which is why he is here.*

He turns and looks at me. He places a hand on my shoulder. "You don't have to answer that right now. Come, have a seat."

We walk back to the desk, and we sit down. I'm still fuzzy about what he is saying, but I do understand that he wants us to stay at his Sanctuary. In exchange, we will work for him. That does not sound like a bad deal, but I will need to see what he wants us to do.

"You asked me what I want from you, but the real question is, what are you willing to do to secure your future? Are you willing to do what it takes to ensure the safety and well-being of your friends?"

"Yes, of course!"

"I understand you are the leader of your group."

"I wouldn't say that. We don't really have a leader."

"Lance, Lance! You're too modest. My scouts were watching you for a couple of days before they approached you, and from what they tell me, your group looks to you as a leader."

"I'm, I'm not their leader. We're just friends."

"Have you offered them guidance, reassurance, courage, and strategized to help protect them? Have you fed them and provided them support when they needed it?"

"Yes."

"Then you are their leader. You see, Lance, most good leaders, are accidental. I didn't seek to be here, but there was a need, a vacuum. I became to these people what you've become to your group. I did not see myself as their leader, but they sure did not feel the same way I did. I guarantee you that your people feel the same way about you. Like it or not, you are their leader."

"I hadn't thought of it that way."

"Now, John tells me that you and your group have some tactical skills, and you know how to handle weapons."

"We had to learn quickly, but we did get some help along the way."

"Most of the people that come here do not have any tactical or combat experience, so it makes you and your group unique. We're in need of people with your skillset. We could use a hand, patrolling the neighborhoods that we now control."

"Are you asking us to stay here and work for you?"

"Yes. I'll give you and your group a house you can share if you'd like to stay together. Food and water would be rationed to you on a daily basis so you can help keep the communities safe."

"Is that all?"

"That's all. It's a mutual relationship. You help us, and we help you."

"What about the gallows outside? Who are you planning on hanging?"

Tyler leans back, and he gives me a sinister smile. He sits up straight and continues. "You don't miss a thing, do you? You're observant. I like that."

"Well, what are they for?"

"Take a look around you. There are no police. There are no prisons. If someone rapes or kills, we need to make a strong example of them. We need to keep our community safe from those who would bring the destructive nature of the old world into our communities. Don't you agree?"

"Well, yes. If someone hurts another person, they should be punished."

"Yes! And that is what we do here. This is why there are virtually no crimes here."

"I can understand that."

"We also make a strong example for the others. We will not tolerate their intolerance! We will not go back into their way of thinking, slip back into the disease of the old world. This is a new world, where we must be forward-thinking. We fought against nature, and we lost. Mother Nature spared our lives. We must now learn how to live in harmony with her, and we must change. But we cannot have change without sacrifice. We have to sacrifice our technology, which polluted the world. She took it all away to show us that there is another way."

"I agree. We do need to make a change. We polluted the

planet with our large carbon footprint. But millions of people have died from this disaster."

"Billions, Lance. Billions, by my estimations."

"Ok, billions. Doesn't that alone reduce the pollution to where we can have the technology to make life easier?"

"Lance, if you don't put in place some form of population control, policies to prevent the industrial monsters that we've seen in the past, in one hundred years, we will find ourselves in the same situation that we're in today. Our children will curse us, just as we curse the leaders and past generations."

"How can we help?"

"You and your friends will be my guests at dinner tonight. This will give you some time to think about my offer. But more importantly, I need you to talk to your friends and help them see the merit of what we're doing here. You're a smart young man. I trust you will make the right decision. Whatever you decide, I will respect it."

"So, we can leave if we decide not to stay?"

"Of course you can. You're not prisoners."

"It sure felt like it, waking up to a gun barrel in my face and being forced into a room under lock and key."

"Let me apologize for that, but we must take precautions with how we approach people. Do you know I almost lost an entire patrol? All but one of them escaped with their lives. As they went to recruit a group of young people like yourselves, they were all slaughtered by those they were trying to help.

This is why we have to take these measures. I have some business to attend to, but John will escort you and your friends to a house with running water. You and your friends can clean up and get ready for dinner tonight, where you will be my honored guests."

CHAPTER SIXTEEN

After our conversation, I leave Tyler's office. I do not know what to make of what he had to say. If anything, he is creating a new world rather than destroying what is left of it. We've been out there for a while, and most people are just destroying what little we have left. *Everyone is just out for themselves. There is no cooperation, no law, and order. Tyler seems to have the right idea: to bring people together and build communities. It's been three months since we left the police station, and we have not seen any place suitable for us to live. This place, this sanctuary, can be the fresh start we are looking for. I know my ragtag band of brothers will have a million questions for me about this place and Tyler. At least we will need to stay for the night to get something to eat and a good night's rest.*

I walk back to the others, who are now standing around talking to each other. I rejoin them, and John leads us out of the building. He no longer has his weapon pointed at us.

"Follow me. I will get you set up in temporary housing so you can clean up for dinner," he says.

As soon as we step out the door, the questions start.

"What happened in there?"

"What did he want?"

"What did he say?"

"What are they going to do with us?"

There are so many questions that I do not know who is doing the asking. I don't want to address them in front of John, but the others cannot stop themselves from asking. I can understand because I would be anxious to know too. I want to tell them everything, but as we keep saying, we can't trust anyone.

"I'll tell you everything when we get to the house."

"I think Tyler likes you," John says, interrupting us.

"Really? I couldn't tell."

"He usually doesn't spend that much time with new guests. You're lucky to get that much time with him. He's a brilliant man."

John leads us a few blocks down to a cul-de-sac where a big estate stands. Whoever built the house must have been wealthy. It looks very lavish from the outside.

"This is our guest house," says John.

"That's a big house," says Emma.

"Only the best for our guests," responds John.

We reach the house, and John stops at the front door. He looks at us and says, "Listen, I know we got off on the wrong foot, but I was only doing what was best for the group and for the Sanctuary by bringing you here safely."

He opens the door to the house, sticks his head in briefly, looks around, and steps back out. "Well, here you go. There's water and snacks inside. Freshen up, but don't eat too much. Dinner is in an hour."

John walks away, and I slowly open the door to the house. We walk in, and like the outside, the inside is lavishly decorated with beautiful furniture and paintings. Everyone is in awe of the beauty of the house. Emma flips the light switch, and surprisingly, the light turns on.

"There's light!" Jeremy exclaims.

"Yes, finally light," says Nate, elated.

Taylor walks straight into the bathroom and turns on the faucet.

"We have running water!"

"I'm showering first," says Jeremy.

We all rush towards the bathroom.

"This is a big house. It has more than one bathroom!" I shout. "Be sure that you're careful not to waste the water, so we don't run out."

"We need to talk about your conversation with Tyler," says Cassie.

"I will tell you everything we talked about, but we should freshen up first so we can be ready for dinner afterward."

Jeremy and Emma disappear from the group.

"There is another bathroom down here!" shouts Emma.

"All of the rooms have bathrooms, and the water runs in all

of them!" shouts Jeremy.

Everyone runs upstairs simultaneously, and I follow Cassie up the stairs. As I make my way up, there is a knock at the front door. Cassie and I turn and look at it.

"You can go ahead," I say. "I'll get the door."

She continues up the stairs, and I go downstairs to the door. I open it, and Kirsten and three other people are standing outside. They have our backpacks and equipment with them.

"I thought you guys might need these," says Kirsten. "Can we come in?"

I open the door wide. "Sure, come right in."

"Where do you want these?"

"You can set them near the couch."

They come into the house and lay the bags near the couch.

"Thanks," I say. "I appreciate you bringing them by."

The three people with Kirsten leave. She closes the door behind them, but she doesn't leave.

"Thanks again for bringing our things."

She walks over towards me. "Listen, I'm really sorry about what happened earlier. I don't like it, but that's the way they do things around here."

"It's ok. I understand you had to take precautions."

She smiles at me and moves in a little bit closer. "I hope you do decide to stay. I could really use the company of a sane person."

"Sane! What do you mean by that?"

She smiles at me and walks away. She opens the door, turns back to look at me, and smiles. "Just think about it!"

My heart was racing the entire time she was standing next to me. She is so beautiful and smells so good, and it's a refreshing change from our new normal. We don't get to shower or wash often, and I imagine we don't smell like flowers. Kirsten has been doing her best to make me comfortable since our first meeting. I have a good vibe from her, and I hope she is someone that we can rely on. I walk to the door to close it, but I do not shut it all the way; instead, I watch her through the crack. As she makes her way down the street, she takes her hair out of its bun, letting it down and running her fingers through it. My heart races even more. I watch her until she disappears around the corner.

I close the door and turn around, and I am startled at the sight of Cassie standing behind me.

"Enjoying the view?"

"It's not like that!"

"What is it like? It looks to me like you're staring at the girl who kidnapped us at gunpoint!"

"Why are you spying on me anyway?"

"I'm not spying on you. I don't trust her, and I don't trust any of them," Cassie responds. "I guess I can't say the same for you from the way you are smitten with her."

"I'm not smitten! When you hear what Tyler has to say, you will see this place in a different light."

She walks to the bags and grabs her backpack. She walks to the stairs, and then she stops and looks at me. "Well, since you like this place so much, you can stay and have fun with Kirsten!" She walks up the stairs.

"It's not like that!"

I pick up the bags and bring them upstairs two at a time. I set them in the common area upstairs, where they can be seen. I go back downstairs and grab my own bag, and I look for an empty bathroom. I quickly find a bedroom that is not occupied, sit on the toilet in the bathroom, and relax briefly. Then I grab my bag and pull out a pair of jeans and a T-shirt and hang them on a towel rack. I take off my shirt and toss it to a corner. Then I take off the rest of my clothes and enter the shower.

The water feels good. No, the water feels great! It has been three months since I last took a shower. Mr. Jenkins had a shower in the bunker, and we were clean as long as we were there. Since we've been living in the woods, we've been washing up in the creek near our campsites, but this water feels like it's the first time I have ever taken a shower. I grab the soap and begin washing up. I wish I could stay in the shower forever, but I do not want to waste the water, so I quickly wash and get out. I grab a towel and dry myself. Then I put on my clothes, place my dirty clothes in a separate pocket of my bag, and walk out of the bathroom.

I step into the bedroom and set my bag on the floor. I sit on the bed and put on my shoes. I leave the room and make my way to the stairs. As I head downstairs, I can hear Ethan speaking. When I get downstairs, Nate, Ethan, and Jeremy are already there. The girls are still upstairs. I walk over to the kitchen area, where the voices are coming from. On one of the counters are snacks, water bottles, and cups arranged neatly in a corner. Nate, Ethan, and Jeremy are each eating from a small bag of chips. Ethan grabs a bag and tosses it to me, and Nate throws me a soda pop. I catch the soda pop and the chips, walk to the counter and lean against it. Nate pulls the cell phone from his pocket.

"Do you think there's a USB cable around that I can use to charge my phone?"

"The phone is fried. Even if you could find a charger that works, that phone will never work again."

"I won't know unless I try."

Nate goes through each of the cabinets, looking for a charger. It is amusing to watch him rifle through the cabinets, one after another, in search of a USB cable. We all have accepted that our phones will not work anymore, but Nate is having a hard time coping with it.

"What did Tyler have to say?" asks Ethan.

"We had a long talk about what he's doing and his vision for the communities in the world. We should probably wait for the girls to come down so we all can talk about it."

Exhausted from his search, Nate sits on the floor and asks,

"What are your thoughts on the place?"

"I don't think that it's perfect, but it does provide food, shelter, and security. Tyler made us an offer that we all have to discuss and agree to when the others get down here."

As we are speaking, the girls walk into the kitchen. They must have found a blow dryer because their hair is done, and they even look breathtaking. After being in the woods with them for so long, I forgot what Cassie looks like. And before this moment, I never knew what Taylor looks like. I glance over at Nate, and his mouth is wide open. He stares at Taylor intently. The way he stares at her is almost comical. He is already in love with her, and this is just the icing on the cake for him. I feel bad for him because she is not into him at all.

Cassie walks over and takes a chip out of my bag. "This place is nice, but I still don't trust any of them."

"Yeah, I can't believe they have a blow dryer," says Taylor.

Nate stops chewing momentarily and stands up. "By the way, Taylor, your hair looks nice. I like it."

Cassie cocks her head to the side and looks at him.

"Yours looks good too, Cassie," he continues.

"So, let's talk," says Cassie.

I began to tell them about my conversation with Tyler, and I explain to them Tyler's vision for the Sanctuary.

"Tyler wants to rebuild all of the communities in the area and provide them with security the same way he's done here. He already has a few other communities, just like this one that he's rebuilt. I think this may be a good place for us to hole up. We would have shelter, food, and security."

"What does he want us to do for us to stay in the community?" asks Cassie.

"Everyone has to chip in with a skill or something that helps the community function properly."

"Chip in how?" asks Taylor.

"It's all based on your skills. Some people are responsible for food, some are responsible for water, and others are responsible for security."

"What would we be responsible for?" asks Nate.

"Before they approached us, they observed us, and John told Tyler that he thought we would be a good fit for security if that's what you want to do."

"Well, I don't know if I'm up to handling food," says Taylor.

"I think whatever we decide, we should stay together as a group," adds Ethan.

"I agree, especially since we do not trust them yet," says Nate. "We need to stick together in case we have to get out of here quickly."

"I'm getting a bad vibe from this place," sighs Cassie. "We can stay, but I wouldn't get too comfortable."

"Tyler said it's up to us if we stay or not. We can leave anytime we choose."

"I don't know about all this," continues Cassie.

"It doesn't hurt for us to give it a try, maybe for a few days, to see how things work out."

"If we can't stay together as a group, I say we leave," demands Cassie.

"I say give it a try, and besides, we'll have food and shelter while we do it."

They all seem to be in agreement with what I said, but I want to make sure that they do not feel like they have no choice in the matter. I do not want to make the decision for them; this is something we all have to decide together.

"Tell you what. Why don't we put it to a vote? All in favor of staying for a few days, raise your hand."

Everyone raises their hand and votes to stay. I'm surprised that even Cassie's hand is up. *This is good for all of us. At least we can have a place to lay our heads at night, and we can stop sleeping in the woods. We've been roughing it for three months in the woods, and that shower sure felt good. I wouldn't mind another one tonight. I'm glad they made the decision that, and it's unanimous. If everyone did not vote to stay and something went wrong, it might break the group apart.*

As we finish the conversation, there is a knock at the door, and it opens. Kirsten walks through the door. She has freshened up and changed her clothes. Her hair is down, and she is wearing a little bit of lip gloss. She's replaced her boots with some medium heels, which accentuate her body. *I am beginning to understand how Nate feels.* My heart is pounding like it is trying to break through my rib cage and fly out of my chest, and I have this weird sensation in my stomach. This is a sensation that I've only felt once before, during an odd moment with Cassie on my birthday when she hugged me. I was confused back then, but I know now what it means. I am falling for this girl, and I am not sure if she will even feel the same way about me.

Kirsten walks into the kitchen. "I'm here to escort you to dinner."

"Is everyone ready?" asks Taylor.

"Yes."

"I'm ready to eat."

"Let's go."

We head out the door, and we make our way down the street. Kirsten and I are walking side by side, leading the rest of the group. She is very chatty, and we talk all the way to the dining room.

"Did you decide to stay, or are you going to leave?" she asks.

"We decided to stay and give it a try."

She gets very excited at that, and she smiles and hugs me. For that brief moment, I feel a sense of calm and happiness. Then she quickly lets go of me. "I'm sorry. I'm just glad you're staying."

"It's ok. I don't mind."

I turn around to look back at the group, and they give me nods of approval. Cassie has a look of disapproval on her face, however. She does not like me being friendly with Kirsten at all. We arrive at the dining room, where dinner is already being served. There is a place set for us at Tyler's table. Kirsten walks us over to the table.

"Well, here you are," she says

"You're not staying?" I ask

"I don't eat at this table." She turns around and points to a table in the far corner. "That's where I usually eat."

I am filled with disappointment at her words. I was hoping to spend more time with her at dinner, and now it looks like that's not going to happen. Tyler looks at me, and he sees the disappointment in my face.

"Nonsense! You stay and join us," he says. He seems elated. He waves down one of the kitchen workers. "Pull up another chair from the back."

We all sit down, and Cassie takes the seat on my right. I slide my chair over from her to make room for Kirsten. We sit down, and the kitchen workers begin to bring out the food. The workers set the food in the middle of the table.

"You must be famished. Here, try this," suggests Tyler.

He hands me a plate of meat. We have not eaten any meat that did not come from a can in the past three weeks. We are lucky that Hector got the burgers for us. I reach and take the plate from Tyler.

"How did you get your hands on meat?"

"We have teams of hunters that go out and capture whatever

animals they can," says Tyler. "They also go out and find farms that have been abandoned with animals that are still alive. They bring back the animals, and we slaughter and preserve some, and the rest is raised right here."

"Wow!"

"So, you see, Lance, we have a lot of different people here with a lot of different functions, and everybody plays a part in keeping the community functioning."

"It's a good thing you're doing here."

"Where are my manners? Please, introduce me to the rest of your group."

"On this side, we have Cassie. Next to her is Ethan. On the other side is Nate, Jeremy, Emma, and Taylor."

"It's a pleasure to have you all here."

"Thank you."

"The pleasure is all ours."

"Thank you for having us."

"Have you discussed what you are going to do?" asks Tyler.

"We decided we are going to stay," says Cassie.

"Excellent!" he shouts.

He stands up and picks up a glass of wine. He raises the glass in the air, and he toasts: "To the newcomers."

Everyone in the room cheers and pounds on the tables. Tyler

takes a sip of the wine and sets the glass on the table. He spreads his arms and begins speaking.

"I am pleased you decided to stay. All of our communities are growing by leaps and bounds. Now you'll stay here for the time being to train and learn. Once training is over, we will have to move you to a different community. This is the first community, and it's already all filled. But don't worry, you'll all be together."

"Thank you. We all appreciate your generosity."

"Yes, thank you."

"We really appreciate it."

"Don't mention it. You are a part of the family now. This is what it's all about, building a new family. We've all lost our own, and now we've found each other. And with your help, we will build a strong family."

He raises his glass again to the air. "To family."

Everyone in the room, with one voice, responds, shouting out, "To family!"

The scene is eerie, a little bit creepy, but I shrug it off. I raise up my glass along with the rest of the group, and I nod my head. "To family!" I say.

"To family!" whispers the group.

Our glasses are filled with fruit punch, and we drink it after making the toast. They pass around plates with different assortments of foods, and we pick out what looks appetizing to us and begin eating.

"How did you manage to get electricity and running water?" I ask.

"I and some others are part of the Army Corps of Engineers. We had the know-how and ingenuity to get basic electricity working again. We made some electric pumps to pump water into the tower to pressurize it. While the technology itself may be affected, electricity is not. The reason devices like cell phones, tablets, computers, and televisions don't work is because they have microchips in them. The microchips are what was fried by the EMP from the solar flare."

"What about cars? Why don't they work?" asks Jeremy.

"Newer cars have computers in them, so they will not work, but older cars without computers will. If you can rewire newer cars to bypass the computers, they will work too."

"Don't you need microchips for the electricity to work?" asks Ethan.

"Electricity can be generated without modern technology. Electricity existed before microchips, but only devices that do not have microchips will work. This is why light bulbs and simple gadgets like electric blow dryers work."

"So, simple motors will work, and computers won't. Got it," I say.

"My crew and I were fortunate. We were transporting wind turbines, which can generate tens of thousands of kilowatts of power when this happened. We were able to rewire the generators and bypass the computerized electronics. It allowed us to create a wind farm to generate electricity, which the communities are using."

"You guys did great work getting this place up and running," comments Nate.

"We only need the basic necessities to survive. We have all we need right here in the community. We will first take back our communities and then our country, street by street, and eventually, city by city."

"That's ambitious," says Taylor.

"Yes, it is. We can build a new world. We can bring peace and tranquility to the world. We have an opportunity for a second chance, an opportunity to remake the world, and we must seize it. This is the only way to make it a better place for future generations."

"What about people who don't want to rebuild the world? Don't they get a vote?" asks Cassie.

"It would be irresponsible of us, here and now, not to take the opportunity to make the world a better place. If each and every one of us in this room does not step up to the plate and make a difference, then we should not complain when things don't go our way. We should not be displeased when we are in distress. But enough talking for now. Eat."

We were all listening to Tyler intently and did not have an opportunity to eat. We begin eating, and the morsels of meats are delicious. I reach for one of the rolls on the table in front of me. Kirsten reaches for one at the same time.

"Sorry!" we both whisper.

"I pick up the basket of bread and hand it to her. She takes a dinner roll and sets it on her plate. She takes a second and puts it onto my plate, and I smile.

"Thank you."

She smiles back at me. "You're welcome."

We stare and smile at each other briefly. I don't know why I do, but I look over at Cassie, and she rolls her eyes and turns her head away from me.

"How old are you?" asks Kirsten.

"I just turned seventeen."

"Wow! Me too. My birthday was in May, May 18. Well, I mean, I didn't just turn; it's been almost five months."

Looking at her, you would think she is twenty years old. She is very mature looking for her age.

"Where are you from?" she asks.

"We're from Virginia, well, except for Taylor and Emma. We met them on the road."

"Really? What are you doing all the way in Pennsylvania?"

"We were trying to get out of range of the nuclear fallout from the meltdown at the nuclear plant near our homes."

"I'm from Pennsylvania. My parents..."

Just then, she looks at Tyler, and she stops speaking. Whatever it is she was going to tell me, she does not want Tyler to hear. I begin to wonder what it is that she's afraid to say to me in front of Tyler, but I do not press the issue. I figure that she will tell me in her own time or somewhere away from Tyler. As I sit there pondering, someone steps onto the makeshift stage and begins announcing the entertainment for the night. I am thrilled that we are going to have some entertainment; it has been a while since we were able to entertain ourselves.

"They made the trip early from one of the Oakwood communities for Purification Day, which is in just a little over a week. Here they are, the Sanctuary's own, The Flares."

The band has three members: one plays the piano, another the drums, and the third is on guitar. The band takes the stage, and they begin playing a song that they wrote about the Sanctuary. The song is a little creepy. It's about Purification Day, whatever that is, and the hard cleansing that has to be done. They also have a verse thanking Tyler for showing them the way. I do not think much about it, though. I am hungry, and getting some food in my stomach is all that matters at that moment. Besides, it is hard to be in the company of Kirsten and not focus my full attention on her. I cannot understand why Cassie is not happy about our mutual interest in each other. I will have to give her some time to get used to the new situation. The band plays a few songs and ends their show.

"We'd like to thank Tyler for his leadership and for allowing us to come over and perform for you guys," says the bandleader.

Tyler stands up and raises his glass. "Thank you for your constant travels to keep all of the communities in the

Sanctuary entertained."

Everyone stands up and gives them a standing ovation. The band takes a bow, and then we sit down and continue eating.

"What is Purification Day?" I ask.

Tyler wipes his mouth and gives me another sinister smile. "This is going to be our second Purification Day. I established Purification Day to be a day on which we celebrate our newfound freedom, freedom from the oppressions of the past, freedom from those who would abuse our trust and have us labor for nothing, freedom from bigotry and hate, freedom from the prejudices and the unfairness of the past."

"So, it's a celebration?" asks Taylor.

"It's good that you can make time to celebrate after what happened," I comment.

"But purification doesn't come without sacrifice. We must absolve ourselves of all the past misdeeds and all the sins of the past so that we will never forget the world that was as we rebuild the world that is. For now, we hold the purification celebration once a month. As the Sanctuary grows, we'll have less and less to atone for, and it will then become an annual observance. You all will have a great treat very soon; Purification Day is in a little over a week. Then you will see what it means to be a member of the Sanctuary and if you have what it takes, if you have the guts, to rebuild this country. No! No! To rebuild this world," orates Tyler.

Tyler's speech gets a standing ovation from everyone in the

room. They shout, whistle, scream, and howl for Tyler after his speech. We eat and drink, and afterward, people from around the room come over to introduce themselves to us and welcome us to the Sanctuary.

Kirsten leans over and whispers to me. "You should take a walk with me."

She gets up and walks out of the dining area, and I get up and follow her. Cassie is ever so vigilant; she looks at me disapprovingly. I exit the room and meet up with Kirsten in the front.

"I misjudged the Sanctuary," I tell her. "It seems like a very nice place."

"Follow me. I know a quiet place where we can sit and talk."

We walk towards the far end of the community and sit on some benches near a manmade pond.

"You're fortunate to have found this place," I say. "We were out there on our own for a while."

"The Sanctuary isn't at all what it appears to be," she whispers.

"What do you mean?"

"I can't say any more. I've already said too much. Tyler likes for newcomers to experience it themselves."

"Why did you stop speaking about your parents inside when you looked at Tyler?"

She gives me a blank stare. "I'm sorry. Like I said, I've already said too much. Maybe we should go back inside."

I convince her to stay, and we talk for a while about other things, but her uneasiness leaves me wondering if we made the right decision.

CHAPTER SEVENTEEN

I slowly open my eyes and roll over onto my back. The sun's rays pierce through the window, almost blinding me. I take a long stretch, and then I pull the pillow closer to me. I lie there for a moment, thinking about all that we have gone through, all the problems that we've had since the day the Burning began. We lost our homes, and we lost our parents, but throughout the whole ordeal, we had each other. There are dangerous people out there beyond these walls who want to hurt others for no reason.

We have an opportunity not just to survive but to thrive in the Sanctuary. We had to grow up quickly out there. Now we have to help secure this place and make a new life for ourselves. I am glad that we found this place, even though they are a bit strange. I cannot get Kirsten out of my mind. She is so beautiful, and I think I am falling for her. The past few days have been magical; it is love at first sight. I thought that Cassie would be happy for me, but I do not know what the deal is with her. She does not seem to like Kirsten. I think if she gives her a chance, she might like her. I have to wait for the right time to tell Kirsten how I feel. I know I've only known her for a few days, but from the moment I met her, I knew I wanted to be with her and that she is the one.

I hear a knock on the door downstairs. I roll over and sit up on the edge of the bed. I stand up to put on my pants and slip on a shirt. I open the door and head towards the stairs. It sounds like everyone is already awake. The door opens, and I hear Kirsten's voice. I walk downstairs and see Kirsten standing in the doorway.

She walks into the house and sets her rifle next to the door. "I've been sent to bring you all in for duty."

"Duty?" asks Cassie.

"Yes. You've had three days to acclimate yourself to the place, and now it's time to learn the ropes. You all will be learning about the community and patrolling the walls with me today."

"Give me a minute to get ready," I say.

"Take your time," replies Kirsten.

I go back upstairs and quickly get ready. I splash water on my face and brush my teeth. I go back downstairs and walk into the kitchen to grab a bite to eat. I pick up a pack of crackers.

"Put that down!" shouts Kirsten. "We'll pick up breakfast in the dining room."

I place them back on the counter. Jeremy and Nate look at their Pop-Tarts and then put them down.

"Breakfast," they say, elated, and then they head towards the door. "Let's go."

Taylor and Emma come downstairs, and everyone gathers at the door. Kirsten picks up her rifle, and we head out. The street is full of kids heading towards the dining room. The odd thing is that I have not seen any grownups. Yeah, there are people in their twenties, but I don't consider them to be grownups. They are very immature. I begin to wonder, *did the radiation kill most of the grownups?* That is the only thing I can think of that makes sense as to why all these kids would be without their parents like us.

"Cassie?" I call.

"Yes."

"Don't you find it odd that there are no adults around? The oldest person I've seen is Captain Tyler."

I don't think she'd given it much thought before I asked her. Kirsten must've heard my question to Cassie. She turns to look at me but, oddly, does not say anything.

We continue to the dining room, and we do not think any more about it as we enter and join the breakfast line. There are eggs, bacon, sausages, toast, and oatmeal out on a buffet. The food smells good and is inviting. We learned yesterday that Tyler has a brigade clearing out the corpses anywhere near the camps. The horrific smell does not exist at the Sanctuary; we are really able to enjoy the smell of breakfast.

As we make our way down the line, the food is rationed, so we are each given a portion of what we want. We get our food and walk to our table. As we are walking, a boy comes up to Kirsten and whispers in her ear, which irritates her.

"You should not be here," she murmurs.

He looks at us, and then he turns and walks away.

"What was that about?" asks Cassie.

"Nothing. That's Quinn. He's harmless."

"You should've introduced us," I say.

"Another time, maybe, when the time is right."

We take a table, and we all sit down to eat. The food tastes delicious. We have been eating canned food for months, and we have not had a real breakfast since the one Hector made for us at the police station, and now this is the third day in a row that we are having breakfast. I wonder, *What happened to Hector? He disappeared in the middle of the night, which scared us into leaving the police station. It was probably a good thing, though, because it got us to move further from the fallout zone.*

We do not talk much while we eat breakfast. We just sit there quietly and dig in. We all clean our plates, and when we are done, we return them to the washing station. We leave the dining room and head back outside.

"I'm going to give you a tour of the compound to show you how everything works," says Kirsten. "Just follow me."

We begin walking towards the back of the compound, in the direction of the field that Tyler showed me in his office.

"Each Sanctuary community is a self-contained, self-functioning micro-city. We already have four communities, and they're in the process of building the fifth one, which is most likely where you will be staying."

"So, we won't be staying here?" asks Emma.

"We bring everyone to this community first, and then Tyler decides where you go from here."

"So, we're not going to be working with you?" I ask.

Kirsten avoids the question by smiling, and she says, "This is the beginning of your tour, so pay attention. We will start in the center of the community, and we will work our way through every station so you can familiarize yourselves with how it functions."

"Where do we go first?" asks Taylor.

"Since you've already been in the dining room, I'll begin the tour here."

We turn back around, and we go towards the dining room.

"We should've just stayed inside for the tour," says Cassie.

"I just thought about it."

We climb the stairs and enter the dining room.

"Not everyone has a skill, and those who do not have any particular skill end up working in the cafeteria. Besides the cooks, who know how to prepare the meals, everyone else in the cafeteria, from the dishwashers to the servers, do not have a skill that can be used elsewhere in the community."

"So, if you don't have a skill, they stick you in the kitchen?" asks Cassie. "What if you don't want to be in the kitchen?"

"While they work in the kitchen, they have the opportunity to learn other skills and get transferred to other areas."

"I guess that's a fair way of doing it," comments Nate.

"If you were not able to use your weapons, you would've probably ended up working the kitchen too."

We walk to the first station, behind the dining room, which is the food distribution station.

"The food distribution center used to give each person their own rations for the week, and everyone was responsible for making their own meals. Eventually, people started running out of their rations quicker than anticipated. Tyler instituted the dining room, with cooks and servers to distribute the food after it's been cooked. This prevents people from running through their rations quicker than they should."

The distribution center is just a plain house where the food is kept in the rooms. We walk through the house, and each room is completely filled with food from the floor to the ceiling. One room has rice, and another has a variety of dried beans. There are three other rooms just like it, which are filled with canned goods. In the back of the house, there are three sheds. Two of the sheds have smoke coming out of the top. She opens the shed in the middle, and it is filled with meat. There is a large fire on the floor to smoke the meat. The third shed is used to store the meat after it is smoked.

"Why do you smoke all the meat?" asks Ethan.

"We have to smoke it because we don't have refrigeration yet. Smoking the meat preserves it, and we can store it for months at a time without spoiling."

She takes a piece of dried meat and hands it to Ethan. "Here, taste."

Ethan takes the meat and eats it. "Hey, it tastes like beef jerky."

Kirsten pulls out a knife. She slices strips of meat and hands a slice to each of us.

We continue on to an empty space behind the house, where there are two barns and the third one under construction.

"What are the barns for?" I ask.

"Tyler is having them built in all the communities to keep the animals."

"Why not just have them stay outside?"

"They would get heatstroke and die. Tyler rigged a water-cooling system using the well water. The water gets cooled at night, and they use it to spray a mist in the barn to keep the animals cool."

We pass the barns and head into another area. This is a large field that they use as a solar farm. It is arranged with solar panels across three or four acres.

"This is part of where the electricity that we use comes from."

"How did he get that many of them to work?" asks Ethan.

"Tyler is a captain in the Army Corps of Engineers. He and his team are trained to get these types of systems running after an EMP blast."

"So, he did all of this?" asks Nate.

"Not just him. Most of his team survived. There are twenty of them. They set up this power station first, and we send power to two other communities. The rest of his team is setting up the electricity in a new community."

In a field adjacent to the one with the solar panels, there are dozens of wind turbines spinning almost synchronously, generating electricity.

"Between the solar panels and the wind turbines, we are able to generate all the electricity we need."

We continue walking until we see five people sitting at the other end of the field.

"It took you long enough," says one of them.

"What, you have somewhere else to be?" retorts Kirsten.

They all stand up and pick up their rifles.

"Who do we have here?" asks another while staring at Cassie.

"This is Lance, Taylor, Cassie, Nate, Ethan, Jeremy, and, and…" She turns and looks at Emma. "Don't tell me. I'll get it."

She stares at Emma for a moment.

Emma places her hands on her hips. "It's Emma!" She stares at Kirsten disapprovingly. "You remembered everyone else's name!"

"And I will never forget it again."

"I'm Tobi. This is Luke, Michael, and Brandon, and it's our job to break you newbies in."

Tobi and Michael look like they are about twenty-one or twenty-two. The others look about our age.

"We're going to take you around the defense perimeter," says Kirsten.

"All right," says Tobi, "today is your training day. You will learn everything you need to know to defend the Sanctuary."

"What is it you expect us to do?" asks Taylor.

"I expect you to be quiet and listen because I'm only going to tell you once."

As he speaks, Tobi walks closer to the wall. "This wall is our only defense against the anus."

"Against the buttholes?" asks Nate.

"Tobi finds it funny to call them anus, but it's a Latin word that is pronounced a-nus," corrects Kirsten.

"The anus is those who mean to do us harm," continues Tobi. "They are those who have destroyed the past world. They are the enemy of the future, and we must do everything to stop them."

"Why do you guys wear the green armbands?" asks Jeremy.

"Because, when you're out there, that is the only way we can tell ourselves apart from everybody else. You wouldn't want me to shoot you by accident, would you?"

"No, I guess not."

"And it also symbolizes that we are one with the earth," adds Michael. "We have accepted living in a symbiotic relationship with the planet so that we don't destroy it like the anus did."

"And none of you will earn one of these," says Tobi, pointing to his green armbands, "unless I say so. Now, move out!"

We start walking along the wall. Tobi gives us instructions on how to do a patrol. The walls must be at least fifteen feet tall and are made of mostly metal and concrete. In between the metal and concrete, at designated points, are cinderblock towers. The wall encompasses the entire compound and is under constant patrol. The towers are manned twenty-four hours a day. Along the metal section of the walls, there are small peepholes that can slide open to fire a weapon in case the community is under attack.

"You see these peepholes? When you patrol, you have to make sure they remain closed. They can only be opened from the inside, and we don't want to give the enemy a chance to take a shot at us."

"Why do you say they are the enemy?" I ask. "We're all Americans, and we should be helping each other."

"You've seen what's out there," says Tobi. "You've been out there. It's lawless. The United States of America no longer exists. Tyler established law here, and the anus rejected change. Now they want to destroy us because we have embraced the new world."

"So, why not just help them see that they're wrong?" asks Cassie.

"Yeah, I'm sure they can be reasoned with," adds Taylor.

"Look at this place," I say. "Tyler's rebuilding society. Why not give them the opportunity and sit down with them and work out your differences?"

Tobi stops. He turns around and looks at me. "Look, they are the ones who destroyed the planet. They are the cause of this, and they are not willing to change the old ways. They cannot be part of our Sanctuary. The sooner you get that through your thick head, the better off you'll be. Trust me on that. So, if you're done talking, we can go up this tower so I can show you what your guard duties are going to be."

We follow Tobi up the guard tower. It's slightly higher than the wall, maybe about twenty feet up in the air. We reach the top of the tower, and Tobi goes to the far end of it.

"Look around," he says.

The tower provides a 180-degree view of the compound and a view of the side the tower is on. You can see for at least a mile, up to a line of trees outside the compound.

"You see the trees?" asks Tobi.

"Yeah, what about them?" I reply.

"The trees obstruct our view, so we devised early warning systems to alert us when people approach too closely. We will need to go outside so I can show you."

The guard towers are equipped with automatic weapons, grenades, and plenty of ammo.

"One more thing. You see this?" Tobi points to what looks like a megaphone attached to the wall of the tower. "This is a World War II-style air-raid siren. If we come under attack, you will need to crank the siren to turn it on. Did you all get that?"

"Yes, sir!" we reply.

We go back downstairs with Tobi, and then we go around the side of the base of the tower, where there is a metal door.

"Every tower has one of these doors, and inside each of these doors, there is a trapdoor in the floor. The trapdoor leads to a tunnel that will take you three hundred feet from the wall. If we are ever under attack, we can use these tunnels to attack the enemy from behind."

"How did you build all this in a matter of months?" I ask.

"This is a gated community, so most of the wall was already built. We added to the wall and extended it," says Tobi. "We scavenge a lot of old farm equipment to run cement mixers. We found an old bulldozer on one of the farms that we used to dig the tunnels. Everyone worked day and night to build the wall and tunnels for safety."

Tobi opens the trapdoor, and there is a ladder that leads down into the tunnel. We grab the flashlights that are hanging on the wall, and we follow Tobi down the ladder into the tunnel. The tunnel is well constructed, but it is long and dark. We make it to the other end, where there is another ladder leading up to a trapdoor to the outside. There is a rope that comes from the trapdoor, and it is tied to a bucket on the floor.

"The ladder leads outside. You have to pull on the rope, which will empty the dirt hiding the trapdoor on the outside. If you don't, the dirt will fall on you. You need to get the dirt into the bucket before you can open the trapdoor."

Tobi pulls the rope, and dirt pours into the bucket like sand in an hourglass. The bucket quickly fills up, and we move it out of the way.

"Now we're clear to go up," says Tobi.

He climbs up the ladder and opens the latch to the trapdoor. He pushes the door open, and we all climb outside. We can see part of the gate through the trees, but most of it is obstructed from view. We all look around to get our bearings.

"As you can see, it's difficult to see you in the tree lines, especially at night from these towers," continues Tobi.

"So, how will we see someone in time to stop them?" I ask.

"You won't. This is why we set up this alarm system."

Tobi walks over to two trees, and very low to the ground, between the trees, is a tripwire that is connected to a beacon on top of one of the trees. The beacon's power source is a solar panel that is at the top of the tree.

"The beacon can't be seen from the ground. It can only be seen from the towers. It gives us a chance to prepare our defenses before the enemy even knows that we know they are here."

Tobi walks closer to one of the trees and points to a mark on the trunk.

"But you need to know where these wires are. These X's are on the bottoms of the trees, so they will not be at eye level. This makes them harder to spot if you don't know they're there. Every tree with an X has a tripwire that will turn on the beacon when tripped. You need to be aware of that for when you are patrolling the outside perimeter."

Tobi walks back to the trap door.

"You two, pull the bucket up and empty it," he commands Ethan and me. We walk over, and we stand above the trap door. We grab the rope and hoist the bucket up. I grab the bucket, and I dump the dirt to the side of the trapdoor.

"Lower the bucket back down," continues Tobi.

I lower the bucket down, and Tobi closes the trapdoor. He spreads the same dirt over the door to hide it.

"Every trapdoor is surrounded on all four sides by tripwires. So, the tripwires are in a square pattern, and they mark the location of the trapdoor from the outside."

We walk around the woods, identifying the tripwires and their locations. The Sanctuary compound must be much bigger than I initially thought, as it takes us over an hour to walk the perimeter. Midway through our second patrol, Tobi stops at an area that they use for target practice.

"Ok, you, big man, come here," Tobi commands Ethan.

Ethan steps forward and stands next to Tobi.

"I want to see what you can do with a target fifty yards away."

Ethan checks his rifle, cocks it, and aims at the target. The target is a tree trunk situated at the other end of the range. Ethan fires his weapon and hits the tree trunk on the outside of the target.

"Let's see what you got," Tobi says to me.

I check my magazine and then place it back into the rifle. I lift the rifle and aim downrange. I fire the weapon and hit the inside of the outer circle of the target.

"Let me try," says Jeremy.

"Ok, little man, let me see what you got," replies Tobi.

Jeremy takes his rifle, and he cocks it back. He aims and fires, hitting the inner part of the second circle.

"Yeah!" shouts Jeremy.

We all high five him, and I rub his hair.

"Ok, you've got potential, kids," compliments Tobi.

Nate grabs his rifle and begins walking forward. "Why don't we let one of the ladies go next?"

"Are you kidding? You are one of the ladies," jokes Ethan.

We all laugh. It is very refreshing to hear Ethan joking. It gives me the feeling that we made the right decision to stay here. Ethan is getting comfortable in a place where we belong.

"Ha ha ha, very funny," hisses Nate. He moves to the back, allowing Taylor and Cassie to move forward.

"How about you?" Tobi asks Cassie.

She shakes her head.

"Don't tell me you ladies are going to let these guys show you up. You're not scared, are you?"

Without saying a word, Taylor walks to the front of the group. She cocks her rifle and aims at the target. She fires the first shot and hits the center of the target. She fires a second and third shot, and both also hit the target in the center.

She turns and looks at Tobi. "Scared? I don't think so."

"Now, that's how you do it!" shouts Tobi.

We are all in shock. I turn and look at Nate, and he is staring at Taylor with puppy-dog eyes as if he just fell deeper in love with her. Cassie and Emma high five Taylor.

She places her arm around Cassie. "You can do this!"

Cassie walks to the front. She aims her rifle and fires. She misses the target altogether and is very disappointed.

Taylor walks to the front to comfort her. "That's ok. You come out here and keep practicing, and you will hit the center of that target. I promise," she says.

Emma runs to the front. "My turn, my turn!"

"Ok, you've got the fire in you. Show me what you got," says Tobi.

"I'm not as good as my sister, but I can shoot too."

She takes her rifle and cocks it. Then she aims at the target, and she fires. To my surprise, she hits the inner part of the second circle on the target.

"Yeah!" shouts everyone.

Jeremy runs to the front and hugs Emma. Everyone gives her a high five. She is thrilled, and she smiles the entire time.

"One of you is a marksman. The rest of you will all need some work. You will need target practice, and fortunately for you, we're a family here at the Sanctuary. We will train you to get better, so don't be discouraged. With practice, you will all become marksmen."

He smiles and points to Taylor. "Taylor."

"Yes," she answers.

"You and Kirsten will be in charge of making sure that the rest of the newbies know how to hit that target."

"Yes, sir," replies Kirsten.

Tobi looks at all of us and says, "I joined the Marines to make a difference. I was on leave when this shitstorm hit. But thanks to Captain Tyler and the Sanctuary he built, I have a chance to serve again. I need you to be confident, strong and to know that there is nothing you can't do. The defense of the Sanctuary is your responsibility. Your new family is inside those walls. The time will come when you will have to do what it takes to protect them. When that time comes, you will be committed, and you will be ready."

He stops speaking and looks at us. "Can I get an oohrah from everyone?"

"Oohrah!"

"I can't hear you!"

"Oohrah!"

"You will need this enthusiasm when the anus shows up on our walls."

"Why do you call them anus?" I ask.

"Anus is a Latin word. I would do you a disservice if I told you what it meant before Purification Day. Luckily for you, that's in four days. On that day, all your questions will be answered. All your doubts will be removed when you pledge allegiance to the Sanctuary. Now, can I get an oohrah?"

"Oohrah!"

After the pep talk, we go around the perimeter to make sure that it is clear and secure. We make it to the front gate and go back into the compound. We walk along the inside of the wall in the opposite direction that we went earlier. We walk through the residential side of the complex. There are many homes in that section. Each of the houses is shared; the number of people in them depends on how large the homes are. We patrol the compound until lunchtime when we eat in the dining room. The lunch is nothing to write home about, but it's nice to be able to sit down for a meal. After lunch, we go back out with Kirsten to the range for some more target practice.

We practice shooting for the next two days. Tobi does not want us to patrol until he is confident that we can use a weapon properly. I spend a lot of time getting to know Kirsten over the two days. I enjoy getting to know and learning about her. The tension between Cassie and I has grown increasingly worse. We've gone from being good friends to her, avoiding me. We've barely talked the past two days, and I don't know why.

On the third day, Taylor works with Cassie, giving her pointers on how to fire the weapon properly. As she works with Cassie, Nate approaches her from behind.

"Hey, Taylor."

She seems a little hostile to Nate when she answers, "What do you want!"

"I wanted to know if you could show me how to shoot like you. Believe it or not, I never held a weapon before all this started."

At Nate's words, Taylor's attitude changes, and she invites him over to practice with them.

After a while, Tobi enters the range. "Everyone gather around," he commands.

We put down our weapons and form a circle around Tobi.

"Now, to protect this facility, you will need some basic combat training. I will instruct you on how to properly conceal yourselves, how to cover from enemy fire, and how to properly engage the enemy and return fire."

Tobi walks out of the circle and picks up a weapon. He walks over to a tree and then turns to face us. "Now, it's imperative that you are aware of your surroundings, first, to make sure you have an adequate cover so as not to be seen by the enemy and, at the same time, to make sure you have a clear view of your target."

He points his rifle up, and he places his back against the trees. "When you are under fire, it's important that you find cover that will protect your entire body. You don't want to leave your arms or legs exposed. This tree here is perfect because it's large enough to give full protection from anyone firing, at least from downrange. However, you will find yourself in situations where you do not have adequate cover. In that case, do the best you can. It's also important to have a clear line of sight, so you do not hit any friendlies. More importantly, you must work together as one cohesive unit. You are not individuals out here; you're a team. People are brought home in body bags, while teams live to fight another day. Communication with your team is paramount to your survival out here. By having good communication through visual hand signals, you and your team will make it home for supper."

As Tobi speaks, John and his squad join us.

"John," says Tobi, "why don't you and your crew give us a demonstration."

John walks up to the circle and says, "In close-quarter combat situations, talking will give away your position to the enemy, and they will know which tactics you're planning against them. I'm going to show you some hand signals that will help you with basic communication without having to talk. In my opinion, the most important one is the 'I do not understand' sign. You do it by waving your palm back and forth. If you don't know what's being planned, you better speak up, or you might just get your squad killed. Next, we have the 'I understand' sign."

John goes over so many signs that it is hard to learn them all that quickly. We spend the rest of the afternoon, learning the hand signals and going over drills and tactics with John. It is fascinating; I never knew that military tactics were so methodical. John also spends the time showing us how to use objects for cover and how to communicate and attack in formation for maximum effectiveness. He shows us how to retrieve the wounded off the battlefield. He also teaches us how to attack by flanking the enemy on different sides. Running around and doing these drills in the heat takes a toll on us, but John tells us that the enemy is not going to care whether we are tired or not.

As night falls, the cool of the evening is welcomed. We are all relieved when the sun finally cools down. We practice nighttime tactics in the low light, and then John stops for the day.

"That's enough for now!"

Everyone stops, and we walk over towards John.

"You all should be proud of yourselves. You did good today. The same spirit you showed today is what we're going to need to protect this place. Now, head to the cafeteria and get yourselves some dinner. We'll continue tomorrow."

CHAPTER EIGHTEEN

We are all exhausted from another day of training. Today was the third day of these drills. I guess it could be worse: at least we are doing this for a good reason. The slow walk to the compound gives me a chance to cool down because the sun has gone down. We walk around to the front of the complex and enter through the front gate. I have to say, although it's been rough, I've enjoyed every minute. I've especially enjoyed sparring with Kirsten. We make it to the front of the compound, not too far from the dining room. *I can't sit down and eat filthy like this. We still have some time before dinner starts. I will go and wash up.*

"I'm going wash up before we eat," I say, and I pull the dirty, sweaty T-shirt off.

"I'm with you, bro. I could use a hot shower," adds Nate.

Everyone agrees with the sentiment, so we all decide to go back to the guesthouse and clean up before dinner.

"I'll see you guys at dinner," says Kirsten.

"Save me a seat," I reply.

Kristen smiles at me, and then she turns around and walks away. I stand there, watching her walk away with John and the rest of his squad until Ethan grabs me by the shoulders.

"Let's go, dude!"

We walk towards the guest cabin, which, thankfully, is close to the front entrance, so we do not have a long way to go. We enter the cabin, and we all disappear into the rooms. I enter my room, take off my clothes, and turn on the shower. I get in and let the water wash dirt off me. The water has changed color, as if it were mixed with mud, by the time it hits the shower floor. We were rolling in the dirt, so I imagine we are all filthy.

I get dressed and go downstairs. The other boys trickle downstairs one at a time.

"I'm exhausted," complains Ethan.

"I think we are all exhausted," I reply.

"Are you kidding me? That was fun," says an elated Jeremy.

"Of course, you would think that was fun," says Nate. "And we have to do it all over again tomorrow."

"Don't know what you're complaining about, Nate," I say. "I saw Taylor's arm around you, showing you how to fire that weapon."

The girls finally came down, and we leave the house and head to the dining room. When we get there, Kirsten is waiting for us outside.

"There you are!" she says. "Tyler's back from his trip, and he wants you at his table again tonight." She grabs me by the hand and begins walking, dragging me along. "Hurry up, guys. They started eating without you."

I turn around and look at everyone. Cassie seems to be

annoyed with me again. I can only assume that it is because of Kirsten. I shrug it off and go into the dining room. Kirsten was right: by the time we get there, Tyler and all his lieutenants are at the table, and they have already started eating. We all walk over to the table, and I pull out a chair for Kirsten. I take the seat next to her, and we sit down.

"Welcome," says Tyler. "John tells me that you had a good day today."

"Yes, it was a lot to learn and process," I respond.

"I had a feeling you would do well from the moment I saw you. I know it's been a long day. Eat!"

We take our plates and utensils, and we begin selecting food to eat. I grab a piece of meat and pass the plate around. As I look around, I realize that only Tyler's table, for his lieutenants and his guests, has this abundance of food. Everyone else in the dining room has to get in the buffet line, where the food is rationed and served. Immediately after I notice this, I get a sick feeling in my stomach, and all of a sudden, I am not that hungry. But to keep up appearances, I take a little bit of food and eat. I must be the only one who's noticed it because, as I look around the table, everyone is filling their plates, talking, and laughing. I look at Kirsten, and it dawns on me that both the last time and tonight, she has barely eaten. I did not notice it the first night, but we skipped dinner the past couple of nights, and Kirsten brought our portion to the guest house on John's orders so that we could get comfortable. I begin to wonder if this is bothering her as much as it is bothering me and whether or not she is happy here at the Sanctuary.

I lean over to her. "Not hungry?"

"I eat very little," she says, "but go ahead. Eat and enjoy yourself."

"I am eating."

"I know you can eat more than that. I saw your plate the other night."

"I overdid it a few nights ago. I had not eaten a meal like that in a long time."

Everyone at the table eats heartily, and some even go for a second helping, but I am already put off from eating and barely manage to get down what I have on my plate. Tyler must've noticed that I'm not eating because he looks at my plate.

"Eat. I promise I won't charge you for it."

"I'm just a bit tired from all the running around today."

"The more reason you should eat. You want to keep your strength up."

I stick my fork into the meat, and I take another piece and place it on my plate. I also grab a biscuit. I do not want to give Tyler any indication that I do not like how he runs the dining room. I eat my share of the food, forcing every bite down as I go along.

Kirsten must've noticed that I really don't want to eat the food. She leans over and whispers in my ear, "You don't have to eat all of it if you don't want to."

"It's ok. I'm fine."

She places her hand in my lap, and she cocks her head to the side and smiles at me. I place my hand over hers and smile back at her. We stare at each other briefly, but we are interrupted when Tyler knocks his fork against his glass. He stands up and begins speaking.

"The Sanctuary has a lot to be thankful for. Every day, we grow as new members make their way to the safety of our compound. This week, it was Lance and his group. Today, it's Jonathan and Susie. Our sister compounds have also reported twenty new members this week."

The cafeteria explodes with cheers. Everyone seems to be happy with Tyler's report. He smiles at the applause, and when it dies down, he continues.

"Now, tomorrow, we will have our monthly day of purification. You will be known as the greatest generation that has ever lived on the planet. This is because you had what it took to hunt the anus and make them pay for their crimes against humanity, for their crimes against this planet. Those who are backward, who do not respect the planet or live in harmony with it, must be moved out of our way to make room for the New World."

Again, the crowd cheers. It goes on a little longer this time until Tyler raises his hands and calms the applause.

"We have grown by leaps and bounds since the last Purification Day. Tomorrow, members of the other Sanctuary communities will make their way here to celebrate with us. We will welcome them with open arms. We will show them that even though we are apart, we are still of one mind, and we are with them always. We will also punish anus for their many crimes and their tyranny, whipping them from the face of the earth. We will have the bonfire tomorrow night, behind the clubhouse, but tonight, you all can enjoy movie night in the outdoor theater."

Everyone cheers. John takes Tyler's hand and raises it in the air. The cheering goes on for a minute before dying down. After the cheering ceases, everyone begins clearing the tables, placing the trays in the cleaning area. Tyler stands up, and everyone at his table stands with him. Tyler and John head towards a back door that leads towards his office, while most everyone else heads out the front door.

"We should probably stay behind and help clean up," suggests Kirsten. "That way, they will be able to see the movie too."

I turn to the rest of the group. "Hey, guys, Kirsten is right. We should probably give a hand cleaning up so they can finish before the movie starts."

We gather the trays, along with plates and utensils. There is a designated wash area, which is set up like an assembly line. Kirsten and I go to the wash area and work at the washing stations. She hands me an apron, and she puts one on too. The cleaning station has two sides, one for washing and one for rinsing. She takes over the side for washing, and she begins scrubbing the plates, passing them on to me to rinse. As we wash, everyone else is cleaning up and bringing the empty plates and trays to the cleaning stations. It doesn't take us long to clean up with all the help. Kirsten sprays a little water on me, and she giggles. I look at her and spray her back. She sprays it at me again, and we both laugh. After we finish, the cleanup crew comes over and thanks all of us for the help.

We take off our aprons and leave the dining room. The movie is just getting started, and there are chairs and blankets all over the dried lawn. Cassie, Nate, and the rest of the gang find a spot in the back and plant themselves there. Kirsten and I walk towards them.

"Hey, my shirt is a little wet from the dishes," Kirsten says. "I'm going to change, and I'll be right back."

"Mine too," I reply. "I'll walk with you."

"We'll be back in a minute, y'all," Kirsten says to the others. "We're going to change these wet shirts. It's chilly out."

We walk away from the field and head to Kirsten's house. I have not been to her place yet. It will be interesting to see how she lives.

"My place is this way."

The house that she is staying in is situated on the opposite side of the guesthouse. We walk through the neighborhood, towards her house, talking as we go.

"You keep telling me that you are from Pennsylvania, but you never say which part you're from."

"My house was actually in one of the other communities. After Tyler took it over, he moved me over here."

"Tyler seems like a good guy. He's doing good work here."

"Look, you and your friends are nice, and I like you guys, so I'm going to be honest with you. Everything that you see here is not as it seems."

"What do you mean it's not as it seems?"

"I shouldn't have said anything. Forget I even mentioned that."

I stop walking and take her by the hand. "Wait, is there something going on? You need to tell us."

She looks around in all directions. "We can't talk out here. Somebody might hear us."

Her concerns begin to worry me. Besides the food situation, I haven't noticed anything else unsavory about Tyler or this place.

"Let's go to your place," I say. "We can talk there."

"The walls of my house have ears. It will be safer to talk at the guesthouse."

I let go of her hand, and we continue walking without saying another word. We reach her house, and she opens the door.

"Wait here. I'll be right back."

I sit on the steps of the front porch, staring at the homes as I think about what could be wrong with this seemingly beautiful community, this sanctuary that everyone seems to be happy in. *I have to remain objective. Maybe Kirsten is being difficult. Maybe she misses home. I guess it doesn't hurt to hear her out. Once I listen to what she has to say, then I can make a decision on what I should tell the others and what we should do.* As I sit there pondering on these things, the door opens, and Kirsten walks out with a clean shirt on.

"Are you ready to go to your place?"

"Yeah, let's go."

I take off in the direction we came. "Follow me. I know a shortcut."

Kirsten and I walk through some backyards until we make it to the back of the guesthouse. We go around to the front and enter the guesthouse.

"Give me a minute to change my shirt."

I go up the stairs and into my room. I quickly change my shirt, and just as fast, I go back downstairs.

"That was fast."

"It was just a T-shirt."

I slow step in closer to Kirsten, and I take both of her hands. "Tell me something you've never told anyone about yourself."

"What? Why?" she giggles.

"Because I want to know all about Kirsten. Here, let me start. When I was ten, my bird died. I spent the next three days after hiding in my room, crying."

"What?" Kirsten giggles. "I would not tell anyone else about that if I were you."

"I went first to break the ice. Now it's your turn."

She slowly slides her hand behind my neck, and then she leans in towards me until our lips connect, and we kiss passionately. It is deliciously electrifying, sending chills all over my body, making the hair on my arms stand. I have never felt this way before. A wave of emotion overtakes me. I have been kissed before, but this is the first time that it felt this way. I feel like I could stay like this forever, but she slowly stops and pulls away.

"Wow," we both say simultaneously and giggle.

"So, what does this mean?" I ask.

"It means from the moment I stood over you with the gun, I wanted to do this. But we can take it slow if you want."

I lean into her for another long kiss. She moves her head to my ear and whispers, "That's all you're going to get for now!"

She tugs on my earlobe with her lips as she pulls away, and then she turns around and steps back slightly.

"What did you want to tell me about this place."

She turns around and takes a couple of steps as if she is thinking of what to say. She turns back, and she faces me. The smile is wiped from her face as she steps in closer. "Do you trust me?" she asks.

"I know we just met, but you are genuine, so I say, yes, I trust you."

She takes both of my hands and looks me in the eye.

"Whatever you do, do not tell Tyler that you do not want to stay."

"Why? He said we can leave anytime we want."

"He does not let anyone leave. That is why I'm still here. He kills anyone who tries to leave."

"No way! He seems like such a nice guy."

"That's why everyone stays until they find out what this place is really about. Whatever you do tomorrow, do not react during any part of the cleansing ceremony. Let your friends know that they should do whatever is asked of them if they want to survive."

"What do you mean by 'do anything'?"

"Besides the crazy soldiers who set this place up, look around you. People do not want to be here. They are all pretending because they know what happens to those who want to leave. Just be careful, ok."

She softly places her hand on my cheek. "Everything is going to be ok. I have a plan."

"Ok, I trust you. We should start heading back to the movie before they miss us."

We leave the guesthouse and walk down the street towards the clubhouse. We go around back to the area where the movie is playing. We look around for Cassie and the others. When we spot them, we walk over and sit in an open area behind Cassie.

Cassie turns around and looks at us. "Where have you been?"

"I'll tell you all about it later when we get to the house."

The movie has already started. It is playing on a vintage projector. I guess it works because it doesn't have any microchips in it. They are playing an old black and white film. I guess the projector is so old it can only play the older movies. I have never watched a black and white film before, and that makes it interesting. I do not know the name of the movie, but we sit through the entire thing. When the credits roll, I get up with Kirsten, and I tell everyone else that I will meet them back at the guesthouse. We've been in each other's way since the start of the Burning. I think it's about time we stretch our legs and get a breather from one another, and being with Kirsten is my opportunity to getaway.

I walk Kirsten home. On the way, she takes my hand, and we hold hands until we get to a quiet place under a tree. We stop under the tree to share a kiss. I don't know what type of tree it is, but the ambiance makes it magical. I only slow down and then stop to tell her what I am thinking.

"You how you said we can take it slow if I want? Well, I don't want to take it slow because you never know what tomorrow will bring."

I lean into her again and continue our kiss. As more people start to walk by from the movie, we slowly stop, and I take her by both hands. "If only we had a cloak of invisibility," I say.

"How would I be able to see those beautiful blue eyes?"

"Come on, I'll walk you home now."

We continue walking and hold hands all the way to her doorstep. We walk up the stairs, and I take her by both hands again. "Are you enjoying our first date?" I ask.

"Date?"

"Well, we rolled in the dirt all day, then dinner and a movie. And we made out! I think it was a date. A great date considering."

Kirsten giggles. "Well, since you put it that way."

She leans in and kisses me, and as we are kissing, her roommates reach the house.

"I guess this is the end of our date," says Kirsten.

I let go of her hands and

slowly head down the stairs. Her roommates reach the stairs, and she goes into the house with them. I turn around and head towards the guesthouse.

I open the door to the guesthouse, and immediately, Nate runs up to me. "What the heck, bro? Do tell, do tell!"

"You don't leave out any details. You tell us everything," adds Ethan.

They are laughing at me, and I am a little bit embarrassed, so I shake my head. "There's nothing to tell."

"So, how do you explain the lip gloss on your ear?" asks Nate.

I rub my earlobe, and there is a little bit of lip gloss on my hand. I don't want to talk about this with them, so I begin to think of any way I can get out of it, and that's when I realize we have not talked about what Kirsten told me about the purification ceremony.

"More importantly, we have things to discuss, very important things," I say, interrupting their line of questioning. I take a seat across from everyone and say, "Kirsten and I got a chance to talk."

Everyone becomes attentive to hear me out.

"She told me that things are not as they seem in this place. Tyler does not let people leave. If he finds out that we don't want to stay, he will have us killed."

"What do you mean?" asks Cassie.

"Yeah, what are you saying?" echoes Nate.

"Well, according to Kirsten, aside from the jarheads who protect the walls, people are not happy here. They are all pretending, including her."

"How can you trust her? We just met her, and you believe what she says?" complains Cassie.

"Well, we haven't known Taylor and Emma very long, and we trust them," says Nate.

"Nate is right. I do trust Kirsten, and I believe what she said."

"And you trusting her has nothing to do with you making out with her?" asks Cassie.

"I trust her, and I believe what she said. Kissing her has nothing to do with it."

"Of course it does. So, what? She kisses you, and you become blind!" continues Cassie.

"Cassie, why are you so hostile towards her?"

"You see, you are blind. I don't like her, and I don't trust anyone here. I'm not going to sit here another minute and listen to any of this!" she rants, and then she gets up and stomps up the stairs.

"Let me make sure she's ok," says Taylor, and she and Emma go up the stairs after Cassie.

Everyone else remains downstairs.

"What did you do to piss off Cassie?" asks Nate.

"Nothing. She's been acting like this since we got here."

"Finish what you were telling us," interrupts Ethan.

"Kirsten said that we should not show any emotion or reaction no matter what happens tomorrow during the cleansing ceremony for Purification Day."

"Did she say why?" asks Ethan.

"She did not want to go into details. She was afraid that someone might overhear. That's why I believe her."

Nate and Ethan seem to understand my concerns and the reasons why we should be careful. Nate gets up and sits next to me. "Come on, bro. Tell me, how was it?" he asks.

I look at him and smile. I cannot contain myself. They can see it from my smile.

He punches me in the arm. "You devil you. How far did you go, third, fourth base?"

At this point, I stand up. "I'm beat. I'm going to go to bed. I'll see everyone in the morning. You guys should head upstairs too. We have a long day ahead of us."

I go upstairs and get into bed. I must have been exhausted because I hit the pillow, and the next thing I know, it is morning.

CHAPTER NINETEEN

I open my eyes and sit up at the edge of the bed. My body is sore from yesterday's workout, so I'm not quick to get on my feet. My shoulders are so sore, I can't do another workout like yesterday's. I reach for my pants, grab them off the floor, and slip them on. I stand up and stretch, and then I walk into the bathroom. I turn on the water to wash my face and quickly brush my teeth. I walk back into the room, put on my shoes, and head out the door. I get downstairs only to realize that I am the first one up. I look at my watch, and it is seven twenty a.m. I go into the kitchen and pour myself a cup of water. I open the cabinet, and I take a Pop-Tart out of one of the boxes. I lean against the cabinets and take a bite into the Pop-Tart, and I quickly realize that it is stale. I grab the garbage can, stick my face in it, and spit out the Pop-Tart.

"She made you sick to your stomach, didn't she? I would throw up too if I had to kiss one of the freaks," says Cassie.

When I hear Cassie's voice, I take my head out of the trash can and look at her. "Cassie!"

She turns around and walks out of the kitchen and into the living room. Taylor and Emma are already sitting in the living room, waiting. As I walk into the living room, Ethan and Nate come down the stairs. It seems that Cassie is still upset at me. I can't understand it; she had an entire night to get over it, and she did not. I want to talk to her and reassure her that everything is ok. As I walk over to her, the door opens, and Kirsten walks in. Cassie looks over at Kirsten and rolls her eyes. Kirsten being here is not making things any easier.

"Come on, everyone," Kirsten says. We've got to get some breakfast. We're on the eight o'clock shift."

"Where is Jeremy?" asks Nate.

"I woke him up. I hope he hasn't fallen back asleep," replies Cassie.

Nate sticks his head up the stairs and shouts, "Jeremy, let's go!"

Cassie gets up and heads upstairs to get her brother. I attempt to follow her so we can talk, but as I walk past Kirsten, she takes my hand and pulls me towards her.

"Where are you going?"

We kiss and smile at each other.

"Did you get to talk to them?" she asks.

"I spoke with most of them, but I did not get a chance to talk to Cassie and Taylor."

"We don't have time to do that now. We have to get breakfast and head out on patrol."

Jeremy walks downstairs. He is barely awake. Cassie follows him into the living room. Kirsten immediately opens the door and asks us to go with her. "Come on, let's go. We don't have a lot of time to eat breakfast and get to the patrol."

She walks out the door, and we all follow her to breakfast. In the dining room, we each grab a tray and then go to get in line to receive our rations. I get in line first, and Kirsten and the others follow.

The kid behind the counter sets some bacon on my plate and says, "Thanks for helping us out last night. We really appreciate it."

"No problem, man, anytime."

"Most people around here only do their own task. We usually end up working the latest, so we really appreciate the help."

He gives me a nod of approval, and I continue down the breakfast line. We all sit down at a table and eat breakfast. Cassie sits at the far end, away from me, so I can't tell her what Kirsten and I discussed the previous night. I can't risk anyone overhearing us and turning us into to Tyler, so we sit there quietly at the table and eat. I look at my watch, and it is ten after eight.

"We need to leave now," says Kirsten. "We only have five minutes."

Nate stuffs his face with the rest of the food on his plate. Everyone else attempts to finish as quickly as possible, but we eventually all give up. We dump our plates and head outside to start our patrol. We walk out of the cafeteria and head for the front gate. We walk until we get to the meeting point. John and Tobi are standing there waiting for us. They turn and face us as we approach them.

"All right, gather around," John says.

We gather and form a semicircle around John and Tobi.

"We're going to split you up into two teams today. Half of you will be on perimeter patrol with Tobi, and the other half will go out scouting with me."

John chooses Cassie, Taylor, Jeremy, and Emma for the border patrol. Ethan, Nate, and I will go scouting with John and his team, which includes Kirsten.

"This is going to be a live training, so pay attention and ask questions if you don't understand. Is that clear?" asks John.

"Yes, sir," we reply.

"You all have your assignments. Join up with the rest of your teams and move out," commands Tobi.

For the first time since we left our homes, we are going to be apart of a situation that is out of our control. I look at Cassie, and she looks back at me. I know that I will have to do something to bring us all back together. She does not approve of my relationship with Kirsten for reasons that I do not yet understand.

"Be safe," says Taylor as she walks away.

"You too," we respond.

We walk away and head out with John. Tobi's group heads towards the main tower, while John leads us to the front gate, where we meet up with the rest of the team.

"Ok, we have some newbies here today," says John, "so I need you veterans to stay sharp, and I need you newbies to pay attention and learn."

He goes into his pocket and retrieves some green armbands, and he distributes them to us. I can't believe that we are joining up with these people. It feels weird to have one of these armbands after being out there all this time and seeing what they are capable of. Now that we are here, we have to participate.

"Make sure you keep these on you at all times out here. You don't want us to mistake you for an anus because, if we do, you won't have a good day."

We take the armbands and put them on.

"It suits you," comments John.

"Thanks."

"Now, we have to cover a lot of ground today, and we don't have a lot of time to do it in. We have to be back here early to provide extra security for Purification Day."

John signals to open the front gate, and they do. We step out through the gate, along with six others from John's squad.

"Lance, you take point with them. You three cover the rear, and you two with me. You watch, and you learn, understood?"

"Yes, sir!"

Kirsten and Michael, who we met with Tobi when they captured us, go to the front. Quinn, Kirsten's friend, goes to the back with Nate and Ethan. There is another girl and two other guys in the middle with John.

"Stay sharp and keep the noise down," commands John.

Kirsten, Michael, and I take the lead and begin walking. We go into the woods, following a trail that they use for patrol. Within a few minutes of walking, the compound disappears behind the trees.

"How wide is the area that we have to patrol?" I ask.

"I don't know, five, maybe six miles," responds Kirsten.

"How long does it take?" I ask.

"Well, it all depends on how many stops we make along the way. Any detours will increase the time," replies Michael.

"What sort of detours?"

"We have to go check out any noises or disturbances. It's usually nothing most of the time, but once in awhile, something will turn up," responds Kirsten.

"Something like what?"

"Hopefully, the anus so I can get my target practice on," replies Michael.

"We'll patrol until about lunchtime, and we'll stop to eat lunch and then come back out for another patrol until dinnertime," says Kirsten.

"We didn't bring anything to eat," I say.

"Those guys back there have enough for everyone."

We continue talking as we walk through the woods. Several conversations are going on behind us with Nate, Eric, John, and the others. The temperature begins to rise as the morning goes by. I look at my watch, and it is about nine-thirty a.m. We've been walking for about an hour, and with the rising temperature, my throat begins to get a little dry. I pull out the water canteen strapped to my belt and take a sip of water.

"Slow down. We just got out here, and we have the whole morning ahead of us," implores Kirsten.

"My throat is a little dry. I just needed to moisten it."

"That's a nice watch. How is it still working?" Kirsten asks.

"This watch belonged to my grandfather. He left it to my dad, but I took it when I left my house."

"Can I see it?"

I hold my wrist out, and she takes me by the hand to look at the watch.

"It still works because of the mechanical movement in it. It doesn't take batteries. The movement powers it."

"I've never heard of a mechanical watch before. I thought all watches used batteries."

"Well, there was a time before electricity, when all timepieces were mechanical. They still make mechanical watches, but they are expensive. My grandfather had this watch for a very long time before he passed away. My dad kept the watch after my grandfather died, but he never wore it. He kept it in a plastic container with some of the old things in our basement."

"I'm going to have to find a mechanical watch for myself. I need to keep track of the time. Who would have thought that keeping track of the time would become such a chore?"

"None of us ever thought that the mundane things that we took for granted, like the ability to tell time, would become so difficult."

Michael puts up his fist and halts the group. "Shhhh."

He listens to the woods. John walks and stands next to him.

"Do you hear that? It sounds like another pack of dogs," says Michael.

"Let's check it out," commands John.

We slowly walk in the direction of the sound. It almost sounds like a pack of wolves growling. We walk a little bit until we are able to see about seven or eight dogs tearing up the carcass of a deer.

"The dogs are roaming in packs now," explains John. "Without people to control and domesticate them, they get together and hunt for food, and they will attack humans. They are very dangerous in this state, and we try to avoid them, but if they attack us, we'll need to take them out."

Everyone slowly backs away into the woods. As I back out, I inadvertently step on a tree branch, which snaps and alerts the dogs to our presence. The alpha male is a Great Dane. He looks up and stares straight into my eyes. Then he growls and takes off running towards me. The other dogs in the pack stop eating. They look up at us, and they take off running behind the alpha male. We all turn and runoff in the other direction.

"Get back to the trail!" shouts John.

The Great Dane is very fast; before we can even take off running, he is already barreling down on me. We try running through the trees, but that only causes us to get separated in different directions. As we split apart, the Great Dane and a Rottweiler are right on my tail. My heart is racing. I'm running as fast as I can, jumping in between trees, trying to lose them.

I look to my right, and I can see Kirsten running with a dog chasing closely behind her. I turn back around and look at the dogs. I have not gained any ground. In fact, they are closing in on me. I cannot keep this up, I think. They are going to catch up to me eventually. I grab my rifle, and while running, I turn sideways and fire a few shots into the ground behind me. The noise stops both the Great Dane and the Rottweiler. They stand there, growling at me.

"Get out of here!"

I take my rifle and fire a few more shots into the ground in front of their legs. They take off and run back towards their kill, howling as they leave. I hear a few shots in the distance, but I'm not sure who fired them off. All the dogs retreat after the alpha male.

"Kirsten, are you ok?" I say as I walk towards her. We are both winded, so we try to catch our breath. She puts her hand on a tree and leans against it.

"Yes, I'm fine. Just out of breath."

We look at each other, and we both laugh.

"Come on, let's find the others," she says.

We make our way back to the trail, where we meet up with the rest of the group, who's slowly made their way there.

"Next time, we need to take them out before they have a chance to chase us," suggests Michael.

"Tyler's orders are to leave them alone until we figure out a way to trap and capture them," says John. "Once we know how to catch and train them, they will be helpful to us."

We continue patrolling the trail until it is almost lunchtime. John decides that we will head back to the compound for lunch. By lunchtime, we have made it back to the front gate. They open the gate as we approach, and we go in for lunch. By the time we reach the cafeteria, Cassie and the rest of Tobi's crew are already occupying a table. I grab a tray, along with the rest of the scouts, to get lunch. We find an empty table to sit and eat. I do not do too much talking at lunch because my conversation with Kirsten from last night dominates my mind. Besides Taylor and Emma, we've all known each other for a very long time and have survived a lot together in these past months. Now my relationship with Kirsten is tearing Cassie and me apart.

Tobi's crew was already about done eating by the time we reached the cafeteria, so Cassie and the rest of the group leave and go back on duty. It is frustrating that I do not get a chance to talk to her, but I figure we will talk tonight.

We barely speak at lunch; we just eat and sit there for a while before leaving the cafeteria. When we finish, we go back out on our scouting detail. We go deep into the woods, and we scout for what seems like forever. We stop to drink water a couple of times, and we switch roles back and forth. Lucky for me, Kirsten and I are assigned to the same details. We talk a lot, but we avoid the subject of Purification Day. I love how she says if we find a genie on the trail, she gets the first wish. She says that she is going to wish for a giant ice cream cone. I don't blame her; I have not eaten ice cream in almost five months, and I miss it.

The afternoon is uneventful until we hear the sound of a pot falling to the ground. Michael raises his fist, and everyone stops.

"Michael and you two, come with me," commands John.

John and the three men leave, and the rest of us stay behind while they check out the noise.

"What do you think it is?" I ask.

"Probably some campers," replies Nate

"Let's pray it's not," whispers Kirsten.

As we stand there debating what it could be, the sound of gunfire erupts: automatic weapons being fired from where John and the men went. We grab our guns and take off running towards them. Not far from where we were, we stumble on the campsite. John, Michael, and the other two are already securing the site by the time we get there. There are two women and a man who looks like they are in their forties lying dead on the ground.

I approach John. "What happened?"

"This is how we deal with the anus. We kill them on sight."

I can't understand why John had to kill them, I think. They had no weapons, so he could have taken them, prisoner. If we'd taken them as prisoners, maybe we could have talked them out of their rebellion. After all, the Sanctuary is a good idea for everyone.

"Grab anything we can use," commands John.

We all search and take whatever useful items they had. It doesn't sit well with me that Tyler's orders are to kill these rebels on sight without giving them the chance to see the good work the Sanctuary is doing. After leaving the camp, I walk with Ethan and Nate at the rear of the group.

"I can't believe they just killed those people," says Nate. "They didn't have any weapons, and they were not causing us any harm."

"I know, but keep your voice down about that. We don't want them to hear," I reply.

"This is wrong! What are we going to do?" asks Ethan.

"We have to think clearly. I'm sure John had his reasons for what he did," I whisper.

"Whatever the reason was, they were harmless, and it was not right! Especially after what Kirsten told you," replies Nate.

We continue patrolling into the evening. After our brief discussion on what happened, we do not say much else. It surprises me how John and others are fine after just killing three people. I was right to worry about putting on these armbands. What does it say about us if we are willing to help murder innocent people? I'm starting to think joining the Sanctuary is a bad idea. What are we going to do? We need to get away from these people. How are we going to getaway? They have eyes everywhere. We need to start planning our escape tonight after the celebration. Maybe Kirsten will come with us since she is not happy here.

Kirsten's demeanor, on the other hand, seems to have changed. She is no longer the cheerful soul she was earlier. I guess it has something to do with the people they killed. She may feel just as we do and does not approve of what just happened. Only someone who is devoid of any emotion and who is mentally disturbed is ok with what they are doing. In any case, I can't talk to her about it now. I am hoping to get a chance during or after tonight's celebration to talk.

As night falls, we stop to take a break before heading back to the compound. We find an area with some trees, which we decide to sit under for fifteen minutes before our final leg of the patrol. We sit down against the trees, and everyone looks exhausted. The heat is finally dissipating, and we can feel the cool breeze of the night on our skin.

"We need to make it back before the ceremony begins. The other four communities are going to be there, so we will need extra security. Pack up and let's move out," commands John.

We get back on the trail and head towards the compound. I'm still uneasy about what John did. How could he be so cold? What kind of a person does this? If they are that cold, they probably will kill us if we try to leave, like Kirsten says. We have to get out here, away from these psychopaths who think it's ok to just kill people in cold blood who don't agree with them. This is insane. We need to come up with an escape plan tonight.

As we walk down the trail, we come across a large number of people from one of the other compounds heading towards ours. I know they are from one of the compounds because of their green armbands. We join them on the trail. There is a sense of excitement amongst them, and their fervor for Purification Day seems almost religious as they talk with each other.

"I cannot wait for the bonfire."

"I hope this one is bigger than the last one."

"I will never forget the look on the anus' faces at the last bonfire. Priceless."

CHAPTER TWENTY

As we approach the compound, we can hear music coming from inside. It sounds like the same creepy song from the weird band about Purification Day that they played our first night. The doors to the compound are open, and people are streaming in. It is odd, though; even in the other compounds, there are no grownups. Everyone that we see is in their early twenties or younger. I look up at the main tower, and I see Taylor, Cassie, and some others posted there. The streets are filled with people who are singing and dancing as far as the eye can see. The arriving crowds bring food and drinks with them. They make their way to the cafeteria to drop off their meals and then join the party.

Kirsten walks closer to me. She leans over and whispers into my ear, "Remember, no reactions!"

"I haven't gotten the chance to tell Cassie and Taylor, and I don't know that Jeremy would've known to tell them."

"You can't say anything now. Can't risk being overheard. Hopefully, when Cassie and Taylor see that you guys are calm, they will remain calm as well."

"All right," says John, "you all did well today. I know you want to join the party, but our work is not done. We're providing security tonight, so pair up and mingle among the crowd. If you see anything suspicious, you come to find one of the other lieutenants or me, and we'll take care of it.

Remember, there is a zero-tolerance for illegal fighting and disorderly conduct. Now, go forth and conquer, and remember, it's a party. Enjoy yourselves out there."

John pairs me with Nate. To my disappointment, he pairs Ethan with Kirsten. Although I am disappointed, I know it will give me some time with Nate. We have not really spent a lot of time alone since the Burning started.

"We all need to be back here before the bonfire," continues John. "The ritual is mandatory for everyone, especially the newcomers."

"I'll catch up with you later," sighs Kirsten. She turns and walks in the opposite direction from me, and she disappears into the crowd. I stand there and watch her until she is gone.

Nate grabs me by my shoulder and shakes me. "You lucky dog, you. I'm happy for you, bro. I only wish I had your luck."

We take off walking in the opposite direction.

"Bro," I say, "I know you like Taylor, but I don't think she's into you."

"I think she's just playing hard to get."

"That's because she doesn't know the real you. Give it some time for her to get to know the real you. She'll change her mind."

"Well, the real me is about to look elsewhere. Just look at all these fine ladies out there. Nothing like an apocalypse to bring out the honey's, right into the palm of my hand."

"How's that been working out for you?"

Nate shoves me, and we laugh. "Well, things are about to change. A few months ago, we couldn't keep the honey's off us, captain of the football team, and the star running back you and me. We were a force to be reckoned with. Now, look at us. We're two grunts in Tyler's army."

"Yeah, we were supposed to go to college together, and now our lives have been ruined."

"No, my life is ruined. Four months ago, we were the most popular guys in school, and now Taylor won't even give me the time of day. But you, you've got that honey Kirsten under your arm. Life is still going good for you."

"I miss my life, our old lives, I mean."

Nate reaches into his pocket and takes out his dead cell phone. He swipes it a couple of times, and then he looks at me. "We don't even have social media. In my opinion, this is hell on earth. The only thing that's missing is the devil."

I laugh. "Why don't you just throw that phone away?"

"You never know. It might just start working again."

"The circuits are fried. It will never work again. Besides, Tyler will not allow any of the old technologies in the Sanctuary. This is a new world, remember."

We see a crowd forming, and we hear them cheering not too far from where we are.

Nate taps me on the arm. "What do you think is going on over there?"

"I don't know, but we're about to find out."

We walk towards the crowd and push our way through. In the middle, two men are fighting. Nate and I run to the middle of the fight to stop it. We're pulled back by two other people.

"Let them fight, newbies. We have money on this."

"Tyler said no disorderly conduct is permitted," I reply.

"You newbies," the man says, "the redemption circle is for sanctioned fights."

"Redemption circle? What the hell is that?" asks Nate.

"That's where you go and redeem yourself when you do something wrong, like failing to take out an anus when you have a clear shot."

He points to a man who looks like a giant. He is at least six foot six and 330 pounds. "So, if you don't want to face Bradley over there, I suggest you leave the fight alone." With that, the man goes back to watching the fight.

The fight seems unfair because of the size difference. Nate and I leave and continue patrolling. The scene is like a carnival. There are small groups of people watching others showcase their talents. It's like one of those reality shows except without the cameras and judges. Everyone seems to be very cheerful. I don't get the sense of dissatisfaction that Kirsten told me about. It may be because everyone is so young, and they are able to hide their emotions well. We continue walking through the festival until we reach the end of its designated area. We turn and head back to the crowd.

We pass by a juggling act, then a human-robot, and eventually make our way back to the fight. Two men are dragging out the smaller fighter, who appears to have been severely beaten and knocked out of the fighting circle. We eventually meet up with Kirsten and Ethan.

"What's up, y'all?" asks Ethan.

"Kirsten, did you know about the fighting circles?" I ask.

"Yeah, it's Tyler's way of having someone who did something wrong redeem themselves and prove their loyalty."

"They beat a kid almost half to death back there."

"I told you, not everything is as it seems."

"All this food is making me hungry," complains Ethan.

"Come on, we can grab some food before the bonfire starts," suggests Kirsten.

We take off in the direction of the dining room. I look for Cassie and Taylor in the tower, but they are no longer there. We walk through the crowd, where we see some interesting acts, like the human pretzel, a girl who can twist every part of her body. There is a fashion show next to a rap freestyle battle.

Kirsten takes me by the hand, and I look into her eyes. "What?" she asks softly.

"I did not think I could be happy in this world. When I look into your eyes, none of this seems to matter."

She leans in and kisses me. As we kiss, I see Cassie in the

distance, watching us. She turns and walks away.

I take Kirsten by the hand. "Come on."

I start walking in the direction where Cassie was standing.

"What is it? Where are we going?"

"Cassie, I just saw her over there. I need to tell her."

I reach the spot where Cassie stood and look around for her, but I can't find her. I'm not sure where they went, but I hope I find her before the bonfire.

"Come on, I'm sure she's going to be fine."

"Yeah, I'm sure you're right. Let's get something to eat."

We leave the area and go to the cafeteria. We bump into Nate and Ethan on our way there.

"What happened to you two? One moment you were behind us, and the next minute you were gone," says Nate.

"I was trying to catch Cassie."

"Where is she?"

"I lost her in the crowd."

We go into the cafeteria. There are tables all over the cafeteria, each covered with a wide selection of food, but there is no room to sit. We go around the tables, picking off the platters. We take our food outside. Some other kids have just finished eating, and they are getting off the side steps, so we sit down to eat. The food is delicious, and Nathan is humming as he eats. It's something that he's done since we were kids when he's enjoying his food.

A few boys go by and tell everyone that the purification ceremony is about to start. There is a mixed reaction from the crowd. Some people seem very excited, while others show no emotion. We finish eating, and we join the crowd, which is heading towards the far side of the grounds, to the Olympic-size pool. The pool is empty and full of ash. I assume the ash is from the last bonfire. Kirsten does not really want to go to the ceremony.

"Is everything ok?" I ask her.

"No, but like everything else around here, we don't have a choice."

The crowd forms several lines leading to the pool. There are dozens of stacks of wood. The wood ranges from two-foot-long sticks all the way to ten-foot-long poles, and they are arranged in the pool area. As the crowd goes in, each person selects a piece of wood.

Kirsten stands there for a while, staring at the wood. "Hey, can we wait a little bit before we go in?"

"Sure, no problem. Guys, let's give Kirsten a minute."

Nate and Ethan come back and stand with us. We stand there for a while, but we do not speak. Kirsten leans on me, and I place my arms around her. She seems very distraught. I can hear people in the crowd talking, but I cannot make out what they are saying.

"Hey, you don't have to go in if you don't want to. We could always go back and hang out at the guesthouse."

"Tyler will be looking for me. He already doesn't trust me. If I don't show up, there will be hell to pay."

We all walk towards the back. When we get to the back, Kirsten walks to one of the woodpiles, and we follow her.

She takes a piece of wood and turns to us. "Just do as I do and repeat what I say."

We each pick up a piece of wood and head towards the pool after her. As I get closer to the pool, I can finally hear what is being said. As each person takes the piece of wood they are holding and tosses it into the empty pool, it forms a growing pile, and they repeat the phrase:

"I purify the past for a better future."

I cannot understand the fear that is coming from Kirsten; the ceremony appears to be innocuous. It is an eerie scene watching person after person throw the wood into the empty pool while repeating those words. Nevertheless, it is part of the ceremony. Especially being new, we have to show solidarity with the rest of the Sanctuary. We continue down the line until we get to the pool, and then we each toss our piece of wood into the empty pool and repeat the words.

"I purify the past for a better future."

"I purify the past for a better future."

"I purify the past for a better future."

"I purify the past for a better future."

After everyone tosses their wood in, Tyler comes and stands on a makeshift platform. The crowd goes wild, cheering and screaming. Shortly after that, they chant Tyler's name.

"Tyler, Tyler, Tyler!"

The chant eventually dies down, and Tyler begins to speak.

"It has been more than four months since the skies burned. For more than a century, our forebears carelessly destroyed our planet until the day when nature fought back. It fought back against the cruelty of man, who would destroy our planet for profit. It fought back against those who are indifferent to the constant pollution and poisoning of the environment, against those who would partake in the destruction through consumerism and negligence. The time has come to make them pay for their crimes. The time has come for us to cleanse ourselves of the sins of the past."

The crowd explodes with cheers, and Tyler raises his hand to quiet everyone down.

"Tonight... Tonight, we're going to let our voices be heard. We're going to let our voices reverberate throughout the planet, to let them know that we will no longer allow them to kill Mother Earth. We will not let them poison, we will not let them rape our planetary resources for profits, and we will protect it and live in harmony with nature."

The crowd goes wild, cheering, and chanting his name again.

"Tyler, Tyler, Tyler!"

It's like something out of a movie, surreal, and yet there is something very ominous about it. The complete support of the crowd gives me a weird feeling, and Kirsten becomes even more uncomfortable. I look to the other side of the pool, and I see Cassie, along with Taylor, Jeremy, and Emma. I point them out to Kirsten. I call Nate and Ethan so we can go over to them. The crowd is packed in tight, so it takes us a while to move to the other side. As we make our way there, the chanting stops, and Tyler continues speaking.

"It's up to each and every one of you to make a difference. And the difference begins here and now when we purify the past for a better future. Praeterita purget."

After he speaks the words, the crowd begins to chant continuously, "Cleanse the past! Cleanse the past! Cleanse the past!"

It is a spectacle, and each time the crowd or Tyler says something else, we stop to watch what's going on. After the chant has gone on for a while, Tyler raises his hand, and there is silence. When the chanting stops, a group of people is led to the front of the platform where Tyler is standing. They have hoods over their heads, and their hands are bound behind their backs. A group of kids come to the edge of the pool and pour gasoline over the pile of wood. Once they finish pouring the gasoline, the hoods are snatched off the heads of the prisoners, who are revealed to be of all ages and races, male and female.

"The aged, or the anus as they are known in Latin, is the cause of the destruction of this planet, and we must cleanse them from the face of the earth. There is no redeeming them. Anyone who reached the age of thirty before the cataclysm must die! Anyone under thirty who would harbor and support them will die along with them."

Tyler takes a long match and strikes it. He tosses the match into the pool and sets the wood ablaze. He then repeats the purification phrase: "I purify the past for a better future."

I can see the fear and the dread on many of the prisoners' faces. I cannot believe what I am hearing. I am mortified, and now I finally understand what Kirsten was trying to tell us. I understand her reluctance to tell us exactly what would happen. She was right to hold back; we might have said something earlier, causing us to be in the same position as these people. I realize at this point that I need to get to Cassie and Taylor fast before their reactions betray them. I begin forcefully pushing my way through the crowd.

"Excuse me, excuse me!"

As I make my way towards Cassie, one of the prisoners turns to Tyler and shouts, "You don't have to do this! This is insane! Stop this madness!"

The person standing behind the shouting prisoner repeats the words, "I purify the past for a better future," and then pushes him into the pool. As he falls onto the pile of burning wood, he lets out a piercing scream. It is one of those sounds that I will never forget. As he screams, others are pushed into the fire, and they cry and scream as they plunge to their deaths. I am closing in on Cassie, and I become mortified as I hear her scream, "You people are insane! This is murder!"

Taylor joins in with Cassie and begins shouting at Tyler, "What the hell is wrong with you? You are killing innocent people. Are you all out of your minds? What would your parents think if they saw you doing this?"

Tyler turns in their direction. The crowd goes eerily silent.

"And those who protect the aged will meet the same fate as they do. Take them!"

A group of kids immediately grabs Taylor and Cassie. At the same moment, Emma and Jeremy begin shoving the people. We rush towards them, Ethan, Nate, and me, and come to their aid. Ethan slugs a couple of guys, but eventually, we are overpowered. I look around, but I do not see Kirsten.

"Seize all of them," commands Tyler.

John quickly walks towards us and relieves us of our weapons. "Put them in the lockup," he commands.

I turn towards Tyler and shout, "You don't have to do this! All of this is unnecessary, Tyler! You said you were going to bring peace on earth, and I believed you! I believed you!"

They drag us away, and as they pull us out of the crowd, I see Kirsten. We look at each other and lock eyes. Then she turns around and walks away, disappearing into the crowd. I cannot understand it; she's abandoned us. I would have never abandoned her. *How could she do this to me?*

We eventually stop struggling because it's pointless. We are outnumbered, and the more we struggle, the more they are injuring us. They take us back to the holding house they kept us in when we first got to the Sanctuary. They put us in the same room and lock us in. Everyone is in a panic. We do not know what to do. The only thing I can think of is that we need to escape before they kill us.

"Oh my God, they killed all of those people," cries Cassie.

"Killed? They murdered them in cold blood!" shouts Taylor.

"We need to get out of here before they kill us," I add.

I go to the window and lift the shade. There are bars on the outside of the window. I lift the window, and I grab the bars. I cannot shake them, though; they will not budge. I stop myself from panicking any further. I have to think about this clearly if we're going to get out of here alive. I turn around and see Emma sobbing. Cassie is hysterical, and everyone else looks stunned.

Cassie turns to me. "Your girlfriend knew about this. She's part of this. She's crazy just like they are."

"No, she came by last night and warned us, but you were upset and went upstairs," pleads Nate. "We intended to tell you today, but we got separated and never got a chance to."

He walks over to Cassie and embraces her. "So, you see, it's not Kirsten's fault, nor Lance's for that matter."

Cassie buries her face into Nate's chest, sobbing, and she wraps her arms around him.

"We need a plan to get out here now!" I exclaim. "When Tyler's done pushing those people into that funeral pyre he built, he's going to send for us."

"We should break the door down and take out the guards," suggests Ethan.

"We don't know how many of them are out there," I reply. "They have weapons, and we don't."

"What other choice do we have? we're going to have to chance it," says Nate.

"That seems to be our only choice at this point," adds Ethan.

"Well, we can't just run out there without a plan," I say. "We need to make sure that we can take out the guards without getting hurt."

Taylor lets go of her sister and steps over towards us. "When we first got here, they only had one guard behind the door, one in the front, and one at the armory. If we kick the door down and act fast enough, we could overpower the guard at the door and take his weapon."

"We'll need to do it in waves," I say. "Ethan, you take down the door, and Nate and I will rush the guard. Once we take down the guard, the one in the front will rush to his aid. This is when you, Taylor, and Cassie will take him out. We need to work fast, and we need to commit. No hesitation. Do you all understand?"

"Yes."

"No hesitation," says Taylor.

We take our position and begin the countdown.

"On three," I instruct.

They all nod in agreement.

"One, two…"

The countdown is interrupted when I hear voices outside the door.

"What's wrong?" asks Ethan.

"Listen, voices outside the door," I say. "Sounds like more of them showed up. we're going to need another plan."

"What are they saying?" asks Nate.

"I don't know," I reply. "I can't it make out."

I hear a sound and then a thump against the wall. We brace ourselves for anything that might come through the door. The door opens, and it's Kirsten. She rushes to me and hugs and kisses me.

"Is everyone ok?" she asks.

"Yeah, we're fine," we reply.

"Come on," she urges. "We need to get outta here before they come for you."

"I'm not going anywhere with her," says Cassie. "I don't trust her. She's one of them, and she's a murderer just like them."

Kirsten knocked out the guard who was posted at the door. The thump that we heard was the guard falling against the wall. He is out cold.

"If I wanted you dead, I would not be here. I'm risking my life, so quit your nonsense." Kirsten turns to me. "We have to go!"

I step out of the door behind her.

"Come on, let's go," I urge.

"Your weapons are in the armory," says Kirsten. "Grab them quickly."

We run to the armory to get our weapons. As we are picking them up, someone opens the back door. We all turn and point our guns at the person. Kirsten walks over and stands between us.

"Everyone, this is Quinn. Remember, I told you I had a plan?"

"Yes!"

"Well, he's part of it. We had to put it into action to save you guys."

"We've got to get out of here. The guards are on their way," says Quinn.

We grab our weapons and ammo, and then we head out a side door.

"This way," directs Quinn.

We all take off behind Kirsten and Quinn. We run through the backyards of the homes. Everyone is at the ceremony, so we are not worried about being seen. Luckily, Quinn was posted at one of the guard towers, so we will be able to use the tunnels of that tower to make our escape. We get to the tower, and Quinn opens the door. Kirsten and Quinn have already collected our bags, and they place them next to the trapdoor.

"We brought your bags for you," says Kirsten, "so strap them on and let's go."

We grab our bags and strap them on. Quinn opens the trapdoor. He grabs the flashlight off the wall, and we go down into the tunnel. Kirsten pulls the door to the tower closed, and everyone goes down into the tunnel. I help Kristin down, and then I am the last one to head out. We run through the tunnel, hoping that they don't catch us before we get to the other end. Emma stumbles and falls, and Jeremy helps her up. Quinn grabs Emma's bag, and we continue running. When we reach the other end of the tunnel, Quinn does not bother pulling the ropes to empty the sand. Instead, he uses his shoulder to push open the trapdoor. He climbs out, and Ethan follows him.

"Give us the bags," says Ethan.

We pass all the bags forward and hand them up the ladder to Ethan. Emma and Jeremy go up the ladder next. We all eventually make it outside, and then we take our bags and run away into the woods.

"Follow me and step where I step," commands Quinn.

Quinn leads the way, and we all follow him, running through the woods. He turns off the flashlight, but there is a full moon out, so we are using the moonlight to see in the woods.

CHAPTER TWENTY-ONE

We run through the woods as if our lives depend on it because it does. We are trying to get as much distance between us and the compound as possible before they come looking for us. *The Sanctuary will kill us if they catch up with us. This is the most danger that we've been in since the shooting at Mr. Jenkins's house. This is truly a life-or-death situation for us. It's a good thing there's already a trail out here, or else we wouldn't be able to make it out of here. I know at some point we're going to have to get off this trail, and it's going to slow us down.* As soon as the thought crosses my mind, Quinn turns off the path and heads into the woods. We run through the woods for a while, and it is not a walk in the park. I look back, and I see Emma is struggling to keep up, and I realize we can't maintain this pace.

I turn to Kirsten and Quinn and ask, "How long do you think before they come looking for us?"

Kirsten looks at Quinn, and he turns around and says, "Hopefully, they'll search the compound first. That'll give us a good ten-minute head start. And hopefully, they'll think that we are dumb enough to stay on the trail and chase after us that way."

"How much further do we have to run?" asks Ethan.

"We don't stop running before we reach the first marker," says Kirsten.

We continue moving, following Quinn for what seems like forever. Ethan trips as he runs in the dark. Kirsten and I stop to help him, but he waves us away.

"Don't stop. Keep going. I'm fine. I'll catch up," he says.

We go to his aid anyway, helping him up, and then we continue running. We've fallen behind a little bit, but we can still see Quinn. After a while, Quinn begins to slow down. He stops, and we catch up to him. We rest there for a minute, trying to catch our breath, and have a drink.

"Are we here?" asks Kirsten.

"Yes, we made it," Quinn responds.

"Where is here?" I ask.

Quinn takes a sip of water, wetting his mouth, and then he says, "There is a point from the towers where we can no longer be seen, the point of convergence where the line of sight ends. To be safe, I set this marker a quarter-mile past it. Now we can use the flashlights without being seen from the tower."

"We'll need to be careful," I suggest. "We don't want to run into that pack of dogs again."

"Good point," says Kirsten. "We will have to keep moving through the night. Stay as quiet as possible and keep an eye out, everyone."

I go into my bag, and I'm happy to see that the walkie-talkies are still there. I'm glad I did not tell Tyler I had them; he would have taken them for himself. *I think this is a good lesson to learn: we should be careful as to how much information we share.* There are only five of them, so I do not have enough for everyone.

"Hey, I need you guys to take the walkie-talkies in case we get separated, but don't turn them on unless we're separated. I do not have enough for everyone, so hopefully, if we need to separate and you don't have one, you'll be with someone who does."

I pick up the walkie-talkies and hand one to Quinn, Taylor, Jeremy, and Ethan.

"Now, these have a twenty-five-mile range, but with the trees and other obstruction, let's cut it down to about eight miles. So, within an eight-mile radius, we should be able to hear you if you call."

"What channel should we be on?" asks Jeremy.

"Let's use eight as a primary channel and five as a backup if eight becomes compromised."

We stick the walkie-talkies into our backpacks, strap on our bags, and begin walking. The woods are not dense at all; Quinn scouted this area before as an escape route.

"Do you two know where you are going?" I ask.

"Yes, we're headed about five miles away," replies Quinn.

"So, what's over there?" asks Taylor.

"There's a shopping mall that we raided a while back," replies Kirsten. "Quinn and I set some supplies in a closet of one of the stores. If I know John, he will look for us in the opposite direction, where there are plenty of supplies."

"If he knows the supplies are there, wouldn't he follow after us there?" asks Cassie.

"We never told them that we left anything there. We knew we would need it to get away one day."

"And what the hell is wrong with that psychopath Tyler?" asks Cassie.

"And why didn't you tell me that they were killing people?" I add. "Why didn't you tell us that they were a cult?"

"I thought you said she told you," says Cassie.

Kirsten stops walking. We all stop and look at her, waiting for an answer.

"There used to be four of us who wanted to leave. We decided to work in pairs so that in case we were ever found out, only two of us would be captured, and the other two would help the captured escape. The other two thought they could trust someone who'd just gotten to the camp. They told him what was going on, thinking that he would join us, but instead, he told Tyler, who had them killed before we could rescue them. This is why I couldn't just tell you everything. I trust you, but I didn't know what everyone else would do if you told them."

Taylor walks up to the front of the group and takes Kirsten by the hand. "Thank you! We appreciate what both of you did for us."

"Yeah, word," adds Nate.

"Thank you."

"We really appreciate it."

"Not that I don't appreciate the sentiments," says Quinn, "but if we keep standing here, sharing our feelings, they're going to catch up to us."

We have a long walk ahead of us, five miles through mostly woods at night. It is not going to be a fun walk, but we begin to make the trip. I hope everyone is up for this journey. We just made an enemy out of the only organized group in the country. They will pursue us hard, and they will definitely kill us if they ever catch up with us.

Quinn turns around and looks at Cassie. "What's your name again?"

"I'm sorry. I forgot you hadn't met everyone formally," says Kirsten.

She stops for a minute and introduces us to Quinn. "This is Cassie, Taylor, Nate, Ethan, Jeremy, Emma, and you know Lance. Everyone, this is Quinn. We lived in the same neighborhood until Tyler took it over."

Kirsten begins to get emotional. "That bastard killed our parents! Quinn and I were out trying to find water when Tyler and his cronies came into the neighborhood. They killed all of our parents. By the time we got back, there was nothing we could do. He killed any of the kids who fought back. We had to pretend that we'd bought into his bullshit for him not to kill us."

"I'm so sorry, Kirsten," I say. "I didn't know."

"Yeah, both of you, sorry you had to live through that," adds

Taylor.

We continue walking, heading towards the store. We are quiet the rest of the way – it's tough walking through the woods, and we have never had to hike this far before. It's nighttime, and it's cold. We have to make it out of the woods to get the supplies, so we push on and do not let the cold or the distance bother us. We are in survival mode, so we are doing what is necessary. After walking for close to an hour and a half, we reach the end of the trees. We can see the road getting closer and closer to us.

"We made it to the road," says an elated Kirsten.

"What road is this?" I ask.

"This road is on the other side of town," replies Quinn. "This is the furthest we came on the road with John. You'd have to walk ten miles to get here from the compound, and we figured out it was a shorter walk through the woods. If John and Tobi are looking for us, they will never think that we've come this far."

"I think we're going to be safe there for the night," says Kirsten.

We reach the edge of the trees and walk onto the road.

"It's not far from here. We should be there in ten minutes," Kirsten continues.

It's a relief when we finally make it onto the road. Walking through the woods in the night was not a pleasant experience and is something I'm not looking forward to doing again anytime soon.

"This way," commands Quinn.

Here we are, a bunch of teenage kids with weapons in hand, walking down a dark road in the middle of the night. Our group has grown by two, and I hope it means a stronger group for us. We need manpower if we are going to survive. We silently walk until we make it to the shopping mall.

"Keep your eyes open," I direct. "Jeremy and Ethan, you two take point."

Jeremy and Ethan raise their weapons to eye level. They walk forward quickly, scanning each of the stores as they go.

"Look at you, Commander Lance," says Kirsten, smiling.

"What? No, no, it's not like that."

"Don't worry. I kind of like it."

"If you two are through molesting my ears, we have work to do," complains Quinn.

Jeremy and Ethan give the all-clear signal, and we enter the supermarket. The place is completely deserted. We turn on our flashlights to look around. Nate trips over a box, and we turn and look at him.

"Sorry, sorry," he apologizes.

"Over here," calls Kirsten.

We follow her to the back of the store, into the employee area.

"We cleaned out the place and brought everything back to

the Sanctuary," she continues, "but there was a small closet full of things that they didn't know about."

We walk to the back of the room, and she opens the closet, but all of the supplies are gone.

"No, no, no, no! It's all gone!" she rants.

Kirsten rips through boxes, one after another. I grab her by the arm and try calming her.

"It's ok. We'll find more supplies somewhere else."

"So, what are we going to do?" asks Quinn.

"It's the middle of the night," I reply. "We need to get some rest, and in the morning, we'll figure out a game plan."

"I think we'll be safe here for the night," says Quinn, "but we'll have to get out of here early in the morning before the Sanctuary tracks us down."

"We need to get some rest," adds Cassie.

"Too bad we don't have our sleeping bags," complains Nate. "Come to think of it, we don't have our helmets or our Kevlar vests either."

"I didn't say you would be comfortable," I say, "but we will need to get some sleep. We'll need to rotate a watch. I can take the first shift. Tomorrow, we can look for supplies."

"I'm usually on the night shift," says Quinn. "I slept all day, and I'm not tired yet. I can take first watch."

I grab a bunch of empty boxes, open them up, and lay them

on the floor. Then everyone else grabs some boxes and lays them out on the floor too. Kirsten places her box next to mine. I lie down, and I use my backpack to prop me up. Quinn takes a chair, puts it next to the door, and sits down. Everyone quietly lies down, and no one says a word. For a few minutes, it's just me and my thoughts until Kirsten rolls over into my arms. I guess she wants to spoon because it's cold. My heart is pounding. She turns and places her hand on my chest and smiles.

"I hope I don't give you a heart attack."

I smile at her. She lies in my arms and curls towards me. I'm tired, and I fall asleep right away.

I am awakened by a noise that sounds like the brakes of a nearby truck. Kristin pulls my wrist closer to her to look at the time on my watch.

"Did you hear that?" I ask.

"Yeah, it woke you up too? What do you think it is?"

"I don't know, but let me check it out."

I turn and look over towards the door. Quinn is asleep in the chair. I quickly get up and walk towards the front. I look at my watch, and it is nine twenty a.m. I stick my head out of the front door, and there is a military truck at the far end of the mall. John and Tobi exit the vehicle. There are about eight or nine other people with them, searching door to door, with Michael at the lead.

"Shoot!" I run to the back and shake Quinn. "Wake up!"

I run around, shaking everyone to wake them up.

"What's going on?" asks Kirsten.

"We've got to go. The Sanctuary is here."

Immediately, everyone wakes up and jumps to their feet.

"We need to leave now! They're searching the entire complex."

I grab the boxes and begin to throw them into a pile.

"What are you doing?" asks Quinn.

"If we leave them like this, they might figure out someone was here, but if we pile them up, they might think it's a bunch of garbage."

"Let's go out the back," suggests Kirsten.

Everyone places their box on the pile. We rush through the back door, and we take off running into the woods. We run for a good five or six minutes to put some distance between the Sanctuary and us. We are deep in the woods when we finally slow down and then stop. We are all out of breath. I place my hand on a tree to catch my breath. *We are going to have to move to another area far from the Sanctuary, or this is how it's going to be from now on. I'm not going to play this cat-and-mouse game with them.*

"Do you think they saw us?" asks Nate.

"I don't think so," I reply. "They didn't even know we were there."

"Now, what do we do?" asks Quinn. "We have no supplies, and the Sanctuary is hunting us."

"We don't know that they are hunting us," I reply. "Let's not jump to any conclusions. This could have been just a routine check."

Quinn and Kirsten look at each other.

"What?" I ask.

"The Sanctuary's policy is that all traitors must pay with their lives at all costs," says Kirsten. "If it was only one person who escaped, Tyler might've let it go, but it was nine of us. He will find us and drag us back alive to make sure we don't inspire anyone else to do the same thing. So, no, they will not stop chasing us, and this is not a routine check."

"We need a game plan, and we need it quick," urges Quinn.

"Hold on," I say. I open my backpack and take out the map. "Quinn, Kirsten, do you know the name of the road nearest to the highway? I need to find our location on this map."

Quinn takes the book and traces back to our location. "The Sanctuary is here. This is the road with the supermarket. We must've run about half a mile from the road, so I would say we're about here."

I stare at the map for a while. I do not quite have a plan; I'm trying to figure out what our next move should be. Wherever we go, it needs to be as far away from this area as we can get on foot. We lost our bikes when John took us, prisoner. Our movement is going to be slow in this heat.

"Is it strange to anyone else that they have a working truck?" asks Nate.

"Tyler had three of his engineers dedicated to getting his trucks working. I guess they finally succeeded," answers Kirsten.

"We can't outrun them in that truck. Whatever ground we cover will be nothing to them in a truck," says Ethan.

"They don't know that we know that they have the truck, so we can use that to our advantage," I say. "We will stay in the woods and go parallel with the road. They might expect us to walk on the road, and they may not be looking for us in the woods. They will eventually get ahead of us and think that they lost our trail and move on to another road."

I turn the map and show it to everyone. "So, here is the plan. This road connects to I-68. We will continue south until we hit I-68, and then we'll go west on I-68 to I-79 to West Virginia. We'll scout for supplies along the way."

"West Virginia is mostly farmland and empty space. Why don't we go to one of the big cities?" asks Quinn.

"There are nuclear power plants all along the Eastern Seaboard that is in meltdown and going critical. All of the big cities are in fallout zones. The safest bet is to go west, where there are a lot of empty spaces we can use to hide out."

"Quinn, he's right," says Kirsten. "We need to stay away from other people. The more people we are around, the more danger we'll be in. I say we head to West Virginia."

"West Virginia, it is then, unless someone has a different

idea?" I look at the others.

No one speaks up with any other ideas, so I take the map book and put it into my backpack.

"So, we'll walk in a direction parallel to the road. We'll need to get closer to the road once we get further down to find places where we can resupply."

We strap on our backpacks and take off westward, walking parallel to the road. The heat of the day has already started by the time we start traveling. We need to pace ourselves, so we do not become dehydrated. I look at my watch and see that it is half-past ten.

"We need to pace ourselves. We should walk for about an hour, and then we'll head to the road to see if we can find water and food."

Everyone nods, and we continue walking. We are all in fear, running from a group of psychopaths who are bent on destroying thousands of years of civilization. I cannot imagine what Kirsten and Quinn must have been through, to have their parents survive the Burning only to be murdered by these zealots. *Look at us; we have all suffered so much loss amid this chaos.* My mother and father were both scientists who were trying to help the world. They worked in Washington, D.C., at a genetic research facility, trying to cure diseases. All of our parents, siblings, friends, and family have perished. We have a new family now with each other. We cannot allow the Sanctuary to take this away from us. We have to survive. We must survive.

After walking for over an hour, we make it to the highway

junction. In the distance, we can see a large shopping center, probably about a quarter-mile from where we are. I am not sure if it's a good idea to go into that particular shopping mall, because the area may be populated.

"How about that shopping center?" asks Cassie. "It may still have some supplies."

"I don't know," I reply. "I can see two different subdivisions from here. The people might've raided it, and we may run into trouble."

"Yeah, but we'll have to take the chance," insists Quinn. "We have no food or water. I don't think we have a choice."

"He's right," agrees Taylor. "We have to take the chance. We're hot and thirsty. We need to at least try."

"Ok, we'll do it," I say. "Jeremy, Ethan, and Quinn, we'll take point and make sure that there are no surprises. The rest of you will follow us in."

We look through the tree line to make sure that it's clear. Then Quinn and I run across the road and into the parking lot of the shopping center. We search the parking lot using the scopes on our rifles. It seems clear, so we signal for Jeremy and Ethan the follow. The four of us continue walking through the lot. It's a huge shopping center with many stores, so the lot is huge. We do not see anything, so we signal for the rest of the group to come. As we move forward, I walk around a parked car, and I stumble on a man lying in front of it. He is bleeding to death. He is still alive, though, so he must have just recently been shot. I go to him and check his wounds. He is breathing heavily, dying painfully.

Quinn comes around the car and sees him.

"He's been shot," I say.

"Who the hell shot him?"

"I don't know, but they may still be around."

I take the man's hand. "It's going to be ok."

The man tries to speak, but I cannot make out what he is trying to say. There's a jacket lying next to him, and I grab it and use it to apply pressure to his wound. He tries to talk again, and I try to stop him from speaking. This time, the word comes out.

"Run!"

As soon as the word registers in my brain, gunfire erupts. The windows of a sporting goods store shatter outwards. Several bullets hit the ground near me. Quinn runs behind the car, and I follow him, and we both hide. The rest of the group gets down and hides behind the cars. The gunfire continues, and the windows of the cars are getting shot out.

"Who the hell is shooting at us?" yells Quinn.

I stick out my head slightly from the side of the car to see where the gunfire is coming from. Immediately, bullets hit the headlight near my head. I drop back down behind the car to safety.

"They're in the sporting goods store."

More shots riddle the side of the car.

"We need to grab him and pull him to safety," I say.

"We have to leave him," replies Quinn. "We'll get shot if we try to save him."

"We can't just leave him to die."

"Even if we do manage to pull him to safety, he'll probably die anyway. There's nothing we can do for him."

As horrible as it sounds, Quinn is right. Trying to save him will only get one or both of us killed, and if we do manage to get him out of there, he will probably die anyway. It's a tough choice to let someone die, but this is the new world.

"I'll lay suppression fire so you can rejoin the group. Once you get there, help me get over."

I wait for a break in the gunfire, and then I stand up and return fire at the sporting goods store. The glass windows of the store shatter, falling to the ground.

"Go, go!"

Quinn gets up and runs towards the others. I run out of ammo, so I drop back to the ground. A barrage of bullets hit the vehicle. I get on the ground and lie flat. I look down the parking lot and see that Quinn has made it safely to the others. They stand up and open fire on the sporting goods store, and I get up and run towards them. I join them and drop behind one of the vehicles. They stop shooting, and they all fall to the ground. More gunfire erupts from the sporting goods store while we reload our weapons. The weird thing to me is that I am not afraid. The only thing on my mind is getting everyone to safety.

"What are we going to do? We can't stay here," shouts Kirsten.

She's right. We are pinned down behind the cars and cannot stay here long.

"Ok, here is what we're going to do. Quinn, Kirsten, and I will stay here and lay some suppressive fire. The rest of you make it to the brick sign at the front entrance. Once you make it there, you lay some suppressive fire for us to join you, just like we practiced at the Sanctuary."

Everyone is looking at me. This is the only plan that I have, but I have to show confidence in it so they will not be afraid.

"Are you ready?" I ask.

"Yes," they reply.

"On three."

I do a three-count, and then Kirsten, Quinn, and I stand up and open fire. The rest of the group takes off running to the front entrance and makes it there safely. The three of us stop shooting and hide behind the car. More gunfire comes from the store. I can hear the sound of the bullets whizzing over my head. I hold onto my rifle tightly, grab another magazine, and reload. Kirsten and Quinn also reload their weapons. Cassie and the rest of the group open fire on the store.

"Let's go!" shouts Kirsten.

We take off running to the front. As I sprint past a car, I see a jug of water sitting in the back seat. The car window is shattered, so I stick my hand into the car and grab the jug.

"To the tree line," I shout.

The three of us race past the rest of the group, and we keep running until we reach the tree line. The rest of the team stops firing and gets down.

"Come on!" I shout.

The three of us open fire at the store, and the rest of the group runs towards us and then into the woods.

"Ceasefire," Quinn says.

We stop shooting, and a few moments later, Tobi and about five other members of the Sanctuary exit the store. We look at each other but do not say a word. We take off running into the woods.

CHAPTER TWENTY-TWO

Here we go again, running through the woods for our lives. Is this what life is going to be like from now on, running through the woods from one place to another? Is this what the world has become? We have been running all day, it is hot, and we are tired and thirsty. We cannot continue like this; something has to give. We can't go on living like this. Society has broken down, and there is no help coming. If we don't stop the Sanctuary, everything we know will end, and life as we know it will cease to exist. Life is not going to be worth living if the Sanctuary has its way. We continue running until, finally, Emma stops. She collapses at the side of a tree and lies on the ground. We run to her side.

"Oh my gosh, Emma!" shouts Taylor.

She drops her bag and kneels on the ground to prop up Emma. I rush to Taylor. I hand her the jug of water, and she puts it to Emma's mouth for her to drink. Everyone is concerned about Emma. As we try to revive her, I realize that we've let our guard down.

"We need to head back," I say. "They were right on our tail. We can at least hold them off."

I take my weapon, and both Nate and Ethan pick up theirs, and we head back towards the mall.

"Wait for me!" shouts Quinn.

We spread out and walk back in the direction we came from with our weapons in hand. We scan the woods, looking for Tobi and his squad. From the way they were shooting at us, I can clearly tell that Tyler wants us dead. We walk for a while, but we do not find any trace of Tobi and his men. They must have lost us when they came out of the sporting goods shop. I don't think they saw which way we went, or else they would have been all over us.

"Do you see anything?" I shout.

"Nothing over here!" Nate answers.

"Nothing on this side, either!" replies Quinn.

"Form up!" I shout. "I think they lost our trail."

We meet up in the middle, and we head back to the rest of the group.

"We caught a break," says Nate.

"It's about time," Ethan replies. "We've been getting our ass kicked out of here."

When we make it back to the group, Emma is sitting up, and she appears to be fully alert.

"How is she doing?" I ask.

"She's dehydrated," replies Taylor.

"We all are," adds Kirsten.

"We need to take a break and rest," suggests Cassie.

"We can't stay here," I say. "We'll need to go a little further and find an area to camp."

"I don't think she should move," says Cassie.

Emma shakes her head. "I'm ok. I can do it!" She gets to her feet.

Kirsten hands the jug of water to me, and I take a sip. I wipe my mouth and pass the bottle to Nate. He takes a drink and passes it on. We reload our weapons and grab our backpacks. Then we continue in the direction we were going, which takes us deeper into the woods. We walk well into the afternoon. I look at my watch and see that it is after three o'clock. It usually does not cool down until after sunset. We have no water, and we are walking in hundred-degree temperatures. It won't be long until someone else succumbs like Emma.

We decide that we are going to take a break every thirty minutes, so we don't overexert ourselves. The jug of water was only half-full when we started walking. Emma is the only one who has something to drink at our first stop. We don't want her to pass out again. We decide that we will each get a sip of water from the jug at every other stop.

We walk for almost an hour, and then we make our second stop. Everyone is exhausted, and with these temperatures, a sip of water is not enough. During our second stop, I pull out the map to estimate our approximate location.

"I think we should start heading south, to stay parallel to the highway. I estimate that within another ten miles, we would cross the road."

We walk for another twenty minutes or so, and then we hear

what sounds like a stream.

"Do you hear that?" I ask.

"Hear what?" both Cassie and Kirsten ask at the same time.

"Water. I can hear it. It's water," replies Jeremy.

"It's probably a creek or a stream," I say.

"We need to find it. It may be the only source of water we will have to use," says Taylor.

We walk in the direction of the sound. We take a short detour, and then we come across a stream. The water looks clear, but these streams always have parasites that can make you sick or even kill you.

"Water!" shouts Jeremy, and he runs towards the creek.

"Don't drink it!" I yell.

Jeremy stops and turns around. "Why not?" he asks.

"It might have parasites," I reply. "We have to boil it first before we can drink it."

I look around and see a flat area under a tree that will make a good campsite. I walk over to get a better look.

"This looks like a good area for us to set up camp," I suggest.

We set our bags down and sit on the ground.

"We need to gather firewood to keep us cool through the night and boil the water," I say to the others. "While you're gathering wood, pick up any empty food cans you can find and bring them for us to use as an alarm."

We all get up and go to gather firewood except for Emma. Taylor also stays behind to watch over her. Once everyone has returned to camp, I take the first pieces of wood that we collected and start a fire. I take a small pot from my bag and fill it with water from the creek to boil. While gathering wood, I found a few empty cans that campers left behind. I take the cans and string them along with the ones I have in my bag that I've been collecting. I tie them together, and then I place them in wood as an early warning system in case the Sanctuary or someone else shows up. Everyone piles up the wood into a single pile. We do not have our sleeping bags, so we will not be able to keep warm as the night grows cold. I boil the water and pour it into the jug, and then set it in the stream to cool it down. The stream won't cool it fast, though; the Burning also heats up the water in the streams. We have to wait for a while for the water to cool down. Once the water is cool enough, I grab the jug and take a swallow, and then I pass it around.

"Drink up, everyone," I say. "I need to put the water that's boiling in the jug."

As I'm speaking, something trips the alarm that I set up.

"What was that?" asks Taylor.

"It's the alarm," I say. "Quick, get your weapon."

We grab our guns and duck behind the trees. I look through the scope and see Tobi and other members of the Sanctuary.

"Sanctuary!" I shout.

I open fire, and everyone else starts shooting. The Sanctuary members return fire at us. I am able to shoot one of them by firing first. He falls to the ground, and I aim at another. I am not sure how many of them there are. I look to my right and see Quinn going around the side to outflank them. I decide to go to the other side and outflank them there as well. When I get to the side, I can see Tobi and three others shooting at us. I fire and take one down. I aim at the second one, and he falls to the ground. I look over and see that Quinn shot him. I shoot the third one.

Tobi looks at his men on the ground. He gets up, screaming, and runs out of the tree line and towards the rest of the group, firing his weapon. He is shot several times and falls forward onto the ground.

"Cease fire!" I shout. "Cease fire!"

I go over to check the ones that we shot in the trees, and they are dead from their wounds. I walk back to the camp.

"We got them all!" I shout.

Everyone breathes a sigh of relief. Taylor lays her weapon down and walks towards Emma. Without any warning, Nate takes off towards Taylor, screaming, "Nooooooo!"

He leaps into the air, grabbing Taylor in one action, and I hear a weapon go off. He spins with her as he falls and just as a bullet passes through the arm of his shirt. He falls to the ground on his back, and Taylor lands on top of him. I quickly grab my weapon and shoot Tobi, who, apparently, is still alive and fired the shot. Nate had already dropped his weapon, and pushing Taylor out of the way was the only way to prevent her from getting shot.

"Ouch, that hurts," he complains.

"Oh my God, you saved my life," says Taylor, elated. She leans in and kisses him passionately.

"Woo hoo!" Ethan shouts.

"Yeah!" I yell.

She slowly stops kissing him and pulls away.

"You mean to tell me all I had to do was take a bullet, and I could've had you all along?" Nate says. "If I'd known that, I could've had Lance shoot me weeks ago."

Taylor giggles. "Shut up before I change my mind." She leans over and kisses him again.

"Ouch!"

"Let me take a look." Taylor looks at his arm. "It's a flesh wound. You're going to be fine."

"We can't stay here," I say. "That was only half of his squad. The others are probably on their way here after all this gunfire."

Quinn walks over to Tobi and takes off his utility belt, which has a water bottle. "Help me get this stuff off of them," says Quinn. "The two over there have on backpacks. They may have supplies we can use."

Nathan and I go into the woods to get their bags and other supplies. We bring everything back to the campsite. We open

354

the bags, and there are snacks, water, and ammo in them. We distribute the supplies. Everyone takes a snack and something to drink. We have no time to enjoy the spoils, though. We pack our things and move on before the Sanctuary can catch up to us again. Tobi was a well-trained soldier, and we all know that we got lucky this time that there were more of us than them. We were able to overwhelm them with sheer numbers. Once Tyler finds out, he will send more, much more, of them after us. If they start to pursue us in large numbers, we will not be able to hold back the tide and survive.

I look over at Taylor, and she is tending to Nate's wound. He looks up, and I smile at him. Nate smiles back at me with a bright smile, and we both nod our heads. This is the happiest I've seen him in a while. He's finally found the affection he was looking for from Taylor.

"All done," she says.

She places her hand on his shoulder. Nate puts his hand over hers. "Thank you," he says.

She kneels next to him. "What you did was not only brave, but it showed me that you really care. I was overwhelmed by emotion because no one had ever done anything like that for me when I kissed you."

"What are you saying?" asks Nate.

"I like you, and I don't want you to get the wrong idea. Let's take it slow and see where it goes."

"Slow. I can do slowly as long as you keep the kisses

coming."

We pack our things and begin walking again. The skirmish with the Sanctuary provided us with sustenance that has given us the strength to continue. Our faces do not look as depressed as they did when we first got here. We have more energy to walk, and we do.

We continue in a direction parallel to the road, heading towards the highway to West Virginia. We walk for the rest of the afternoon, stopping every thirty minutes to rest. We do a lot of resting, but it helps us to go further in the sweltering heat. I look at my watch one more time and see that it is now after seven. We have been walking for hours. We will need a place to settle down for the night and use the daylight we have left to find firewood to last us through the night.

"We need to find a good spot to settle down for the evening," I suggest. "We need to get firewood while it's still daylight."

We continue walking until we find a flat area that goes on for about fifty yards in all directions. It is full of dry grass that we can use for bedding. It's perfect, and we decide to use this area for the night. We also realize that if we turn in early, we can get up at dawn, while it's still cool. This will help us cover more ground and increase the distance from the Sanctuary hounds.

Everyone goes out to look for firewood. We will not survive the cold of the night if we do not have a fire and enough wood to keep it going through the night. While everyone else looks for wood, I start setting up the tripwires for the alarm. I select the best possible location on either side, and I attach the string of cans between the trees. While I set up the alarm, a pile of firewood builds up. I find an area that does not have any dry grass to start a fire.

As I drop the firewood on the ground, I hear a boom. I must have blacked out then because the deafening ringing in my ears is the first thing I remember when I come to.

I lie on my back, trying to regain my composer, but my system is in shock. It must have been a rocket-propelled grenade that hit us!

"Aw!"

That hurts. I try turning to my side, but I cannot move. I lie back down, flat on my back, and look up at the sky. The beautiful blue that I remember is all but gone. This haze is everywhere. I cannot even remember the last time I saw green on the trees or saw any grass. Everything I took for granted is gone. *I have to get up!* They must be closing in on us right now.

I try to turn to my right this time, but the pain forces me to lie back down. My hearing is slowly returning. I can hear gunfire all around me. It sounds like we are being attacked from the opposite direction from where we came. *I have to get up*, I think again.

I turn to my left again, and my vision clears up some. In the distance, I see Jeremy firing his SKS rifle from behind a tree. He loves that gun, but he is only thirteen. We're all children. We should be playing video games and texting. Instead, we're shooting at each other. We are just kids! I have to get up, I have to help, and I have to survive. I cannot let them down, and I have to be strong. Everything hurts, I cannot move at all, but I have to move. *They might launch another grenade in the same position.* I have to move. I try getting up, but then I fall back down.

As I lie there thinking, I hear a deafening burst of gunfire. I become afraid, afraid that my friends, the only family I have left in the world, are possibly all dying around me and that there is nothing that I can do about it.

The gunfire dies down and eventually stops. A man walks over and stands over me. I cannot see his face because the sun blazes behind him, blinding me. Nate and Ethen ran over to me, and they each grab an arm and lift me off the ground. I grab my ribs, and I turn to look at the man who stood over me. It's Hector, the man we saved in the police station. He has about two dozen other people with him; they showed up just in time to save us from the Sanctuary.

"You just couldn't stay one more day for breakfast," he says, laughing.

I smile and stick out my hand to shake his. As he puts out his hand, the sound of a shot rings out, and a bullet hits him in the head.

"Sniper!" shouts Ethan.

I stand there, motionless, watching Hector fall backward to the ground. Nate runs to the tree line. I want to reach for Hector and catch him, but I am frozen, not because of fear, but because something else is wrong.

I fall to my knees and touch my chest. I look at my hand, and it is covered with blood. *I've been shot.* I can do nothing else but stare at the crimson red that coats my hand.

I look up and see Hector's men firing their weapons and running to the trees while others fall to the ground dead. I see Cassie screaming, reaching for me with one hand while Jeremy tries to pull her back into the trees with the other. I stop staring at my hand, and I extend it to Cassie, reaching for her as far as I can. She is mortified. The distressed look on her face sinks my heart into my stomach. The gut-wrenching pain that I feel staring into her eyes at that moment overshadows my gunshot wound. The pain of seeing her is too great, so I dig deep into my memories of her and begin to remember the day when Nate took me down, and she kneeled over me, her golden hair flowing across her face.

I fall on my side and hit the ground directly in front of Hector. His eyes are open, and blood trickles from his head wound.

I cannot move, but I see Hector's men, the ones who are still alive, running into the woods. Cassie is being dragged away by Jeremy and Quinn as she screams over and over, "Lance! Lance! Lance!"

The gunfire stops, and I hear Russian being spoken. A pair of boots steps into view, but the uniform is not an American military uniform. I feel a sharp pain and a burning sensation in my chest, which takes away my attention and keeps me from focusing. I can no longer stay awake; everything is fading. *Am I dying?* I ask myself. I begin to shake uncontrollably, and the world fades into blackness.

Part two of the series
"The Escape"
Available Now

Part three of the series
"The Rescue"
Available Now

New Spinoff Trilogy Book I
(Can be read as a stand-alone story.)
Book 4 of series
"The Third Age"
Available Soon

Peacekeeper Origin Story from The Third Age Series
"Dawn of The Peacekeepers"
Available Soon

Join my mailing list: https://www.pjpnovels.com/newsletter
.

Join the discussion on my Facebook page and group at
Patrick Jean-Paul - Author
Follow me on TikTok
and social media platforms @PJPNOVES

www.ingramcontent.com/pod-product-compliance
Lightning Source LLC
Chambersburg PA
CBHW070045120726
47909CB00002B/300